THE GUARDIANS OF FOREVER

HOWARD O. FISCHER

First Edition

PAGE PUBLISHING
Conneaut Lake, PA

First originally published by Page Publishing 2023

ISBN 979-8-88654-004-8 (pbk)
ISBN 979-8-88654-013-0 (digital)

Printed in the United States of America

"The universe seems to me infinitely
strange and foreign:
at such a moment I gaze upon it with a mixture of
anguish and euphoria; separate from the universe
as though placed at a certain distance outside it;
I look and see pictures, creatures that move
in a kind of timeless time and spaceless space…"

—Eugene Ionesco

THE GUARDIANS OF FOREVER

The End of Eternity 1
Knowledge 3
Histories 11
A Variety of Devils 19
Star Bright 27
Man As Machine 45
Good and Evil 59
The River of Life 72
Universes 81
Death and Taxation 96
The Ruins of Men 110
Grains 120
Tests 131
Odysseys of the Soul 144
King of the Jungle 156
The Labyrinths of Living 167
Wonderland 177
A Darkness of the Night 192
Armageddon 201
Morning 212

The End of Eternity

Nothing appeared on the farthest reaches of the final Hubble Ultra Deep Field view except a complete cosmic barren blackness, an infinite dark void, devoid of a ray of light, a chance of life, and even the dust of dreams.

Dr. Solomon Sage was more than frantic, staring at the last photograph again and again. The mystified man methodically searched for any remaining remote points of light. But the oldest galaxies, those dwarfs and tadpole-shaped asymmetric morphologies, had disappeared into a celestial darkness. Only the younger galaxies, those spiral and elliptical symmetrical shapes, stayed as the only sunny sentinels to be found. Nothing else except a cold clutch of an emptied edge of the known universe remained to be seen. Hundreds of faraway galaxies had disappeared. Trillions of vaporous stars were gone. They had been completely extinguished like immense distant candles. Not even a single shimmer survived.

The Hubble Ultra Deep Field view from years earlier had clearly shown those wondrous gleaming galaxies in that far scope of space. This 2004 telescopic image was a portion of the north celestial hemisphere about the size of an end of a large soda straw. First photographs had taken almost four months to absorb any faint light from a distant blink of sky. These farthest masses of billions of suns were once clearly seen in that tiny hunk of the cosmos.

Dr. Sage hunched over his desk and rubbed his forehead. He and his Cal Tech colleagues had sole retrieval authority for this astronomical data from the Space Telescope Science Institute in Baltimore, Maryland. They had breathlessly awaited an image created from extremely feeble glimmers gleaned from a furtive fringe of space. Now even the most renowned astrophysicist among them was far more terrified than he had ever been.

Three decades of astronomical observations at the Jet Propulsion Laboratory had not even slightly prepared him for such a heavenly cataclysm. He wracked his brain to find any possible explanation for the obliteration. Perhaps the impossible had become possible.

Hubble Telescopic Fine Guidance Sensor settings and guide stars had been confirmed; satellite transmissions from White Sands, New Mexico, to Greenbelt, Maryland, and then to Baltimore had been verified; both twenty-five-foot solar panels were firm and functioning, without any of the shuddering which had caused earlier resolution problems; the ACS camera with multi-megapixel detectors was properly cooled and operational, capturing almost every photon received at a rate one hundred times more efficient than any photographic film; the half a dozen nickel-hydrogen batteries were still operable, turning out over two thousand watts of power; no yaw, roll, or pitch problems were present; no gas clouds were obscuring the view; all of the computer equipment and downloading software had been checked. Nothing else of consequence remained to be verified. An elusive error must still be hidden in a system, a fatal flaw existing within an ever more flimsy existence.

Something had to be beyond his frail man mind, some thing far outside any known knowledge. Such an annihilation on such a massive scale should not be feasible. Each faraway star bright was being destroyed at a fantastic rate of speed. Overwhelming oblivion madness would eventually engulf every worldly and otherworldly sense of being. The vast and ageless universe known to the human kind was starting an incredibly fast and violent dissolution.

Here was the end of eternity and everything ever held by a fading forever.

Knowledge

The careening car fled down the middle of the two-lane desert highway like the Devil was close behind. Nearby salt marshes spread out less and less to the south of the black asphalt as if surrendering any efforts to keep the vehicle on the road. These efforts must have finally failed as the left rear tire began to tear apart. Tread peeled away like a dark rubber rind.

Two Nevada state troopers trying to closely follow the fleeing car were relieved. Their high-performance Dodge had reached speeds of one hundred and forty during the past half an hour. Somehow a silver Charger still kept falling farther behind a gray Chevy Cavalier. Now only a receding metallic blur was silhouetted against dusty rays of a setting sun.

Pursued and pursuers had reached the foothills of the White Mountains. Starting hills held a last of daylight for a moment as the Cavalier faded to the far shoulder. Then a crazed car began to flip over, rolling on and on. Eventually it rested on the passenger side of the vehicle.

Both troopers were certain the driver must be nearly as dead as a near desert. Their trooper car was driven as close to the wrecked vehicle as training and terrain would allow. Three additional following trooper cars quickly pulled off of the road. One following news helicopter also circled overhead. Quite a caravan had formed over the last thirty-five miles.

"This lunatic got just what was deserved," said one of the troopers. He still drew his gun. His pursuit had already been a dangerous chase. No unnecessary chances should be taken.

"Let the dog go first," said an arriving sergeant. He frantically motioned to the canine handler who was the last on the scene. Man and dog had too many strange feelings about an ever stranger situation.

The large German shepherd raced over the rough ground to within several dozen feet of the wrecked car. But an anxious dog swiftly stopped and started to howl. Anguished wails told of things wondrous and taboo. Canine knowledge sensed something far beyond the scent of man. Then a usually determined dog quickly sat on a grainy ground.

Furious fists punched through the crushed roof of the tipped car. Rough reaching hands firmly grabbed an edge of the ragged steel opening. Fanatical fingers yanked with a steady grip. Surrounding metal was torn to pieces with a screeching ease.

All of the troopers had drawn their guns. Seven apprehensive men watched as a figure of a man stepped out of the wreckage. One solitary dog started to whine.

"Get on the ground!" yelled more than one of the troopers.

The figure of a man leaned against the wreck for a few seconds. His crazy crash had seemed to temporarily disorient him. Deep lacerations were on the left side of his forehead and neck and shoulder. No blood flowed from any of these wounds.

Troopers were frozen in amazement as the figure of a man suddenly raced toward a slope of the nearest hill. Up and up and up it sprinted, so fast that only the German shepherd was ordered to pursue. Quietly the police dog only lay down with a wise gaze. No canine chasing would begin for such a futile pursuit.

"Have the helicopter follow!" hollered the awed sergeant.

Hurriedly the Channel Seven helicopter banked over a narrow arroyo which flanked an upward path of the fleeing thing. Already its infrared camera had been turned on, recording an ever more eerie chase. Then a figure of light ran ever faster, disappearing in the distance.

The airy hunt would end a half of an hour later about ten miles into ever higher mountains.

* * *

"I don't believe it," said Albert Chester Mitchell.

The director of the Federal Terrorist Task Force was a solidly built older man with a firm expression. His always-resolute appearance also held an ever more weary heart. He had seen an enormous amount of human madness over the passing years. But plane hijackings and car bombings and other plots of deranged minds seemed almost normal in comparison with what was now being told. The world of a Wednesday afternoon was becoming ever more otherworldly.

"We've got the infrared film, all thirty-one minutes of it. Fortunately no live television feeds were broadcast so late on a Friday," said Special Agent Adam Hanson. "Nevada State Police confiscated the camera after the helicopter finally landed back in Reno. Attorneys for Channel Seven have already filed a lawsuit to have it returned."

"Let's take a look at what was filmed," said the director. He motioned for Adam to flick off the overhead lights. The office monitor had been hooked up to the digital camera, its wide screen starting with a silent clearness.

"Here is the end of the car chase on Route Six," started Adam.

Two jaded men watched as the tire on the Chevy disintegrated. Soon a gray car began a death roll and started to struggle to a stop. Finally a battered car tipped on its passenger side, staying as motionless as a dead derelict. Swirling clouds of dust slowly settled to earth.

"The news helicopter was on the chassis side of the wrecked car for the next minute, so we can't see what happened immediately after the crash," continued Adam. "But I have sworn affidavits from seven troopers who say the thing ripped the car roof off with its bare hands to get out of the wreck."

"Nonsense, a group of state guys are probably looking for more special funding," said the director. "Who knows what kinds of equipment these various agencies still want."

"Here is where the infrared film begins. You can see it was becoming dark very quickly on the lee side of the mountains."

The figure of light stood next to the wrecked car for a few seconds. Then a fast figure ran to a slope of the nearest hill with ease. Nothing seemed to hinder its pace in any way. It took rhythmic strides at a steady speed, hopping over several high boulders like garden rocks.

Adam glanced at his small notepad. "This first hill is a thousand feet high. It's a run of almost two thousand feet from the wrecked car to the top of the hill, considering the angle of the slope. He does a mostly uphill sprint over rough ground in thirty-six seconds."

"That's impossible!" said the director.

The figure of light reached the top of the first hill and just continued ever onward. Other higher hills were raced over with incredible speed. Then a narrow ravine was jumped without any breaking of stride. No step was missed after a perfect landing.

"We measured that site of the ravine at just over forty feet wide."

"What are we dealing with here?"

"I don't know, sir, but it covered about ten miles into the White Mountains in half an hour, a mile over hard terrain every three minutes."

They watched several more minutes of the racing figure. But it still moved with a repetitive powerful monotony. Obviously it was nothing that could be called truly human.

"What happens next?"

"There are another twenty-six minutes like what we've just seen, and then the helicopter got too low on fuel to continue a pursuit. The news crew had already been in the area doing a story on solar power. They had to make an emergency landing in Tonopah to get refueled."

"Do we have any idea where this thing is now?"

"No, not yet. It was driving a 2005 Chevrolet Cavalier owned by Carl Shenk, who lives with his wife in a small ranch house behind the Starlight Motel in Tonopah." Adam glanced at his notepad again. "Carl is seventy-eight years old and his wife is seventy-five years old. He stated that the Cavalier was parked in the driveway, like almost always, and then it was gone. Their car was reported stolen and a chase was on."

"I don't understand how an old Chevy Cavalier reaches speeds of a hundred and fifty. Has Harold's group found out anything about the car?"

"The car was damaged very badly. They're still sorting through the wreckage."

"Was anything of consequence found in the car?"

"Nothing, but computer equipment was found in the motel room, a standard laptop with a modem and a printer, and no serial numbers. We couldn't trace the gear or the user."

"Do we know who rented the motel room?"

"Cash was paid for the room, no identification required. The motel is one of those places with rates by the hour, but has high-speed internet access. We did get a rough picture of him from the lobby surveillance camera. We're running the photo through facial recognition software now. Also a burned Chrysler was in the back motel parking lot with a busted front wheel bearing. I think that's how this thing got to the motel, but can't be certain."

"It makes sense, after the Chrysler breaks down, another nearby car is stolen when NASA security protocols were breached via the internet. He had to make as fast a getaway as possible. Have you found out anything about the abandoned car?"

"The car was owned by a shell corporation located in Delaware. We're still checking out the company. It seems to be a subsidiary of another shell which is a subsidiary of yet another shell. Charlie has our financial forensic people working on the case. They should be able to trace an ultimate owner fairly quickly."

"So we're dealing with something with no name that might work for a shell corporation owned by a bunch of other shell corporations, a something that can hack into NASA from a cheap motel room to steal just about any available astronomical file, take an aged car and make it reach speeds my Escalade can only dream about, and then run a bunch of three minute miles and break the world running broad jump record by more than ten feet. Hell, I can only wonder who could create such a thing."

"Technological geniuses are scattered all over the world."

"Yes, but exactly what world are we talking about anymore?"

"What do you want me to do now?"

"Get out to Tonopah and talk to the brass at the test range there. Find out if anybody knew this man, or this thing that looks like a man. It seems strange to me that such a thing would be working at a remote town like Tonopah to hack into NASA. It was probably also involved with the DOD in the area. Squadrons of F-117 stealth bombers are still stored by the air force at the nearby base. I'll make a few calls and let them know you'll be making a visit."

"Then what?"

"Then go to Pasadena and talk to that NASA scientist at the Jet Propulsion Laboratory who discovered the computer breach last Friday. What was his name?"

"Dr. Solomon Sage. He was working on the final Hubble downloads when a breach was uncovered. It's my understanding that the entire episode has been quite a shock to him."

The director arose from his desk, looking out his office window to the Washington Monument in the distance. Melded hands were clenched together behind his back. Meshed fingers tried to make sense of a growing madness.

"Maybe a science guru can point us in the correct direction. I'm only feeling my way along on this one. Just when you think you've accumulated a hunk of real knowledge in your life, you suddenly realize a lot more is out there than could ever really be known."

"Do you care if I take a side trip to San Antonio this weekend to see Angelina? I haven't been with her in over a month."

"Not as long as the trip is on your dime. Why don't you hurry up and marry her before she gets away? Women as smart and polished as she is shouldn't be kept waiting too long."

"Angelina won't leave her mother for any extended time until… well, you know."

"I understand."

"What do you want me to do with this camera? Those corporate lawyers will be all over us."

"Warehouse it with the other lost items. That video won't ever see the light of another day."

* * *

For a moment, the thing that looked like a man stopped upon a low ledge of a mountain in an attempt to stabilize his bearings. Ever more struggling hours had become ever more disorienting as his internal positioning capability had been severely impaired. He had not even been able to use any stars for guidance over these passing nights. His wanderings had stayed within the rocky reach of the White Mountains for each and every night and day. Cloud cover on the windward side of the range had seemed to follow him continuously for nearly a week.

The ugly truth was that a thing which had once been a true man was dying. His intellectual coordinator had been damaged by the grave gash in his forehead. Steadily a machine man was losing any ability to readily reason. When a being could no longer think, it ceased to really be.

He stumbled upon a Bristlecone Pine tucked within a fissure of rocks. Hardened stones had kept watch next to the tree for thousands of years. Now those years spoke to all of them.

"I know that you are old," said the thing. "You are ancient, like me… I can feel it."

There was a faint blink of memory as failing right fingers felt along the weatherworn smoothness of the tree. Affectionate remembrances were held from centuries ago. Soft maternal caresses or other touches still lived within him. But any such remembrances were slowly and surely disintegrating. All of his memories were falling into a pit of nothingness.

"I wish you could speak also. I suppose that you do talk, in your own way. I still have much knowledge to tell. I still have wondrous and taboo things to say, but they are leaving me too quickly. They are fading away."

The ancient thing felt the smoothness of an ancient tree.

"I must go now. I have almost failed, but I will try to remember you. I will try to remember something. I will try to remember *anything*."

Finally he patted the tree in a silent farewell. He stumbled down a steep grassy slope toward the start of a wide valley. Early morning sunshine enveloped him as a few wary cattle grazed in the distance. Then he fell to his knees to try to understand what should next be done.

The thing did not yet sense a pair of true men walking toward it.

Histories

The San Antonio River flowed past as it had done for thousands of years passed. Paleo Indians had once waited for game at the near aquifer fed springs; Bidai and Tonkawa and Kawakawa tribes had hunted and fished along these sandy banks; Apache and Comanche had raided the villages along those banks; Spanish missionaries had stayed and struggled to convince nearby Mission Indians that faith was more than a personal well of belief; Americans and Mexicans had fought along these shores from the Alamo to Concepcion. Now the seventh largest city in the United States straddled those shores. An ancient history existed which could never be completely known. A river had so many stories to tell.

Angelina Herr sat with her mother on a restaurant patio near this river of thousands of years. They stayed beneath one of the large cypress trees which clung to the banks of the river like more than grateful children. How those waters did quench a continuing thirst.

"Do you truly love Adam?" said Mrs. Rachel Herr.

"Yes, Mom, I love him more than I should love any man," said Angelina.

"You can never love a man too much, only too little."

"Is that what happened to Dad? We didn't love him enough."

"Your father was a fine man who only had three loves, his wife and his daughter and his archeology. I think sometimes archeology got an upper hand."

"I can remember too many times when archeology got an upper hand."

"I cannot be too critical. I had sometimes put everything aside for my geology."

"You were always available for me."

"The good mother is always obligated, a firm lesson in biology. I still know that your father would have been very proud to see his little girl grown up and with her own doctorate. I wish you had married Adam several years ago and had the grandchildren we always craved. I wanted to hold at least one of your babies on my lap before I die."

"Don't talk like that anymore. Something might happen to cure your disease."

"Let's face a cold and hard fact, dear. No real remedy exists for T-cell prolymphocytic leukemia. I have accepted such a simple truth and hope you will do the same."

"I still don't want you to talk like that anymore. Miracles can happen by the end of the year."

"Let's change to a happier topic of conversation. I want you to forget about me when Adam arrives for this weekend. Three is more than a crowd when only two days are available."

"You know how Adam enjoys seeing you. We should meet for at least one meal."

"Fine, let's meet Sunday morning. But a brief brunch will be our only necessary get together."

Their concerned waiter walked toward the glassed table. He saw two women who had only slightly nibbled at two of the specialties of the restaurant. "You did not care for your entrees?"

"Our food was excellent," said Angelina. "We'll take the rest with us."

"Could I get either of you a dessert or something to drink?" said the waiter.

"Thank you anyway, just the check when you get a chance," said Rachel. "We're going to stay and talk for a while."

The waiter cleared any remaining dishes with a rehearsed efficiency. Then he quickly returned with a check. He waited patiently while both women handed him the needed money. Each of them insisted on making a total payment.

"Senora and senorita," he finally said, "never put a man in a situation where he must disappoint at least one of you."

Both women laughed at his comment. Angelina relented and let Rachel pay the bill. An anxious daughter wondered how many more meals she would share with an ill mother. Any shared days seemed to be slipping away too quickly. A river was flowing past much too fast.

"I would give about anything to be able to have a margarita, but alcohol and chemo don't mix very well for me."

"Or anybody else."

"Here is what everything finally boils down to in the great river of life, a very small wish that still might be made true. For me, it is only a meal with a big chicken-fried steak and a large margarita."

"I don't know about the steak, but I still think you will be drinking your margaritas again on this very patio."

"My daughter, the eternal fortune-teller…and how did you reach such a conclusion?"

Angelina felt the warm breeze that rustled through the cypress trees. She listened to the soft flow of the nearby water. "The river told me this will be true."

* * *

Tonopah was a sleepy town of several thousand people tucked around Route 6 in the Nevada desert. It was a town once known for its silver mines, but such a luster had worn off years earlier. The solar industry was currently running experiments in the area even as the mining had long ago run out. Brilliant sunshine was no stranger to this part of an earth except at night. Yet most nights were so clear that Tonopah was considered one of the best locales in the country for stargazers.

The air force test range stayed near the town as its own isolated complex. Its sprawl of support buildings maintained the fifty hangars which stored active and inactive military aircraft. There was also a hardened runway which was more than two miles in length.

Tonopah suddenly seemed to be a much more intriguing spot on the map than Adam Hanson had first supposed.

Adam was ushered into the office of a Colonel Wade. An anxious colonel was spit and polish for such an important visitor from Washington. Anyone who knew anyone important realized that Adam Hanson was the favorite of Director Mitchell. But Hanson was also a very capable favorite who deserved respect as much as wariness. His boss was noted for using sticks and carrots better than almost anyone else in the massive federal security apparatus.

"The base has had no known computer security breaches, but we did have a security breach of another kind on the afternoon of the date you mentioned," said the colonel. He pulled out a thin folder from his desk drawer, a report waiting for resolution quickly retrieved. "An unidentified man was found in one of the storage hangars for a mothballed F-117 Nighthawk. Our military police tried to detain him without success."

"Was this the man in the hangar?" said Adam. He held out a small photograph taken from the lobby surveillance camera at the Starlight Motel. The grainy photograph was set on the desk of the colonel. "I know his photo is pretty rough, but it's the best I could get."

"We have much better photos. Several of our security cameras got clear pictures of the intruder." Colonel Wade showed a photograph with a frontal view of the man. He set the photo next to the photo offered by Adam. "It looks like a match to me. Who is he?"

"I was hoping you knew. I'd like to talk to the military police who tried to detain him."

"You can speak to one of them. Officer Ricelli is on base and waiting in a conference room down the hall, but Officer Henderson is still in the hospital. He's got a broken jaw."

"How did that happen?"

"I will let Officer Ricelli explain everything to you."

Adam accompanied the colonel to a near conference room. Officer Ricelli stood at attention with more than a little nervousness. Ricelli gave Adam a scribbled note when the colonel left for his office: *Ask me to go outside—whispers can be heard in this room.*

"Let's go for a walk, I need a smoke," said Adam. His cigarettes had really been given up almost two years earlier. Such a smoking surrender had been done at the request of Angelina.

"Yes, sir," said Ricelli.

Officer Ricelli led the way to a far exit. He knew where the safest spots to speak on the base were located. Conference rooms were certainly not any of those spots.

Adam and the officer walked to a shady side of a nearby building. The stifling shade was still too hot for Adam. He had been born and bred in central New York State; a summer of his youth had been mild with a chilly autumn, a winter had been cold with a brisk spring.

"We can talk now, there is no video or audio nearby."

"Is this a photo of the man you saw in a hangar with a mothballed F-117 Nighthawk?"

"That's him, all right. Who is he?"

"We don't know." Adam saw a sudden skeptical look. "No, honestly, we don't know. I ran this motel photograph through our facial recognition software, but without a hit."

"If you ever find out, take my advice and don't get too close to him. I think he's a martial arts expert. My partner found that out the hard way."

"I thought Henderson only had a broken jaw. Anybody in decent shape could have done it."

"Is that what they told you? Frank was first on the scene and got the right side of his head shattered. His jawbone is in half a dozen pieces and he lost twice as many teeth. He's also got a fractured skull, and his injuries were from only a single punch."

"You saw the assault happen?"

"I was a couple of hundred feet away. Frank had detained a guy in the far F-117 storage hangar and even had him cuffed with his hands behind his back. He was marching the guy toward me when…I don't know…the prisoner somehow got out of his handcuffs. The guy turned around and took Frank out with a single open hand slap. It was like watching a professional boxer knock down a kid."

"What happened next?"

"That is an excellent question. This guy ran around a corner of the last hangar, so I figured nowhere was left for him to hide. More than a lot of open ground is beyond the hangars. I spent only a few minutes giving first aid to Frank until help arrived on the scene, but by then the guy had disappeared. It was like he ran off into oblivion."

"You couldn't help what happened."

"Yeah, you should try telling any excuses to the brass. I got busted down a pay grade for helping my partner instead of trying to immediately apprehend an intruder. But to tell the truth, after what I saw that guy do to Frank, I couldn't have stopped him with my bare hands. I should have just shot him."

"Take my word for it. You probably couldn't have done anything."

"Our latest incident was just another chapter in a long history here, except my partner got his head bashed to pieces. We have had glimpses of unauthorized people in the hangars, shadows of someone in the support buildings, missing files, and so on. But you didn't hear any of this stuff from me."

"I will just say you were reluctant to give me any details unless so ordered."

"None of this craziness really matters anymore. I've got almost a dozen years in the service, but I won't re-up. I'll be out of here in a couple of months. Then I can go back to Abilene."

"I hope everything works out for you."

"You know that old movie saying… *We sure aren't in Kansas anymore.* Well, I sure haven't been."

* * *

"I didn't know we would be spending our Saturday morning at a Book Mart," said Adam.

"It's only for a few minutes," said Angelina. "I'm going to lure you into the used book section and seduce you."

"That won't take much effort."

"I promised my mother that I would pick up a certain book for her. We can give the book to her at Sunday brunch for an early birthday gift."

"When is her birthday?" Adam had asked his question far too quickly. Immediately he realized that such an inquiry had probably been a mistake. Her mother only had about three months to live. Now a month was July and days were slipping away.

"March 15, so beware the Ides of March. I suppose we should beware the ides of every month."

"I'm sorry."

"Don't worry about it. My mother has accepted everything just fine. I seem to be the only person who is having a problem with this whole death experience. She wants to be with my father again, but I would like at least one of my parents to stay with me. I suppose that is just being selfish."

"I don't think so. I wish either of my parents were still alive. I would give anything to see both of them and my brother again. Such a wish is just a normal human want."

Two affectionate people walked quietly among the many rows of books. Private pages held them ever closer. Secret sentences spoke to them in special ways. Yet so very many of their words had not yet been written.

"The book I want is at the far wall," said Angelina.

They stopped in a quiet secluded alcove. Angelina pointed to a long set of books titled *The Story of Civilization* by Will and Ariel Durant. She pulled out a book titled *The Age of Reason Begins.*

"Mom is up to volume seven, only four more volumes to go. She always wanted to read the entire set and now has the hours to almost do it."

"How long is the set?"

"It's quite a history, about ten thousand pages over eleven volumes. The Durants worked together for almost fifty years to finish those millions of words. It's too bad the set was not completed past the early nineteenth century."

"I guess a few histories are not quite over." Adam kissed her in the quiet of the alcove just as his cellphone began to ring. How he did not want to answer its persistent buzz.

Angelina had tried to become immune to such regular intrusions during their irregular meetings. Distance was taking its toll on an ever more distant relationship. She pled a caring case with her eyes.

"I've got to take a call from my boss." Adam held her in one arm even as he held the cellphone in the opposite hand. "Yes, I'm in San Antonio… I understand… I'll get there as quickly as possible." His phone was shoved back into his pocket.

"Bad news?"

"It is for us. I have to go out to Napa, California."

"When do you have to leave?"

"Director Mitchell has a military plane waiting for me at Lackland. Please give your mother my regrets."

"I have to give two lectures next week in Los Angeles. Maybe we can meet there."

"I hope so." Adam kissed her again. Then he hurriedly ran down the aisle and quickly disappeared around a corner crammed with paperbacks.

"So long, amigo," said Angelina to an empty store around her.

She slowly walked to the front of the store with her hardcover book in hand. The nearest cashier was an older woman with salt and pepper hair. Her carefully coiffed strands held much more of the former than the latter.

This wizened elder read the title as she rang a total with the tax. "*The Age of Reason Begins*," said the cashier with a slight smile. The passing years had brought more than a bit of cynicism.

Angelina handed over her credit card and waited for a receipt.

"Makes you wonder when it ended," said the cashier.

A VARIETY OF DEVILS

Dr. Solomon Sage had become far more subdued than frantic.

He opened another bottle of Heineken while sitting on the steps of his terraced patio. Deep swallows of beer were drunk as he deeply pondered an impossible predicament. Dr. Sage wondered if another night of deep sleep would ever be available for him. His incessant insomnia over the last week had become ever more unbearable. Attempts had been made to sleep on the living room couch to avoid disturbing his wife. Harriet had always been a more than reasonable woman, but every person had their limits.

Solomon had struggled through these past days with a knowledge only held by a handful of his colleagues at the Jet Propulsion Laboratory. Serious scientists had strained themselves to find a reasonable answer for an unreasonable circumstance. Nothing on any cerebral horizons as yet made any sense to anyone. Their own human limits were becoming far too apparent, far too quickly.

The final Hubble Ultra Deep Field view was hoped to be only a strange anomaly. This photo was a very limited image, a bit over three arc minutes, a speck of space about a thirteen-millionth chunk of the entire sky. Recreating this initial photographic slice of the universe had been completed to commemorate the launch of the Hubble Space Telescope in 1990. Such a recreation could be the last official act of the Hubble as its orbit was inexorably reaching for a wanting earth.

Solomon's intellectual companions had originally thought a blackened something might be temporarily obscuring that tiny part of the universe. Dark matter and dark energy certainly existed among those vaporous stars, but who knew what composed such stuff. A devil was still lurking within an unseen detail.

Nothing could be immediately completed except a spectral analysis of a thousand selected galaxies. Also another Ultra Deep Field view could be created again. The former could be done quite quickly. The latter could be verified using the Webb Space Telescope launched to replace the Hubble. But another deep field view on the newer telescope would have to be expedited through the selection committee, and that process would take longer. Yet he wondered if time really mattered anymore. Solomon sincerely believed the entire universe was actually disintegrating. Unknown forces seemed to be breaking the universe into newly formed nothingness.

How could anything destroy something so vast and ageless!

He looked straight up to a night sky. All individual stars visible to an unaided human eye were in the Milky Way Galaxy. An ancient galaxy was 100 thousand light-years across, or 600 thousand trillion miles. At least 100 billion stars were in this beauty of a celestial spiraled mass. A sphere of humanity swam like a dot of dust in a reaching arm of a sun-laden swirl.

Our observable universe was 94 billion light-years across with at least several trillion galaxies. Estimates of the immense number of stars held by these galaxies were as high as 200 billion trillion. There were more stars than the number of grains of sand on every desert and beach on the earth.

There was also the problem of speed. The initial Hubble Ultra Deep Field view had been created in 2004. Faraway galaxies shown in the original photograph might look very close together, but these galaxies were actually millions of light-years apart. Nothing known to a modern mind could move such enormous distances so quickly.

The speed of light had always been thought to be the one and only celestial speed limit. Such a speed of 186 thousand miles per second was the fastest rate at which anything could travel in the universe. But even at such an incredible speed, most interstellar travels in the Milky Way Galaxy would be impossible to complete during an earthly human life. Any trip across only this single galaxy would take at least one hundred thousand human years. And any intergalactic trip was also beyond reasonable human imagination.

Then there remained the problem of religion. Solomon Sage was an extremely devout man. His philosophy had always included a kind and benevolent God. How could such a god allow such a terrible event to happen. He recalled Einstein's quote: "God is subtle but not malicious."

Omnipotent handiwork had made a wondrous, expanding creation. Celestial guidance had provided the light and heat and elements for a joyous explosion of life. Now it was being destroyed at a hyper light speed.

The universe known to the human kind was very rapidly ceasing to be.

* * *

The senior psychiatrist at the State Mental Hospital in Napa was a robust, jovial fellow. This physician had long ago accepted the travails of the mentally abnormal as a normal portion of the human condition. He seemed strangely out of place in these subdued surroundings. The doctor still made occasional analytical glances at Adam Hanson. Two inquisitive men walked down a long hallway which fairly sparkled with cleanliness.

"Why did Washington send a special agent for such a common case?" said the doctor.

"We had requested the county sheriffs bordering the White Mountains to get in touch with us in the event of anything that was, shall we say...unusual. That's about all I can tell you. What can you tell me about the patient?"

Now an accepting psychiatrist nodded. His report was scanned on a casually held clipboard. No sense was served pushing for any more information on a very sensitive matter.

"We don't have much of a history on him. His name is Juan Martinez...was transferred from a hospital in Bishop...brought here by Mono County sheriff deputies…was found wandering in the Chalfant Valley saying he had seen the face of the Devil. He was working on a cattle ranch with his best friend, Roberto Salina… both men were rounding up strays for the owner of the ranch when Roberto was killed."

"Did Mr. Martinez say what happened to his friend?"

"No, a couple of county deputies had found the body, but it was completely ripped apart. They told me it was probably an attack by a mountain lion."

"Do you know exactly where the attack happened?"

"Not exactly, but I'm certain the Mono County Sheriff would be glad to fill in any more of the necessary details. I assume you have his phone number."

"Yes, I do. So how is Mr. Martinez now?"

"It's difficult to say. He seems to be slipping into an almost catatonic state, but such a mental seclusion is probably only a temporary episode. He saw his best friend killed in a horrible way. Occasionally a human mind needs to hide away, at least for a while."

"He's not violent?"

"He's been as quiet as a mouse. Do you want me to stay in his room with you?"

"No, I suppose that won't be necessary."

"I'll have an orderly wait outside the door, so if you need anything, just ask him."

"Okay, thanks for your cooperation."

The psychiatrist motioned to a brawny man at the end of the hallway. Then he peered through a reinforced glass window at the top of the door. He swiped a key card across the electronic sensor.

"Mr. Martinez seems especially subdued. You won't have any problems."

Juan Martinez was huddled against a wall of the room, motionless on his knees at the far end of a bed. He was bent forward with both palms of his hands held protectively against his face. His left eye was completely covered, his right eye partly visible through an opening in a clutch of otherwise clenched fingers.

"I'm Special Agent Hanson...and I'd like to ask you a few questions." His words had been spoken in a very soft voice. He started to sit on the near end of the bed very slowly and quietly. Nothing abrupt should be done around this undone young man. "I want to speak to you about what happened in the Chalfant Valley."

But Juan stayed motionless on the bed. Not even a flicker of his single visible eyelid was seen. Such an approach was going absolutely nowhere. Much more personal tactics would be necessary.

"I would like to talk to you about Roberto."

Still nothing seeped from the young man except a mostly hidden stare.

"Roberto's family needs to know what happened to him. Roberto was your friend. He should be allowed to rest in peace."

Reluctantly Juan pulled the palm of his right hand away from the partly visible eye. He held this hand against his heart with a remembered affection. His left hand stayed temporarily over his other eye.

"Yes...Roberto was my very best friend."

"Will you tell me what happened to him?"

"No... I know the devil that looks like a man would not want me to say what was done to Roberto."

"Then just tell me what you want to say."

Juan steadily lowered his left hand from his face. He stared off to a faraway sky seen only by himself. His best friend was completely gone from his life. And Juan had not been able to do anything to help him. A person could be far beyond a saving.

"I told Roberto to leave him alone. He is not a real man, look at his wounds. No red blood is there, only dark streams of something flowing down his face. This devil was sleeping, resting on his knees, like I am doing now."

Then a temporarily freed young man looked at Adam with opened eyes. The apprehensive man did not want to tell his story, but a fast friendship can often overcome any slowing hesitations. His words began to be spoken ever more readily, an inflection in his voice trembling.

"Look at the jade, said Roberto, look at the jade. Roberto reached for the jade, but then the devil awoke. He was an angry devil that looked like a man, but I understood why there was anger. Roberto should not have touched the jade choker."

"What happened after Roberto touched the choker? I mean, what happened after he was killed?" Nothing would be gained by again asking Juan how his friend had been ripped to pieces in front of him. Adam already knew far too much about the physical abilities of this particular creature.

Juan looked directly at Adam with a piercing stare. Now a bewildered young man only smiled a bizarre smile. His opened pair of hands was raised to a still seen overcast sky.

"The devil that looked like a man stared at me. He looked into the most secret, sacred part of me. Then he held a palm of a hand to his forehead and staggered off…and I said goodbye to the devil that looked like a man…"

Juan Martinez started to revert to his former state. His hands steadily moved to his face, fingers slowly covering his eyes. Soon only a same slit of a right eye remained visible. His recent experience would soon enough only be a failed vision.

"And wished he could never, ever find me again…"

* * *

Even a grassy side of the foothill was very steep. Adam and the Mono County Sheriff almost fell down more than once during their ascent. Several deputies above eventually waved them over to a more hospitable part of the terrain. Ponderosa pines in the area were their only other nearby watchers.

Finally the pair of struggling men reached a rough path already made by the deputies and the local coroner. Slowly the last of a stark slope was ascended to a wide meadow bordered by patches of trees. More than a few bloodstains remained on the grass.

"This is the spot where my deputies found the body, or at least most of it," said the sheriff, pointing to a faded chalky outline. "Like I told you on the phone, only a single leg was still attached to the torso. His other leg and both arms were found within a radius of about thirty feet."

Three other markings were spread around in a relatively tight circle.

"I hope your men are keeping a firm lid on the killing," said Adam. Nothing was worse than a real truth revealed about a really gruesome event. Too many mainstream and tabloid reporters would be smothering everyone and everything if any secrecy was broken.

"My deputies are as solid as these mountains and so is the local coroner. We did everything just like Washington told us. Our cover story about a mountain lion was the best we could do. Most people don't know only about a dozen such attacks have happened in California over the past century. But it's all we could make up on such a brief notice."

"Your story will probably be believed. Nothing quite flies with the press like a puffed lie with a kernel of possibility."

"We put our two bloodhounds on the trail after the body was taken to the morgue. Duke and Maxie would always follow a trail to the moon if needed, once they got a scent. But something strange must have affected them."

"Let me guess, they refused to go after the suspect."

"You got that more than correct. Both dogs started to whine when they got a whiff off the victim's clothes. We had a devil of a time trying to get either of them to do much of anything. Old Duke just lay down and refused to get up again. Maxie is the younger of the dogs and we coaxed him toward that far grove of pines. Then he led us for a hundred more yards and just sat down. He raised his snout to the sky and gave the most incredible howl I ever heard from any animal around here. That wail was almost like a human cry."

"Maybe it was a cry for something once human."

"I sure don't know what it was, but that howl made me and my deputies cringe. I still get the shivers thinking about it. We taped off the entire area like your boss asked and nobody has been past the tapeline. I sure don't want to get much closer."

"I'll take a look."

Adam walked toward the grove of pines. An ever more wary agent pulled out his nine-millimeter Glock from its holster. A wandering man wondered if a fifteen-shot clip was enough. He also wondered if the thing next to a tree was really dead. Such a thing might only be playing a bizarre game of possum. Maybe a few creatures in this earthly life could not really die.

He circled to his left to put as many trees between himself and the motionless figure. Sudden thoughts of a faking figure furiously firing an advanced weapon also circled in his brain. Laser beams would vaporize tree trunks just before sending him to a fiery hell. But nothing moved as he approached the dead thing from a side. Time had finally ended for this wrecked creature.

Adam Hanson suddenly had the strangest feeling that time was also ending for him.

The frozen figure of a man was on his knees, clutching a thick ponderosa pine like an ancient friend. His left arm was stretched as far around the pine as could be reached. His right hand was pressed against the tree close to a downward tilted head. His eyes were closed, but a make-believe mouth was slightly agape as if screaming a silent scream.

Dark fluid had flowed from the left side of his forehead and neck and shoulder. Thin rivulets from the forehead had circled the eye socket and continued along the cheekbone to the chin. Similar rivulets from the neck and shoulder had followed the fabric of the shirt. Jagged drops had dripped upon a waiting earth, congealing as soiled tears.

"What is it?" said the sheriff from beyond the surrounding tape.

"I don't know..." said Adam, "part man...part machine...part monster..."

Now Adam stood next to that ancient thing. He could see a light-green choker, tight around the neck. Also there was a glimpse of a thin black prism held in the hollow of the reaching left hand.

Star Bright

Dr. Solomon Sage awaited the arrival of Agent Adam Hanson. Dr. Sage had so much on his mind that a meeting with a Washington bureaucrat was the last thing on his mind. But his work had always required substantial federal funds. No escape was available from such responsibility. There would too quickly be no escape available for anyone from anything. It was almost impossible to accept the absolute annihilation of everything.

The ever more cynical astrophysicist had been drinking ever more heavily. His favorite beer had been switched to his favorite cognac. But even the Courvoisier had not soothed his aching soul. Harriet had tried to console an inconsolable man, knowing something was very wrong with her husband. Yet she was not aware of the gravity of the situation.

Solomon laughed at his last thought. "The gravity of the situation…" he muttered to himself.

It was a statement which neatly explained an entire problem. Everything in the universe was going to be pulled back into an incredibly tiny singularity. Anything which had ever existed was going to cease to exist. Nothing would be left except a small speck in a dark void.

He had never believed those faraway galaxies had just been obscured. His colleagues had reluctantly agreed with his conclusion. They unanimously thought these galaxies had been squeezed by an overwhelming something which was accelerating toward a center of everything. Their once ever-expanding universe was now ever more contracting. An eternity of existence had changed. And such a change had happened so very rapidly.

The spectrographic analysis had been completed for a thousand galaxies. Each and every one of these galaxies were no longer red shifted. Each and every one of these galaxies were blue shifted. Such a color change meant they had encountered a celestial U-turn sign, turning back from their expansive path. Eventually they would congeal into a single dense blackness from which not even light could ever escape. Such an annihilation was too depressing for Solomon Sage to completely accept. He did not even have the emotional energy to answer the sudden knock on his office door.

"What do you want?" said Solomon.

His greeting had not been very cordial as his entire demeanor was becoming extremely rude. Not much meaning could be found in continuing any seemingly meaningless pursuits of a life. Solace might be found in soothing alcohol.

"I'm Agent Hanson. We spoke on the phone."

Adam opened the door and extended a hand which Solomon apathetically accepted. Any grip of the astrophysicist was more than weak. Already it was a grasp of a man who had scientifically surrendered.

"Have a chair, if you want one."

Adam was taken aback by Dr. Sage's appearance as much as his attitude. He was a scientist almost as disheveled as a hobo who had just hopped off a freight train. His level of interest in the present situation was as indifferent as his clothes. Too many of his words had also seemed too slurred. A faltering man was falling apart.

"I'd like to discuss several subjects with you," said Adam. "The first is the recent computer breach you reported. I understand NASA security protocols were compromised."

"Oh, yes, apparently somebody hacked into our system and took whatever astronomical observations were wanted."

"Do you know specifically what data was taken?"

"No, not specifically, but any lost data doesn't really matter anymore."

"The lost data matters to me. It may give a clue as to where I'm going on a particularly important case."

"Really…and what case might that be?"

Adam was taken aback even more. Now an insistent agent felt like he was trying to speak to an indignant drunk in a neighborhood bar. He might as well continue onward to the second subject of his visit. Later in a conversation he could return to the first subject.

"Do you have any idea what this device is?" Adam held in his hand a thin black rectangular prism.

The slender dark mechanism was about as large as an oversized deck of cards. Five indentations in a black metal shell formed a small *X* matrix. Each indentation had its own unique mark. Every marking shimmered in a strange way.

"I don't know…a new smartphone in Sanskrit?"

Such sarcasm was almost too much for Adam. He was lost within a case which did not make much sense to him. But there was not yet a realization that Solomon Sage was just as lost. Their mutual sense of direction might be found together.

Then Adam walked under the dual rows of ceiling lights and switched them off. He pointed the dark prism at the nearest empty wall as its upper left shimmering indentation was firmly pressed. Solomon had just begun to voice an objection when any words were suddenly stuck in his throat, for a more than wondrous happening had occurred.

Now a continuous arc of light emanated from the end of the prism. Galaxies began to form in sequence within the brilliant beam. Glowing galaxies formed as perfect holographic images, flowing away as a streaming extraterrestrial 3D movie. Immediately an amazed astrophysicist recognized these starting galaxies.

Solomon arose from his chair like a man resurrected. He stood in awe as the arc stopped expanding outward, but still stayed as a steady stream of light. Earlier shown galaxies steadily faded in sequence at the end of the beam as new galaxies continued to readily emerge in sequence at the start of the beam. The continuing view was a relatively narrow celestial roadway which went on and on.

Solomon Sage stood open-mouthed not far from his chair. A belligerent adult had become almost a docile child. An incredible flowing celestial road continued before his stunned eyes.

"Where did you get the device?" finally said Solomon.

"I found the device in the White Mountains, and that's all I can tell you," finally said Adam. "Everything else is beyond classified."

The tone of Solomon's voice told Adam there could now be real communication between the men. Adam needed an astronomical expert to explain what exactly such a thin dark prism represented. Its brilliant beam looked like a slender slice of the universe duplicated as a miniature pathway. But such a path went onward to who knew where. Solomon Sage was just such a person who could tell him about a final destination.

"This star map is absolutely astounding. I have never seen anything like it."

"Why is only a narrow path of galaxies shown? Shouldn't a more complete map be presented, with many other galaxies and other phenomena?"

"No, that is the simple beauty of such a map."

"I still don't understand."

"Okay, let's say you live in Portland, Oregon, but want to drive directly to Portland, Maine. You would not need a map of the earth or the United States or even any individual states. You would only need enough of a map to plot a single route to your destination, a solitary path so to say. Everything else outside such a route would be a completely unnecessary complexity, and the complexities of our universe are mind-boggling. This map is just such a direct route, only it goes from earth to…let's see where."

Solomon took the offered device from Adam. Then an excited astrophysicist held the first indentation down hard on the dark prism. Galaxies flowed past at an increasing rate of speed.

"Shouldn't more space be between these galaxies? Even I realize that galaxies are many light-years apart."

"Absolute distances between these galaxies have been truncated, or we would be seeing a lot of empty space between the galaxies. Such a truncation exponentially speeds a vision of the map, otherwise we would mostly be seeing a very lengthy movie of a dark void."

"If you say so."

Solomon let up on the first indentation. He pressed the upper right indentation to see what would happen. Now the beam started by the first indentation stopped. But this bright beam still held a last shown galaxy motionless in its light. Entire arrays of data spread out next to this single galaxy. All of the arranged statistics were color coded.

"The device is not only a map, but also a kind of astronomical encyclopedia. Information is displayed about whatever galaxy is isolated on the beam...black holes, magnetic flux, supernovae, and gravitational fields. You name it and it's in here."

"I can't name much. I was never an astronomy buff."

Then Solomon pressed the lower left indentation. Other arrays of data appeared on the wall.

"There is also a great deal of information we can only dream about ever knowing."

"Like what, for example?"

"Like the exact number of stars in a galaxy, the exact number of planets in a galaxy, and the constantly changing distances between galaxies and stars and planets. Specific symbols are allocated to certain planets, but I don't recognize any of them." Solomon pressed the lower right indentation. Long lines of additional symbols appeared. "I'm not familiar with any of these symbols...how about you?"

Adam also looked at the symbols. He was fluent in five languages and fair in two more, yet could make next to nothing out of these codes. One of the symbols looked like a triangular tree. Nothing else was apparent to him but a rapidly growing uncertainty.

Now Solomon returned to the first indentation and the arc of flowing galaxies continued. Arrays of adjacent data disappeared. Then he pressed down ever harder on the indentation, trying for a superfast forward of the process. And many more galaxies went on and on. Finally Solomon sat back in his chair to continue an attempt to reach the end of the route.

He stared at that flowing beam ever more intently until an edge of the observable universe faded into complete blackness. An extended length of darkness was seen for several minutes. And more galaxies appeared as the physicist almost fainted.

"Dr. Sage, are you all right?"

"I don't know, this star map is nothing short of incredible."

The bright beam of light suddenly and completely stopped after another minute. Only a black splotch of a galaxy remained in the holographic beam. No starry brightness was visible in the very irregular mass. A cloudy blackened entity looked very much like an interstellar Rorschach inkblot. An interuniverse route ended in what appeared to be a swirling center of a dark vortex.

"This dark galaxy looks like the end of the star path," said Solomon. "To a very edge of our observable universe and far, far beyond."

"You don't think the device is only an elaborate hoax?"

"No, I don't think it's a fraud. The star route begins in our own Milky Way Galaxy, goes past several of the nearby galaxies of the Local Group..."

"The Local Group?"

"Yes, the Local Group is a cluster of forty relatively nearby galaxies. Our own Milky Way Galaxy is roughly at one end of the group and the Andromeda Galaxy is roughly at the other end, a distance of almost three million light-years. This star route goes past the Andromeda Galaxy and exits the Perseus Cluster, which is three hundred million light-years distant, passes Quasar 3C48, which is four billion light-years distant, and just keeps on going."

"How far does it continue?"

Now the fifth and middle indentation was pressed. Distances and times flowed past like fleeing exponential figures until the last array of data was reached. Innumerable numbers were neatly categorized.

"I would say, taking the cumulative distance in the final table, that the star map extends more than ten times further than our observable universe. That is about a trillion light-years, assuming that light still travels at a rate of six trillion earthly miles per earth year within interuniverse space-time."

"*Inter*universe space-time?"

"The route definitely shows a path far beyond our universe, demonstrating a supposed existence of other universes. Such a concept of multiple universes is not as strange as it might seem. Less than a century has passed since other galaxies beyond our own were discovered. Before then, we thought the Milky Way whirled through space in solitary."

"How can such a device even be possible?"

"I don't have the slightest idea, but a bottom line is that such a compilation is an absolute miracle. Existence of such a map is a wonder of an intellect far beyond our own."

"So you believe all of it?"

"Yes, but this star map has made me feel humble, primitive, even more than a little afraid."

"Why should you feel afraid?"

"Don't you see we're dealing with something so intelligent, so knowledgeable, that it makes our human race seem almost inconsequential. Whatever has information such as this star map is as far removed from us as we are from a clump of algae, or maybe even a lump of clay."

"You may be correct, but this particular lump of clay will try to find out who, or what, could possibly make such a map of space and time. But I still have the strangest feeling that time is running out for me."

"Let me explain another strange thing to you. Time is running out for *everything*."

* * *

The afternoon lecture hall at UCLA was more than packed. Students and faculty and interested others sat in aisles or leaned against walls. Dr. Angelina Herr had become a rising star on the college and corporate lecture tours of the world. Her father had long ago sowed a seed of her success. He had been a brilliant man whose strong opinions and forceful voice more than often carried a day. His words had still not completely faded from view.

Now Angelina often found herself defending her self against her father. She had tried to deny many of his opinions to make her own voice be heard in an often hearing-impaired academic world. Such a denial was not a task which she particularly enjoyed. But she could not allow his past brightness to obscure her own ready light on a variety of topics. She still loved him so very deeply. But she then thought no eclipse of a reputation would be at her expense.

"Let me conclude by saying what a privilege it has been speaking to this audience on such a sunny afternoon. Many of you will not accept my straightforward conclusion that absolutely no archeological evidence exists to substantiate extraterrestrial visitations to this little planet. Our earth is only ours, shaped and scarred by the struggles of human successes and failures, marred by humanity alone without any aid of aliens from a faraway star system.

"Many myths have become stories which have become science fiction for the masses. Such terrific tales have made a variety of aliens our friends and enemies, our dreams and nightmares. They have made us both aware and afraid, aware of what might have happened and afraid of what might still happen. This fiction is just that, made-up stuff to stuff us with nonsense. Any assumptions remain endless while any evidence has no remains."

Unenthusiastic applause was heard. Her audience was firmly in the camp of her father. Many members of this audience were already involved in more than a few of their own unfriendly discussions. It had been a rocky presentation.

One of the sponsors of the lecture series walked to the lectern. He was a portly chancellor who enjoyed more than his share of verbal jousting. "Thank you, Dr. Herr. I think we still have about twenty minutes for questions. Please line up at the microphone in the center aisle."

An inquisitive young man was first in a long line forming at the microphone. A crowd quickly quieted as he began to speak. "Dr. Herr, your complete lack of belief about extraterrestrial visitations to earth completely contradicts the theories of your own father about such visitations. How do you explain his strong acceptance of such visits to various sites, such as the Nile Valley in Ancient Egypt and the Nazca Plain in not as ancient Peru?"

"I believe my father was a sincere man who was a victim of his time," started Angelina. "It seems clear now that an explosion of technologies in Ancient Egypt, technologies which built the Great Pyramid of Khufu, the Temple of Karnak, Abu Simbel, and many other impressive pyramids and monuments and obelisks, was the consequence of a vast climactic catastrophe in the Northern African continent. This climactic disaster was probably due to a change in the Atlantic Ocean conveyor currents caused by a variation in our earthly orbit.

"The resulting desertification forced many scattered peoples eastward to the waters and security of the Nile Valley. Such a relatively sudden concentration of a broad variety of technologies and skills made possible a veritable ancient Renaissance, many results of which we can still watch in wonder, but understand they were built only by our earthly kind."

An aggressive audience again became restless. A majority of the crowd in the lecture hall were devoted fans of the Pharaohs. They wanted to hear about laser beams easily cutting huge stone blocks and antigravity devices just as easily lifting such blocks. Supposedly the Great Pyramid of Khufu was built in twenty-two years with more than two million stones. Many people believed such a construction could not have been completed solely by human hands.

"It also seems clear to me that those large outlines of images on the Nazca Plain were readily made by men and women of our planet. These animals and birds and plants seem to be simple representations of fauna and flora which still live in the adjacent rain forests, and might again be lured back to a mystically rejuvenated part of South America."

"So you do not believe that any of the outlined images at Nazca were a kind of greeting to any extraterrestrials who had once landed there?" said the young man at the microphone.

"You mean such outlines were constructed as a kind of interstellar welcome mat?"

"Yes…or something similar."

"Then I would have to loudly say *no*! These outlines of a variety of animals and birds and plants only represent to me a form of sympathetic magic, an attempt to revive things which once were. Any past of what has passed has always enthralled our species. We want to regain lost histories. We strive to set our clock back to an earlier time. Such a desire is no more than a wish to control time itself."

More unrest rippled through the crowd. This youthful generation had been raised on more than its share of false promises. Video game ghosts and goblins and warlocks had taken a firm hold in their heads. A Loch Ness Monster and a Bigfoot and a yeti had rambled through their brains for years. Any gallivanting group of intergalactic aliens could not be far behind.

Now there was a brief disagreement near the microphone. Two young women next in line squabbled over who was second in the queue. Finally a truce was made between a pair of companions. Their choice was almost as quickly agreed.

"Dr. Herr, you have not discussed this afternoon your father's strongest belief in an extraterrestrial relationship between Chaco Canyon and Puma Punku," said the first young woman. "I wonder if you could elaborate more on your father's theory about this relationship, a topic which he had often mentioned but never explained in any significant detail."

Angelina cleared her throat with more than a little annoyance at a topic which never would seem to fade away completely. She had been involved in many conversations and even a few arguments over the years. Her undergraduate and graduate debates had more than primed a ready response.

"My father was like any archeologist or any other person from any scientific field. He often had his own individual view of a relationship or a phenomenon or a conflict of facts. I am not personally aware of a single credible published account of *any* relationship between Chaco Canyon and Puma Punku.

"These two cultures were not involved in any direct trade. Their architecture and the building methods used for such architecture were radically different. Their ceremonies seem to have varied widely in the degree of violence used, and so on and so on. The very obvious fact that the two sites, Chaco Canyon on a desert plateau in northwestern New Mexico and Puma Punku upon a high mountain in western Bolivia, are about four thousand rugged miles apart, should tell us much about any possibility of such a relationship."

"What about their mutual and sophisticated interest in astronomy, especially as represented by Sundagger Butte in Chaco Canyon and the Gateway of the Sun in Puma Punku?" said the companion of the first young woman. This second young woman had briefly edged her first friend to a side. They still remained side by side.

"I do not think a sophisticated interest in astronomy for any group of cultures is an indication of a relationship between or among such cultures. Both the inhabitants of Chaco Canyon and China of almost a thousand years ago documented the supernova in 1054 AD which produced the Crab Nebula. Should we then assume there was an extraterrestrial or any other kind of relationship between Chaco Canyon and China? I think not.

"Many of these ancients and near ancients looked to the skies with varying degrees of awe and skill—the Mesopotamians, Babylonians, Greeks, Persians, and Mayans to mention only a handful of sky scholars. Stars were wonders which they could not wholly comprehend, but how they tried to do so. We should also look to the stars, but not for any belief in seeing others, only for the benefit of broadening ourselves."

The first woman again edged her way past a secondary friend to the microphone. Many following questioners behind the pair of women were becoming more than irritated. Almost mute mumbling became ever louder.

"How can you so easily dismiss the advanced building techniques used at Puma Punku? Surely the long-ago movement and intricate carving of stones which weigh forty to fifty tons cannot be readily explained wholly in human terms."

"Constructions of the Puma Punku complex and the entire city of Tiahuanaco are certainly engineering marvels of their era. But a few of the approximate contemporaries of the inhabitants of Puma Punku, and I'm thinking primarily of the Romans, also completed elaborate constructions of equivalent complexity and weight. Yet I have never heard a person speculate that the Coliseum or the Tower of Trajan were built with any assistance from extraterrestrials."

Scatterings of applause were heard throughout the lecture hall. Still a minority of an audience stayed on her side of such a provocative subject. Maybe she could change a minority into a majority. Her will would prevail.

"Let us assume that Puma Punku and even the rest of Tiahuanaco *were* constructed with the skilled aid of extraterrestrials," continued Angelina. "We can speculate that these aliens readily revoked the cardinal rule of cultural noninterference as often presented on the old *Star Trek* television series…"

She waited for a substantial laughter from the audience to lessen.

"If such an interference is so, why did these advanced aliens allow this city state to become a predatory state? Why did they allow human sacrifice to be institutionalized? Why did they provide no clearly written language? Why did they not prepare protections against an unknown catastrophe which tossed those immense stones about like paper toys? If these were indeed extraterrestrials, they must have been quite an unethical and uncaring bunch of galactic travelers."

She again waited as a somber silence had descended upon her audience.

"Even if we accept such a premise, how can we fairly compare the complexity of the Puma Punku constructions with the relative simplicity of the Chaco Canyon constructions? Both sites would have held a long-ago viewer enthralled with their differing magnificence, but no such early viewer has ever existed. If Puma Punku must be birthed as a prime example of extraterrestrial interference, then Chaco Canyon must be cradled as a prime example of extraterrestrial noninterference. Such a contradiction is a very strong contraindication of any relationship.

"I will state this as my final comment on the matter: absolutely *no* extraterrestrial or *any* other direct relationship has existed between the sites of Chaco Canyon and Puma Punku."

Her audience had been completely subdued. A majority had been successfully sought and found. An impotent minority no longer had a strong voice. Waiting arguments had withered under her words. Deflated deniers began to steadily flow out of the expansive hall.

Angelina hoped her lecture tomorrow would be just as decisive as her lecture today. But she realized most people held onto their beliefs without much reason. They clung to anything which gave them a feeling of intellectual or spiritual solace. Salvation awaited in many different ways for many waiting people. Often a salvation was not waiting in any form.

Two men approached the lectern even as the remainder of the audience ebbed out of the hall. Both men were dressed in suits with ties and were immaculately groomed. The man in the lead was of average height, with a dark moustache and goatee. He moved like someone who was in charge of others, a confident spring in a step.

The following man was taller, with a lean and powerful physique. He stayed behind like a servant follows a master. But there did not seem to be too much of a difference between their strides. Leader and follower were almost perfectly in step.

"It was a most interesting lecture," said the lead man. "I am Mr. Levid Lanicrim, and this is my personal bodyguard, Mr. Thax."

"I'm glad you enjoyed it," said Angelina, packing her lecture notes in a slim valise. Suddenly she felt chilled. She might be coming down with a cold.

"I was wondering if you could travel to New York City, at my expense of course, and give a similar lecture."

"I'm very busy right now with personal commitments. I will probably not be traveling for the rest of this year. Perhaps we could agree on a lecture date for early next year."

"Such a day is much later than I had hoped, but Mr. Thax will contact you via the phone number on your website." Lanicrim reached out and grasped Angelina's right hand, kissing her skin ever so lightly. "I will see you at this future day."

Now Angelina almost fainted as the pair of men walked down a near aisle. Nearly overwhelming coldness had spread over her stunned body. She felt almost fast frozen, not even hearing Levid Lanicrim speaking to his bodyguard.

"She is an angel only for insurance, Mr. Thax. We must always prepare for a worst possible scenario."

Still Angelina felt temporarily overcome. Her head began to clear as she held onto the lectern. Finally she opened her purse and pulled out her cellphone. There were the usual phone and text messages from people who agreed or disagreed with her lectured opinions. And there was a personal text message from Adam:

> *My dearest Angelina, I apologize again for not being able to meet you in Los Angeles, but I have other immediate obligations which cannot be delayed. I am sending an artifact to your mother as she is the very best geologist I know. I would more than appreciate both of your opinions when you return to San Antonio. Love, Adam*

Soon Angelina read the message again to make certain her temporary confusion had not caused any part of his texted words to be misread. Then she convinced herself that his most recent departure was just another detour on a winding trail of love. How she did wish their relationship could be an ever more straightforward journey.

"Hanson is as Hanson does," she said to herself.

* * *

Herbert T. Ross intently scanned the exterior of the large brick colonial house. He worked in darkness as there was no visible phase of the moon for tonight. Then he thought his entire existence had been in almost complete darkness for too many days and nights. But such a lengthy existence could finally be nearing an end. He thought of Rigel's death in the White Mountains and realized even beings as powerful as themselves could perish.

Now the security system inside the house was evaluated. Such a system was more than sophisticated. It looked like a silent alarm built directly into the house structure and hooked into every possible point of entrance. Connecting electric cables could be ripped out, but he was more than reluctant to do so. Electricity was a technology he had learned to avoid since its development in the late nineteenth century.

He had searched for an open door or window around the perimeter of the house without success. His breaking and entering should be avoided if possible. He was another machine man which had kept a low profile during his existence and wanted to continue such a profile. Nothing was as secure as staying beneath any radars of a world, but his sketchy life was becoming ever more pronounced. Necessity was a relentless and remorseless master.

His decision should be made as quickly as possible. He could easily tear off the pedestrian door to the attached two-car garage. Nobody would see him at that far part of such a heavily landscaped lot. But he was wandering within a wealthy neighborhood with many prominent people. Packs of police would arrive almost as fast as you could say Jack Robinson.

"Solly, are you sleeping upstairs or still staying down on the couch?" said Harriet Sage.

Harriet had already put on her pink night blinder. She had always been a light marital sleeper, but had found her sleep even more elusive without her mate. A wife wanted a husband to return to her solitary side. Any peaceful slumber could not be found without his presence. He had at least promised to stop drinking his beer and cognac.

Solomon should sleep with Harriet and not on a living room couch. Yet sleep had not seemed to bc a high priority for the astrophysicist over these passing days. He had tossed and turned to a point where she had earlier agreed to his downstairs exile. But she regretted her previous decision and hoped her mate was willing to accept a truce.

"Did you say something to me?" said Solomon.

He leaned out beyond an opened door of the master bathroom. Steady streams of water had been running loudly in the sink for his evening shave. Two handfuls of cooling fluid stuff were held to rinse his face.

"Yes, are you going to sleep in our bed tonight?"

"I'll talk to you in a minute."

"Famous last words."

Then Harriet adjusted her night blinder and turned over on her side. She did not see a stranger enter the bedroom. An intruder had walked up the stairs in complete silence.

Solomon did not hear any of her parting remark. Finally he shut off the water and looked in the mirror. His meeting with Adam Hanson had completely changed his outlook on the present situation. Answers must be available even when there appeared to be no solutions. Sets of confused equations in his life had often been suddenly salvaged by an overwhelming insight. Solomon hoped he could find the intellectual strength to solve such a saving.

He turned off the light and exited the bathroom, walking right into the outstretched left arm of a waiting Herbert T. Ross. Irresistible fingers grabbed Solomon by the throat. Clutching digits were beyond hard. They felt like a steel vise within a thin fleshy covering.

"Give me the Traveler," whispered Ross.

"I don't know what you mean," whispered Solomon in an equally low voice. He could barely speak with a hardened hand almost crushing his larynx. But he clearly recognized his attacker.

Herbert T. Ross was a more than dependable maintenance employee at the Jet Propulsion Laboratory. Usually a capable middle-aged man had been seen changing a fluorescent light bulb or fixing a secured door lock. Sage and Ross had exchanged nods over the years, but not much else. Their only known common bond was that they had both started work at the laboratory in the 1990s, although several years apart.

Now Ross became even more angered after such an answer. He lifted Solomon by the neck against the wall. The struggling scientist was suspended in space for a few moments. Strenuously sought breaths were reedy and needy.

"I read the daily emails to and from the Jet Propulsion Laboratory tonight, much as I do every night. You apologize profusely to Adam Hanson for your initial rudeness and also thank him for *lending you the astonishing device found in the White Mountains.*"

"You mean the star map?" gasped Sage.

"Do not play the scientific fool with me!" grimaced Ross.

"Who *are* you talking to?" said Harriet, sitting against the headboard with her blinder still on. Then she reached awkwardly to turn off the lamp on her nightstand. "Solly, just put your cellphone away and go to bed...okay!"

But Solomon could not speak anymore. His face had turned bright red with trapped blood and his eyelids fluttered. He was on the verge of passing out.

"My little lamb shall not yet be sacrificed," said Ross, throwing Solomon across the bedroom. The tossed man landed on the mattress with a resounding splash of springs. All anyone could hear for a moment was Harriet screaming.

Solomon held his wife as she quieted. Harriet was softly sobbing now. She thought this intruder must be a murderer or who knew what else. Nobody was safe anywhere anymore. Such a lack of security was just another sad fact about the pathetic state of the planet.

"I will order you again, give me the Intergalactic Traveler!"

"I don't—"

His response was not completed. Heavy fingers struck Solomon ever so slightly with an open hand slap. Harsh pain still reverberated through his skull. He knew a second strike would be much harder. Such a slap would be an end to his earthly existence.

"Wrong answer, now give me the Intergalactic Traveler. I will not ask again."

"I'm telling the truth. I don't have it."

Ross was ready to make a final strike when he saw a book on the nearer nightstand. A Hebrew Bible seemed to stare back at him, its bright gold Star of David embossed on the cover. An ageless star glimmered to him like the signpost to a long ago and faraway almost forgotten place.

"The Lord of Life," softly said Ross.

Still Solomon and Harriet clung to each other in the near dark of their bedroom. They watched as Ross was transfixed by their Bible. He knelt in front of that golden star like a desert wanderer who had found a lost oasis, staring at it with remembered reverence. Now he turned from the nightstand with saddened eyes.

"Forgiveness, I need forgiveness," said Ross.

Red lights from a pair of patrol cars suddenly swam against the front curtains of the master bedroom. Prompt police had arrived even faster than had been expected. Ross glanced at the lights and stared at Solomon and Harriet for several more seconds.

Then he quickly ran toward the nearest back window. He jumped through disintegrating glass without hesitation. Ross dropped a dozen feet to the terraced patio and raced through the yard. He hopped a five-foot-high fence and disappeared into a darkness of the night.

"Who was that man?" said Harriet, holding Solomon ever more tightly.

Blood was just beginning to return to ashen faces.

Solomon held the Bible from the nightstand. He looked at the golden star. "I don't know if he was a man, but I hope he finds forgiveness."

Man As Machine

"How were the sunny shores of California?" said Director Mitchell.

"I don't know what we've stumbled onto, but it's something that is very quickly going beyond me," said Adam. "What did Harold find out about the 2005 Chevy?"

"Not too much. His crew took the car apart piece by piece and found almost nothing unusual. One important difference was a slight radioactivity around the engine block, not enough to harm anybody but enough to be detected by our scintillator."

"How about the abandoned Chrysler found in the motel parking lot?"

"The Chrysler was owned by a corporation ultimately controlled by Lanicrim Industries."

"I never heard of it."

"I hadn't either. Charlie is trying to prepare a report on the entire group for us, but says there is not a lot of information available. I personally spoke to their head of security, a Mr. Erik Thax. He told me the Chrysler was stolen from a company parking garage in Los Angeles a week before this whole crazy episode started. Mr. Thax also told me the theft was the reason he was out in California. His office is in Manhattan at headquarters."

"I would bet no police report was filed about this supposedly stolen car until after this whole crazy episode started."

"You hit a nail directly on the head, and that's why I want you to speak to him face-to-face. Mr. Thax said he will return to New York City by the end of the week. You can give me your opinion of the guy when you return from interviewing him."

"I've got more news about the machine man found in the White Mountains, but it's news I don't really understand. I had the thing analyzed at Cal Tech as you instructed. Everyone involved has a very high security clearance, so we won't have to worry about any leaks. I guess these slides will have to mostly speak for themselves."

"Just fire away. Now I definitely plan to leave this job after the next presidential election. Our little world is just becoming curiouser and curiouser. I am going to spend the rest of my days working in a country garden back in Iowa."

Adam set up the projector and flicked off the overhead lights. Then he placed a color slide of a normal-looking man on the projector. The man was laid out on a large stainless-steel table.

"No record of this machine man exists that we know about, no name, no address, no nothing. If he had a wallet, it was probably lost somewhere in the mountains. We probably won't be able to trace him to a creator as there are obviously no fingerprints, no dental work, no scars or tattoos or other marks. I suppose we could post his face on the internet and see what turns up."

"I don't want to go public yet. Let's not let the lunch out of the bag until we're really hungry."

"Okay, let me show you what we've found out so far." Adam pointed to the first slide on the screen. He shook his head a few shakes before starting to speak.

Curiouser and curiouser were certainly the correct words to describe the situation.

"Any exterior of this machine man is completely synthetic, but you wouldn't know it unless you eyeballed it from about an inch away. There are no pores or real hair or, as I already said, no fingerprints. However, there do seem to be external nerve endings for a mild sense of touch and feeling, but we couldn't figure out how exactly these nerves function. They don't seem to be hooked into anything else but the false epidermis."

"Why would anybody build such a thing and give it any sense of feeling?"

"I'm not sure. Maybe this anybody didn't want the thing to completely become a machine. We've all read science fiction stories about a logical robot that goes berserk and turns on its maker. Or maybe a slight level of touch was needed for the thing to properly function."

"Go ahead."

"This second slide shows the internal sensory system necessary to detect overheating and severe damage, which we do not fully understand. The system is hooked up to an alloyed skeletal structure shown on the slide by a power relay system, which we also do not completely understand. We couldn't identify any of its alloys or its power source. Slight residual radioactivity was found around the bone joints, maybe similar to what was found on the engine of the crashed Chevy Cavalier."

"I can see we're going nowhere fast."

"The best is yet to come. This third slide shows three coordinators, or the black boxes for lack of a better term." Adam pointed to a trio of small black rectangles shown on the slide. None of these rectangles appeared to be connected to anything else.

"A first coordinator is located in the left hip and controls lower body movements. We're already very familiar with the running and jumping abilities of this thing. A second coordinator is located in the left shoulder and controls upper body movements. I guess the remains of Roberto Salina speak volumes about these capabilities. A third coordinator is located in the left side of the forehead and probably controls intellectual function. But as I stated before, we couldn't find any kind of power source which would run any of these three coordinators."

"Maybe a power source is inside the coordinators."

"That's exactly what the guys at Cal Tech thought, so they tried to take one apart. This turned out to be impossible, so they finally just bored a hole in the top with a diamond-carbide drill. They didn't see anything inside at first, so they put the hole under an electron microscope. Only a group of very tiny, irregular strings was in the coordinator and seemed to run the entire mechanism. Half of the scientists were elated and half of them were depressed."

"I don't get it."

"I didn't either, but then I got a brief lecture on string theory versus the standard model of physics. I don't want to know any more than what I already found out."

"What's left?"

"Our scariest part of all, let me show this last slide." Adam put a fourth slide in the projector. Then he just stood quietly for a moment, tapping his fingers on an edge of the table. His throat was cleared with a hard effort. "Living tissue is contained within the core of the artificial skull. Several parts of an adult brain much like our own were located there. Similar hippocampus and hypothalamus cells were identified, the centers of memory and basic reactions such as fear."

"Good Lord, somebody was killed to make this thing. But why would any parts of a living brain be needed?"

"All we could surmise is that the hippocampus provides a basic framework for such a machine to operate. In other words, memory tells us how to talk or open a door or walk down a road. If not for such a primary database previously prepared, programming becomes an incredibly complex project. Not that this mechanism isn't already complicated enough for me."

"What about the hypothalamus?"

"Here again is only speculation, but fear is a fantastic motivator. You can get almost anybody to do almost anything if they are fearful enough."

"Fearful of what?"

"Who knows? The number of fears is uncountable, from a fear of dogs to a fear of doorknobs. There are probably more potential fears than there are people."

Then the phone on the desk of the director rang as Adam switched on the lights.

"This is Mitchell...huh, huh...better hit the alarm." He pulled out his service Glock from a desk drawer. "We've got a big problem in the lobby, and it's probably coming upstairs."

Adam pulled out his own Glock from its shoulder holster. He and the director headed for the hallway. Intermittent whines of an alarm followed them toward the nearby stairwells.

* * *

Herbert T. Ross had entered the lobby of the building several minutes earlier. Security systems in the lobby were quickly scanned. Neither of a pair of primitive walk-through metal detectors would be able to sense his alloyed bones. But his weapon would be identified, even though its energy source was entombed in a leadlium casing. There was also no way to avoid those many security cameras. These cameras provided a live feed to a secure room in the building. Now any clean and easy acquisition of the Intergalactic Traveler could not be done.

Already Ross had searched the house of Adam Hanson in Fairfax. Insides of the home had been ripped to pieces without success. Insides of the car of the true man had also been searched without success. His vehicle had been parked in a secured garage. Two bureau garage attendants had to be killed to allow such a search to be completed. But what needed to be done would always be done.

Now only an obvious and simple truth remained. Hanson was probably hiding the Traveler somewhere at his office. Yet his office was tucked away in the headquarters building of the bureau. More than a few casualties would be caused by such an escapade.

Suddenly Ross lifted the nearer walk-through metal detector and tossed it upon the nearest guard. Immediately he shot another guard standing next to the other metal detector. His blazing laser gun burned a hole the size of a nickel through the chest of the man. Two remaining lobby guards drew their handguns. They hunkered down behind a nearby reception counter. Four elevators behind the lobby were quickly shut off. Two steel doors leading to adjoining stairwells were already locked.

Following resistance in the lobby was brief. The third guard was shot when he showed the top of his head to gain a better view of the situation. Then Ross jumped over the counter in a running leap, partly landing on the fourth guard with a more than heavy weight. Ross looked like an average man, but his synthetic body weighed more than three hundred pounds.

Repetitive whines of an alarm began to throb throughout the building.

This final lobby guard had been knocked into a temporary stupor. Ross knelt over the guard as he partially revived. Cold fingers clutched a warm throat.

"I need to know where the office of Adam Hanson is located," said Ross.

"I can't tell you," said the guard.

Casually Ross grabbed the nearer hand of the guard. He twisted off the little finger like it was only the top of an extremely narrow jar. Then a fleshy finger was tossed aside like an unused cigarette. The guard writhed in agony at such a savage assault.

"I need to know where the office of Adam Hanson is located," again said Ross.

An amazed guard groaned to catch his breath. Any acceptance of what had just happened could not yet be found. Streams of perspiration began to form on his face. Shock was seeping into his body.

Ross quickly grabbed the ring finger on the same hand.

"It's on the top floor," cried out the guard. "I don't know the office number."

"Thank you very much," said Ross. He grabbed the head of the guard in both hands, twisting the skull not quite as severely as the little finger. It was still a more than fatal force.

Now Ross raced toward the bank of elevators. He quickly saw that the elevators had been shut off. Up and down and floor light indicators had blinked out. Dual stairwells stayed as his only possible upward paths. Both steel doors looked like hardened reflected twins.

The locked steel door to the nearer stairwell was ripped away. But it still half hung within a sturdy frame as a wavering watcher. Ross raced up nine flights of stairs like a machine man on a mission. He reached the top floor in a third of a minute.

Adam and the director and nine other agents were waiting for him. They poured a barrage of gunfire at Ross as a tenth floor door was torn off. Ross used the steel door as a heavy metal shield, most of a barrage of many bullets avoided. His odds were also quickly bettered by shooting two of the agents; a male agent fell with a wound through his neck, a female agent fell with a wound through her shoulder.

How the battle for survival continued to rage.

"I know what this thing probably wants," yelled Adam, pointing to the star map retrieved from a pocket.

The map had been buried in a small plastic baggie within a large potted office plant. This device had been hidden after Dr. Sage had warned Adam about the attack at his bedroom. The Intergalactic Traveler had to be more than wanted. It had to be sorely needed.

"What is it?" yelled the director.

"It's a kind of cosmic map that must be very important to somebody or something."

"Then let's go to the roof so this thing can't get it. An army helicopter has already been notified of the intruder, so we might be able to save the map up there."

Three more of the agents had already been killed by Ross, a toasted trio falling with a variety of wounds. Several hallway security mirrors were being used to bounce beams of laser light onto the agents. Polished mirrors made a deadly game of blinding billiards.

Adam and the director ran toward the maintenance stairs to the roof. Ross watched their retreat, but could not yet follow. Four more agents were still in his way. None of these agents would hinder his quest very much longer.

The broad roof of the building was not completely barren. There was a large concrete block hut which protected the top of the maintenance stairs. Here were also two small metal enclosures holding ventilation compressors. These outcroppings were only three tiny hills on an otherwise flat asphalt plain. A man-made trio roughly formed a large isosceles triangle.

"Let's get him in a crossfire!" said the director.

"Aim for his three coordinators!" said Adam.

Then Adam ran to the far compressor while the director ran to the near compressor. True men waited for a machine man to race up a set of steep maintenance stairs. They also waited for an army helicopter to fly out of a mass of deep billowing clouds.

Herbert T. Ross did not disappoint either of these adversaries for very long. He had blasted his way through any remaining agents with a relative ease. Many killed and wounded stayed behind as a trail of human wreckage. Ross had been hit by at least a dozen of their nine-millimeter bullets, but any impacts seemed to have no significant effect on him.

Soon Ross bounded up that last set of stairs like a determined lion. Then the heavy door to the roof was smashed apart. Adam and the director started firing at Ross as the door was put to pieces. But only a few of their bullets had found their marks. Ross moved like an incredibly fast jackrabbit. It was almost an impossible task to get a clean shot at him.

Only the director was attacked during Ross' brief jagged run. Ross raced toward the near compressor without hesitation. He hopped upon the metal enclosure like something which would never be stopped. Director Mitchell was quickly shot once in the upper abdomen. His gun was dropped as he collapsed on the rooftop and stoically awaited a final fate.

A machine man stood over a true man like a haughty hunter stands over a dying prey. An old trophy in the hand could still be a valuable commodity. Such a prized specimen should not be immediately killed. Pretense of a trade could end almost any present situation.

"Hanson, I've got your pal!" hollered Ross. "Now give me the Intergalactic Traveler!"

Adam put a second clip into his Glock. His first clip had been emptied with possibly a single hit. He had noticed that Ross had only shot at the director. Evidently there was a concern that a blast might hit the Traveler. Such a concern could be used to an advantage.

Now Ross pulled the director to the top of the compressor enclosure. Director Mitchell was slumped headfirst over the metal top. Ross pointed the laser at the back of the skull of a dying man, its bright circle of light staying fixed just above the top of his spine.

"I would give that Traveler to me mighty quick, unless you want to see your friend with a large hole through his brain!"

"I'll shoot the Traveler if you shoot him!"

"Go ahead and shoot it with your puny weapon. You'll be in for quite a surprise!"

But Adam did not really want to shoot at the star map. Such a map was a most incredible device. He also thought the last statement by Ross was not a bluff. Nine-millimeter bullets would probably not have any significant effect on the dark prism. Same small-caliber bullets did not seem to be having much effect on Ross.

Sudden sounds of a rapidly approaching helicopter were heard, an Apache gunship looming behind Ross like a big bird of prey. A machine man was much too preoccupied with getting the Traveler to notice much of anything else, a star map becoming an unholy grail.

The thirty-millimeter cannon of the helicopter swiveled between its front landing gear like an ominous arm. Descriptions of the intrusion and the intruder had already been clearly communicated to the gunship. He was an intruder ready to be terminated at an earliest opportunity. Such a chance was near at hand.

"Okay, you win. I'll trade the Intergalactic Traveler for the director!"

"Just put your gun on top of the compressor and slide the Traveler to me!"

Adam placed his Glock on top of the compressor. He removed the Traveler from his shirt pocket. Then he purposely slid the Traveler beyond a reach of Ross. Such a smooth device seemed to have almost no kinetic friction, sliding on and on upon the rooftop like a hockey puck along an ice rink. Finally it stopped against the low perimeter wall of the roof.

Ross had walked toward the perimeter wall when the gunship began to fire at him. Bursts of thirty-millimeter bullets blazed down upon him. Many of the large-caliber bullets found their marks, ripping Ross to staggering pieces of what had been. This nearly destroyed machine man picked up the Traveler as he stumbled to his knees. He arose to his feet with a grimace as his laser gun was dropped near the wall.

Now Ross struggled in a ragged circle with the Traveler in hand. He looked at a body reduced to synthetic ashes, a few final words hollered. "Armageddon awaits!"

Then he fell beyond the low-perimeter roof wall toward the sidewalk far below.

Adam ran over to the wounded director. He gently lifted the man off the compressor and set him on the roof with care. A laser blast had gone completely through his body, an angry tiny tunnel seared through thick pale flesh. His severely blackened wound had been partially cauterized by the heat.

"Hold on, boss, help has almost arrived."

Soon a medical helicopter was landing on the rooftop pad. Swirling rotors began to slow to a stop as two doctors and two stretcher-bearers hopped out of a wide open doorway. The quartet ran toward the wounded director like a whitened mass on a mission.

Director Mitchell looked at Adam with fading eyes, coughing several bloody coughs. "We sure stepped through the looking glass on this one." Then he grimaced and fainted away.

* * *

"It's only me," said Angelina as she unlocked the front door to the house of Rachel Herr. Angelina saw her mother sitting in a favorite reclining chair. Rachel was looking ever more tired. No child expected any parent to become so old, so quickly.

"Hi, Mom."

"You must have booked an earlier morning plane from Los Angeles than expected."

"I got on a seven o'clock flight, but not by much." Angelina glanced at a package on the coffee table. "I can see you received your present from Adam."

"You won't believe it, but an armed special courier arrived early this morning. I was almost afraid to open the door. It was so very official."

"Didn't Consuela answer the doorbell?"

"No, she's staying home for the rest of the week. Her husband badly sprained his ankle."

"I hope he's okay."

"I'm sure he will be. You know the way Consuela dotes on him."

"Consuela dotes on everybody. She is one of the most compassionate people I have ever met."

"The woman is aptly named. Consuela does mean *consolation* in Spanish."

"I suppose that takes care of my lesson for the word of today. I can also see that Adam was true to his word of the other day. He told me an artifact would be sent to you."

"Do you have any idea what it is? There was only a note asking for both of our opinions."

"I don't have a clue. Adam only texted that he was sending it to his favorite geologist."

"Your fiancé is a real sweetheart."

"Yes, but he is a sweetheart I rarely see." Her words had been stated with a growing resignation. A slight frown was added as an afterthought.

"Adam must be the man for you. I can see that he is driving you crazy even when you're not within a thousand miles of him. Your dad had exactly the same effect on me."

"That's probably one of the reasons why I like Adam so much. He reminds me of Dad so much. Both of them put their job before most everything else. They're like bulls in an arena, head down and full speed ahead."

"I don't know about Adam, but your father sounds just like what you described. But I have no regrets."

"*You* don't, but how about *me*?"

"You are the fortune-teller in the family. All I will say is that when I met your father in college, east Texas and west Pennsylvania merged. We only had twenty years together, but that was better than no years, and you were the result of our relationship. I can't be sad about anything when I can still remember him and still see you. I hope you and Adam have many more years than we did."

"We'll see what happens. What else can I say about a guy who sends a special courier to his future mother-in-law instead of his future wife."

"Now that you're here, let's take a look at what he sent." Rachel slowly opened the small package. She tore past fragile paper into a thick box. Several dozen packing pellets fell onto the floor. Plastic chunks struck the carpet with only a silent sound.

"I'll get them," said Angelina. She dropped to her hands and knees, gathering the scattered plastic chunks. Then she heard her mother gasp.

"Look at this!" said Rachel.

She held up a magnificent choker made of perfect light-green rectangular stones. A dark image was grimly held at its center, an ancient glimmer of things wondrous and taboo in a black ∞ symbol. It looked like that symbol had always existed.

"This symbol is very well known as a mathematical sign for infinity," said Angelina. "It probably means eternal, or maybe *forever*, in such a cultural context."

"Such a symbol is the same kind of symbol your father found years ago at a pair of archeological sites. He was convinced there was a connection between the two sites, but his colleagues thought he had spent more than a few too many afternoons under a blazing sun."

"You mean Chaco Canyon and Puma Punku?"

"Those sound like the places, but you should read his daily diary for such details."

"I didn't even know Dad had a diary. But I've already read everything he ever had published or had prepared and was waiting to have published."

"Your father wrote entries in his diary that he would never write anywhere else. They included his secret ideas and dreams, his deepest fears and affections. I suppose most people have to write such stuff at certain points in a life."

"Why haven't I ever heard anything about his diary?"

"It's my fault you didn't know about the diary. Specific intimate details of our marriage are included which I didn't want anybody to know but ourselves. I'll loan you the diary if you promise to be a nice girl and respect our privacy. Every couple has its secrets."

"I promise to quickly skip over any racy parts."

"Let's take a look at these stones."

"The stones look like jade to me."

"They're definitely not jade. Please get my monocular in the top drawer of the credenza."

Angelina went to a nearby credenza to retrieve the monocular. She at first thought the monocular was not in that particular drawer, but the magnifier had only been pushed to the back of that drawer. Such a nearly hidden location was probably due to a lack of recent use. A daughter handed a magnifier to a mother.

"They're not a light-green turquoise either." Rachel started to rotate various stones under the magnifier. She continued to view ever more of the rectangular stones. "I'd say…what we have here…is a type of stone similar to the Scarab Beetle found as the centerpiece in Pharaoh Tutankhamen's burial necklace."

"I know about the burial necklace of the Boy King, but you will have to enlighten me as to the stone of the centerpiece."

"We all know the story of the discovery of Tutankhamen's tomb in the Valley of the Kings. But unlike you, most people do not know that a very ornate necklace was among the many treasures found there. What more than most people also do not know is that for more than seventy-five years, from 1922 to 1999, the carved light-green beetle in the center of that necklace was thought to be made from a chunk of chalcedony, a type of crystalline quartz."

"I remember now, the beetle was a sacred embodiment of the Egyptian God Khepri."

"Yes, but the discovery which interested a geologist like me the most was that the beetle was not carved from chalcedony. This beetle was made from desert sand fused into green glass by a large meteorite. A long-ago meteorite had crashed in an area later named the Great Sand Sea in western Egypt. An impact site had finally been located near the Libyan border, and other ancient glass found there matched that from which the sacred Scarab Beetle had been carved."

"You're saying the stones from this choker were also formed by a meteorite?"

"That's what they look like to me."

"How old do you think these stones could be?"

"I don't have any idea, but the crash of the meteorite in the Great Sand Sea was found to have happened about twenty-eight million years ago. Any cataclysm which formed the stones of this choker probably happened millions, or even billions, of years ago."

"What about this symbol, it looks like obsidian."

"No, it's not anything I have ever seen before."

Rachel began to rotate the choker under the magnifier, but a strange feeling emanated from that dark symbol as it brushed her cheekbone. Then a terrible darkness suddenly reached out for her. The choker dropped to the carpet.

Angelina saw an abrupt change in her mother. She grabbed for Rachel as the older woman slumped forward. Now she steadied her and reached for the telephone on the coffee table.

"You don't have to call for help. I'll be okay, just keep that monstrosity away from me."

Good and Evil

Adam drove the rental car upon the rough dirt of a remnant of a road. Angelina sat next to him in the red Camaro. Together they watched the slowly passing scenery of Chaco Canyon, a sprawling place of past settlement which had been abandoned centuries ago. Dazed dust settled behind them like specks of an almost gone reality. Airy drops of earth fell as almost forgotten tears. A once bountiful canyon had dried to now deserted desert.

Angelina had read the diary of her father with care and affection. She was amazed at what he had discovered years earlier at Chaco Canyon and Puma Punku. Yet she wondered if these were only musings of a man intent on proving his own theories. Available proof was in the field as far as she was concerned. Adam had accompanied her with his own care and affection.

"Are you sure this road really goes anywhere…and I'm using the word *road* very loosely," said Adam.

"Just keep on going, hundreds of miles of roads used to lead to this canyon," said Angelina. "People traveled from very long distances for the ritual and trade activities here. The canyon was a sacred ceremonial and economic center with fifteen major complexes, as high as five stories with hundreds of rooms."

"What happened?"

"We think the rain stopped."

"Stopping sounds like something we should think about doing. It looks like we are quickly going into the middle of a nowhere."

"My father's diary was very clear. Follow the canyon past Sundagger Butte, which must be Fajada Butte. Then he wrote: '*The symbol shows itself north at noon and never soon, south and east and west are never best.*'"

"Your father was quite a poet."

"Not really. He quoted from an elderly Navajo man who told him a story about a god that fell to earth somewhere near the canyon. The Anasazi who first settled this area, *the people of long ago*, had no written language but supposedly developed a strong bonding with the sky. Navajo and Hopi and Ute peoples only have tales of what might have been."

"Do you believe their stories?"

"I suppose they are like most ancient stories, half true and half not so true. Words often cannot accurately describe what a people see or hear or feel, and then a story becomes a bit distorted with each generation. Any telling of words is not an easy way of conveying, often over many centuries, a perfect picture of a happening."

"It's twelve minutes until noon." Adam parked the car on the north side of the following high butte.

Somehow this butte looked unnatural to him. Shimmering rocks still seemed to be baking in an ever-hotter August sun. Air-conditioning had to be one of the greatest inventions of the human kind as far as he was concerned.

"I have a strong feeling we will find something important."

"Your mother had told me that you were a fortune-teller."

"She probably didn't tell you how I got my reputation."

"No, she didn't give me any of the details."

"When I was seven years old, I saw one of those old werewolf movies from the forties. I think Lon Chaney Jr. was in it. The movie nearly scared my Little Mermaid underwear off, but an old gypsy woman was in the film who absolutely enthralled me. In any event, my mother put together a Halloween fortune-teller costume for me. My outfit included a wide skirt and a blouse with stars and moons sewed on it. There was also a scarf for my head and even a little crystal ball. I told a lot of fortunes for a couple of months after donning those clothes. The neighbor kids had to fork over a whole dime to see their futures before I gave it up."

"You sound normal to me. I guess you slowly but surely got tired of it."

"No, I just suddenly stopped one day."

"Why?"

Angelina bit her lip hard. She winced and tasted a bit of blood. "I told my father's fortune. It was the Christmas just before he left on his last of many expeditions. I blurted out that he would never return home again. I cried my words from the blue, and you would never guess in a million years what he said to me."

Now Adam could only shrug. Already he regretted bringing the topic of fortune-telling into their conversation. "You don't have to tell me."

"I want to tell you. I don't know why, but I finally need to tell somebody." Then she hesitated a few more seconds before continuing to speak. "My father said it did not matter if he never returned home again. Dad told me that he would always be with me no matter what happened, and he would love me and my mother beyond the end of time."

"Do you want to say what happened to him?"

"He died in the mountains of western Bolivia at a site named Puma Punku. He was working on an excavation near the Kalasasaya Wall of Heads. Several of his laborers found him early one morning not far from the wall. He was torn apart."

Adam was stunned by such an explanation. He wondered if there was a connection between the death of Angelina's father and the thing found in the White Mountains.

"Do you know what killed him?"

"Not really, but the Bolivian authorities reported it might have been a puma."

"You mean a mountain lion?"

"Puma or cougar or mountain lion, they're all the same. Puma Punku does translate to *Door of the Puma.*"

"It doesn't sound like they really had any idea what happened to him."

"I guess it doesn't matter. My father would not have fought back. He would have never tried to defend himself no matter what attacked him."

"Why do you say that he wouldn't defend himself? Anyone would fight if their life was in the balance."

"My father would never have done any such defense. He was raised by Quakers in western Pennsylvania and believed all of life was to be treasured, essentially worshipped. His belief was probably reinforced by many travels to archeological sites around the world.

"He had seen the evidence of a hard journey of humanity, the butchery and burning of a lengthy caravan of centuries. He had also seen the evidence of science and art advancing, a reach of human thought ever greater. I suppose he always wanted to help the former perish and the latter prosper."

"It sounds like he realized humanity has always been good and evil."

"We are a species which can annihilate a Carthage and organize a holocaust, yet also create the Lascaux cave paintings and construct the Enterprise Space Shuttle. Somebody a lot smarter than I am will have to figure out such contradictions."

"Only two minutes until noon."

"By the way, how is your boss doing?"

"He's still in and out of a coma, lost a left kidney and a few other parts of him. I spoke to the doctors at Bethesda when I returned from Manhattan. They told me he will pull through."

"I hope everything turns out okay."

"I do, too. Director Mitchell is one of the few men in my line of work who can be more than trusted, and trust can often be almost everything in this life." Then Adam turned off the ignition and exited the Camaro.

Angelina retrieved the light-green choker from the glove compartment. She also left the car and stood next to Adam, glancing at the dark symbol. A hopeful couple quietly watched the north face of the butte for a similar sign.

There was a sudden crystal-clear moment made by a high noon sun. Here was a small rocky alcove with perpendicular walls which reached toward the sky. Flickers of a petroglyph showed far up a face of the cliff. The symbol ∞ stayed for only a handful of seconds. Such a secret symbol quickly faded as the now slightly falling sun pulled its rays beyond that perfect clutch of a craggy cliff. Then there was nothing but a barren breadth of stone.

* * *

Adam and Angelina stood at the ragged north cliff of the butte. Adam looked for any kind of a way to ascend any part of the steep cliff. He did not think anyone would ever try to trek up such a perpendicular precipice except maybe a world-class rock climber or an energetic religious zealot. Angelina held the choker in her hand with more than a vague apprehension. She glanced at the symbol of forever and waited for something else to happen.

"Where did you get that choker?" suddenly asked a soft but steady voice.

The couple turned to their right to see a thin fissure in the rock. They had not noticed any such opening before, but there it was anyway. Here was a very old man swathed in a pure-white robe which covered most of his head and all of his body. He looked like a Bedouin of the surrounding buttes and canyons.

Now a confused couple stood almost completely stunned. Their supposed speeches had become speechless. The figure of a man had just seemed suddenly to materialize at an opening which had also seemed to suddenly materialize. This elderly looking man wore a green choker similar to the choker held by Angelina. But a same symbol on this choker looked like bright diamond instead of dark obsidian. Yet a vibrant symbol still shimmered with secrets.

"And you might be?" said Angelina. She did not understand what this man was doing near a secluded stony butte. But she did sense that something about this rocky tower seemed very unusual.

"I *might* be anything, but I *am* and have always been Aurelius, a guardian of forever, a disciple of the Lord of Life."

"And how did you arrive in this middle of a nowhere?" asked Adam. He did not see any other cars or trucks anywhere in sight. Only a completely barren terrain spread out around them. This entire situation was becoming curiouser and curiouser. A stranger seemed more than delusional.

"I fell to your earth after battling Sargon, a fanatic follower of the Prince of Death. The struggle between good and evil had reached an involuntary pause in our eternal conflict."

"You're speaking of God and the Devil?" asked Angelina.

"Name them as you want," answered Aurelius. "I have pursued Sargon since the beginning of this cycle of Time. We finally fought near the dark side of your moon before mortally wounding our starships. I arrived at this place as recorded on the stone petroglyph more than two thousand of your years ago."

Adam could only shake his head in disbelief. His entire case was going far beyond his acceptance of reality. Angelina had become a more accepting student. Mention of the famed petroglyph had piqued her interest.

"You mean the famous petroglyph of a bright star near our crescent moon with the handprint is a representation of your landing here?" said Angelina.

"Probably the petroglyph is a representation of my starship exploding and vaporizing. I know the belief today is that the petroglyph is a symbol of the 1054 AD supernova which formed the Crab Nebula, but I was here more than a thousand years before that date."

"Why would you stay in such an isolated location?" asked Adam. Any tone of his voice was extremely skeptical. A limit had been reached as to what his brain would readily absorb.

"Where should I go? The small shuttle within which I had escaped was all that remained. But this shuttle is not powerful enough to completely escape the gravity of your planet."

"What happened to your adversary, this follower of the Prince of Death?" said Angelina.

Diary entries of her father had so far been far beyond correct. Finally his prophetic words were being heard by her. She had been deaf to them for too many years.

"Both of us plummeted toward your planet at different locations. Sargon's large shuttle was intact when I last saw it spiraling down. Perhaps it was destroyed, but perhaps it was salvaged. Sargon and his trio of slaves might have survived."

"I thought slavery was a vice of the past," said Adam. "Even our western world outlawed it more than a hundred and fifty years ago."

"Others will always try to enslave others, such is the way of existence," said Aurelius. "This triumvirate of Sargon's slaves are enslaved in both body and mind. The choker you hold once held the neck of one of those slaves. Their choices are rarely their own. Sometimes a border of the nearly good cannot avoid crossing into a country of the absolute evil. No return can be made from such a passage."

"Maybe your sought Sargon could already have escaped to someplace else," said Angelina.

"I do not think so. Your technology has only recently advanced to a sufficient level to aid him. These last decades of human thought have probably brought him to the brink of an escape. Your knowledge will provide the eventual means for an end to his earthly stay."

"Why couldn't this Sargon use his own technology to escape?" asked Adam. His complete lack of belief was evident in the tenor of his question. Any spoken words were more than telling.

"For the same reason I cannot. If your plane crashed among a tribe of hunters and gatherers in New Guinea, you would have no materials to repair or construct a plane. You would be stranded, looking to the skies like a member of a Cargo Cult."

"I guess it makes sense," said Angelina. Many memories of her father had become too strong within her. She could not seem to remove his influence from her orbit. Now she thought any eclipse of a reputation would only be a passing shadow.

"I don't believe any of your story," said Adam. Such a tale sounded like a crazy concoction created by a man who had lived too many years by himself. Desert sun could desiccate a brain as much as a body. Adam had begun to think that his own mind was already partly gone.

Angelina found herself ever more readily believing Aurelius. A daughter was finding the buried beliefs of a father. Somehow his voice was so clearly heard after so many years.

Aurelius sensed their differing reactions were sowing the seed of conflict. He motioned for them to follow into the narrow gap in the stone. "Let us ascend together," finally said the elderly figure of a man.

Adam and Angelina followed like children behind their father to waiting stairs. Those winding stairs were more rocks than steps. Up and up and up, these rocks did take them. Adam stopped counting any of the steps after a hundred. After more minutes, a partly trudging trio reached a crater at the top of the wide butte. There was a small oasis in a large desert before them. Here was a secret paradise which glimmered with a basic beauty.

"Welcome to my secret Eden," said Aurelius.

A spring-fed waterfall on the north side of the crater fell to a clear pool; a little pueblo was tucked under a layered ledge on the south side; chinquapin oak and western catalpa and other territorial types of trees ringed a reddened perimeter; colorful shrubs and ferns and flowers speckled much of any remaining ground. And a strange tingle of tension was in the air.

The trio of beings entered the pueblo of stucco fieldstones and shown timbers. Pieces of rough furniture were scattered around: a circular table made of planks held the center of the room; low chairs were close to that table like moons near a planet, but no bed or other creature comforts could be seen. An isolated monastic life was being lived upon a very high butte.

Angelina was somewhat stunned by the simple splendor of the place. Adam remained ever more on guard, as if both of them were being slowly led into a bizarre trap. His law enforcement experiences had made him more than wary.

"And are you still a doubter?" said Aurelius, staring directly at Adam. His unique grey eyes seemed to look right through a person. They were a pair of steel ellipses.

Adam said nothing, but his demeanor told everything.

"What is your full name?" said Aurelius. He continued to look at Adam with those piercing eyes. Yet he was not angered or even mildly upset.

"Adam Hadrian Hanson." Now Adam expected a cheap parlor trick, a staged event similar to a reading of tarot cards. There would be a generalized introduction of a person, followed by a summary of the mundane. Significant details would be sadly lacking.

"Adam Hadrian Hanson..." repeated Aurelius. He stayed motionless for several seconds in the shade as if retrieving data from an internal supercomputer. Then a steady stream of information flowed from his lips like remembered secrets. "You were born and raised in Syracuse, New York. Your father was a tort attorney and your mother a school librarian. Your first name was taken from your father's father, your middle name from your mother's affection for the Roman philosopher kings. You were the valedictorian of your high school class and attended the University of Pittsburgh on a full scholarship to study foreign languages. Your German and Russian are excellent, your Arabic and Mandarin are very good. You initially joined the Bureau as a translator..."

"Stop!" said Adam.

"But transferred to covert operations after your parents were killed in the World Trade Center attacks. Your father was in the north tower to sign off on a final settlement with an insurance company for an automobile accident. Your mother had accompanied him as they were going to have lunch at the Windows on the World. They had planned to spend several more days in New York City on a short vacation..."

"Please, stop."

"You successfully completed the ordered assassination of Heinrich Bauer in Rostov. You successfully completed the ordered destruction of an arms cache in the Beqaa Valley. You successfully completed the ordered assassination of the Abou brothers in Baghdad. Even your own brother has..."

"*Please...*"

Now Aurelius ceased his brief recital of a life.

Adam silently shook his head back and forth with shakes of resignation. More than a few images of his father and mother and brother wafted about in his mind. It was often much too difficult to be a human being.

But Angelina also stood in silence, having learned more about Adam in these past few minutes than she could have imagined. She was aware her fiancé had a dangerous role at the bureau, but she was not aware he had been cast as a danger to others. Ordered assassinations were as far removed from her world as a distant star.

"Let us speak of kinder things," said Aurelius.

* * *

Time went by unseen. Seconds became minutes which accumulated into hours. Hours became invisible vapors which disappeared to an unknown place. Adam and Angelina told what was known to an ancient man. Aurelius told what could be known by men and women and their kind. Finally a talking trio tired the sun. Several hours earlier its fiery orb had slowly disappeared behind a far horizon.

"You must stay the night, an hour is late and a journey long," said Aurelius.

"It's almost midnight, neither of us wants to drive now," said Angelina.

"You realize the choker brought here must be annihilated," said Aurelius.

"Why would we want to destroy the choker?" said Adam. "It looks like a valuable artifact."

"Too much pain and suffering have been wrought by such a choker," said Aurelius. "Neither of you nor any other human being can imagine the eons of torment caused by such a symbol."

"These stones and symbol look almost exactly like your choker," said Angelina.

"Yes, these stones are identical, formed in the same fire of the first Armageddon," said Aurelius. "But our symbols are fraternal twins with very different masters."

Adam and Angelina looked at the deep grey eyes of Aurelius. Now those eyes appeared as if they could burn down a mountain. Fiery ellipses were fueled by their own inside devotion.

"Then you must do what is best," said Adam.

"Yes, I can understand your need," said Angelina, handing the choker to Aurelius. She recalled much too well what had happened when the dark symbol had touched her mother's face. "And I hope you will understand my need for sleep."

The dismayed woman started for the distant corner of the pueblo. Angelina wanted to maintain a temporary distance from Adam. How she did hope her silent plea for privacy would be respected.

"I would like you to leave with me and Angelina as early as possible tomorrow," said Adam. "I want you to meet a Dr. Sage in Los Angeles. He is a scientist far more knowledgeable about certain topics than I could ever be."

"I will let you know of my decision in the morning. I must have a vision from the stars before a choice is made."

"Fair enough."

The young man watched the ancient man leave the open doorway of the pueblo. Adam saw Aurelius walk to the other side of the broad pool. Then the white-robed figure knelt and reverently reached for a night sky. Adam thought he might be watching a ritual far older than humanity.

Aurelius held the choker to a midnight moon. Words wafted as if caught in a rhythmic chant. Sentences went on and on with a simple sincerity. An eerily wrought whirlwind formed in these outstretched hands, a doomed choker swept into that whirling wind. Green stones and dark symbol steadily disappeared in a swirl of dust.

"Ashes to ashes," muttered Adam, staring in wonder for a moment more. Now he was almost completely caught by a looking glass world. Another existence was waiting for him.

Adam walked toward Angelina at the far corner of the pueblo. He could see she was anxious when near him. Yet he wanted to tell her an almost entire truth about himself. The desperate young man was fearful his true love was not seeing the true man.

He sat next to her, but did not try to touch her. His words were soft, unlike the burdens they carried. His heart was being crushed.

"So you realize I have been living another life, that I have taken other lives. I would have told you about myself, but then I would have seen my Angelina as you now look."

"I suppose naivety should be my middle name."

"I was once like you, but the senseless deaths of my parents changed me. My father and mother were looking forward to their retirements. Now I retire the kind of people who took them from me."

"*Retire*...is that what you call it! You hunt people down and kill them, and it sounds to me like you have been very skilled at your profession."

"I never killed anyone who had not killed scores of innocents. I never harmed anybody who had not harmed many others."

"Yes, but their end is the same. They're *dead*!"

"You cannot compare what I do to what terrorists and arms smugglers accomplish."

"Why not? A terrorist to one country is a freedom fighter to another country. An arms smuggler to one country is a loyal supporter to another country. An instigator can also be a patriot. A vicious saboteur can also be a devoted revolutionary."

"You are becoming too involved in wordplay. Both good and evil exist in our world. A security guard cannot be honestly compared to a street enforcer. A skilled soldier cannot be compared to a serial killer. If such comparisons are ever accepted, then nothing will have any real moral meaning. Any ethical value of any life would be gone."

"I just don't understand how anybody can deliberately kill anything else. It's just not a part of my personal philosophy. Perhaps I have been too sheltered."

Adam touched Angelina very softly. He lightly held her hands with his hands. But she pulled away from him. Her body slightly trembled with its own doubt.

"That's okay, I need to hide from the rain."

* * *

Solomon Sage was back on his back on the leather living room couch. He and Harriet had again agreed to his downstairs banishment. Their frightening incident of an alien intruder had left his wife a temporary emotional wreck. Now she cared for her wreckage with an ample supply of sleeping pills. She wandered into any such forced sleep with a blinder always off and a lamp upon each nightstand always on.

Such perpetual bedroom brightness was too much for Solomon. An anxious astrophysicist still tossed and turned on brown-colored leather in semidarkness. A dozing man would only take an intermittent nap for a half of an hour or so. Then he would awake for a roughly equivalent period. He wondered how such a continuing lack of deep sleep would finally affect him. More than sudden wonder was within him now.

Solomon abruptly sat completely upright on the couch. He had just dreamed the most wonderful sleepy vision. An ancient man glided down from a mountaintop to speak to him, looking like he was as old as a universe. There was a flowing white robe which appeared to be everywhere. Here was also a voice which seemed to echo from anywhere. It held a purity which was difficult to explain.

"Do not despair, I will be with you," said the voice.

"What do you want of me?" said Solomon.

"To be what you have always been, a devout and dedicated man."

"For what purpose?"

"To preserve good, to make an effort to destroy evil. These tasks should be the purpose of each and every life. Those goals should become the philosophy of anything and everything which has ever existed."

Then an ageless white robe began to shimmer away into nothingness. Any remaining whiteness glimmered for a moment and was gone. Grateful relief suddenly prospered within Solomon Sage, his fears wafting away like forgotten secrets. Failing fears had been exiled to a deep darkness which was no longer held within himself.

THE RIVER OF LIFE

The morning sun rose beyond a rim of this earth like it would always exist. Radiant rays flowed over the east wall of the crater as lovely light. Waters of a clear pool shimmered with their early touches of brightness. Oak and catalpa and other territorial types of leaves waved in a slight breeze. Shrubs and ferns and flowers gratefully held their ground. An oasis of living was being temporarily left behind.

Adam had awakened before Angelina. She had resisted his holding of her, but Adam had silently persisted. Angelina had somewhat relented to his advance. Yet she had not completely allowed a distance between them to be closed. It was a growing gap.

Now Aurelius was arising from a kneeling position. The white-robed figure rose from the ground like nothing could ever keep it down. This whiteness glided back toward the pueblo.

"I have decided to go with you on your journey," said Aurelius.

"I am pleased to hear of your decision," said Adam.

"Those nearby stars spoke last night and told me to leave. These vaporous beings warned that this cycle of Time is ending for your universe, but far too quickly."

"And that is why you must speak with Dr. Sage."

"I will, if you will allow me to drive to Los Angeles."

"I don't plan to drive anywhere except to Albuquerque and book a flight for us. It's almost 800 miles to Los Angeles."

"It is a 787-mile drive, but otherwise there would be a three-hour drive back to Albuquerque, plus at least a two-hour wait for a plane, plus an hour-and-a-half flight to LAX, plus another hour and a half to rent a car and drive to see Dr. Sage, or a total of eight hours."

"And?"

"And I can drive us there in half of those hours."

"Drive with what, a jet motorcycle?"

"I took the liberty to make several minor adjustments to the internal combustion engine of your Camaro."

"When did you make these changes?"

"While you slept."

"And?"

"And you and Angelina are not familiar with the effects of such unusual adjustments to properly drive the car. I would therefore advise you to allow me to be the driver. You will quickly realize there is no better choice."

"This does not sound like a sensible idea to me. We can spare a few extra hours."

"Then let me be blunt. I do not have any form of identification which would allow me to board a commercial airplane."

"Now *that* is something I can understand. I suppose we will have to drive the entire way."

"Then you must still allow me to be the driver."

"It's fine with me," said Angelina. She had walked from the pueblo without Adam seeing her approach. "I can accept almost anything now."

Adam shrugged with his own resignation. Not many situations were more frustrating than loving a woman who did not agree with you. "Then we should be getting ready to leave."

"Please give me a moment," said Aurelius.

The white robe glided to a cleft in the perimeter wall of the crater. There was a broad view of the surrounding canyon and mesas and buttes from a wide opening. Here also was a near start of the rocky steps of the stairs.

Aurelius spread his arms as if to embrace an entire cosmos. "Once the river of life flowed in the canyon," said Aurelius. "This vibrant river watched a people striving to be and build and prosper. Their many kivas sang with songs and laments. Their great houses celebrated joys and mourned sorrows. Their hundreds of rooms laughed and wept. Their constructed creations echoed with a splendid labyrinth of living. But the river went to another place in another Time. Perhaps it will again return to this place."

Now Aurelius stood at a very edge of the butte. The white robe reached to a cloudless sky. This whiteness looked upon the large canyon with its steep cliffs and broken arroyos. Any surrounding close land and many surrounding distant stars still spoke to that pure white.

"Adios," softly said Aurelius.

* * *

The Mojave Desert spread out far and wide around Interstate 40. Four lanes of highway flowed across the nearly deserted landscape like a tarred river of moving life. Sand and scrubland held fast and firm as shores of a pretended river. Not much else was staying in the vicinity except an occasional snake and an even more occasional tortoise.

Two Arizona state troopers sat in their Ford Interceptor and awaited an end to another shift. Joe and Larry worked midnight to eight in a morning and were more than content with their hours. Both of the troopers were hardened veterans of the force with more than forty years of service between them. These men had seen the worst of the human condition spread over those years. They had learned to embrace a night as so many nights had passed.

This part of a nightly nation had a speed limit of seventy-five miles per hour. But a broad expanse of a desolate desert seemed to bring out the fast side of humanity. Too many drivers sought this section of an interstate as just a very lengthy drag strip.

These troopers had lost count of how many speeding tickets had been written during their careers. They had once kept a tally on a bulletin board in the office of their captain. But then an investigation into ticket quotas and ticket fixing had been completed. Their bulletin board and their captain were taken down.

There had also once been a monthly contest to see what trooper caught the fastest speeder. The present record was held by a Houston oilman who opened up his Lamborghini near the Kelso Dunes. This particular oilman was even faster than a Lamborghini. He had a lot of political pull and the big ticket disappeared. His car had been clocked at 180 miles per hour.

"Hey, we finally saw that movie *Bullitt* you're always talking about," said Joe.

"How did that happen? I thought Tammy didn't like old cop movies," said Larry.

"She usually doesn't, but now my wife is in love with Steve McQueen."

"Your wife and my mother."

"The movie was excellent, real street-smart stuff."

"How about that car chase?"

"Yeah, it makes me want to drive to San Francisco and try out a few of those hills myself."

A reddish blur went past the parked troopers. An eerily quiet red car disappeared down a ribbon of asphalt in several blinks of an eye. Anxious troopers barely saw it flee past.

"Did you get a read on that guy?" said Joe. Already he had driven the Interceptor onto the interstate. Loud squeals of rubber were heard as he gave the large V8 the gas.

"Two, two, seven," said Larry. But he looked at the radar gun in amazement. "Something must be wrong with the computer."

"Two hundred and twenty-seven! Is our equipment busted again?"

"Tell me about it, but I'll call the speeder in anyway."

The blue Interceptor chased the red Camaro toward a western horizon. Amazed troopers could just see a red glint of a car far ahead of them. Fading glimmers continued to glide away at an extremely high rate of speed. Veteran troopers quickly thought the radar gun might be working just fine.

Adam and Angelina had sat in the Camaro for the first half of an hour in eerie silence. Slowly an astonished couple had gained an acceptance of the speed at which the car could travel. Five hundred miles of New Mexico and Arizona desert had been finished in less than two and a quarter hours. Both of them felt fortunate there had not been much early morning traffic. Solitary cars and trucks had been left behind in an ever more distant disbelief. The State of California looked like it was just around a cactus corner.

"I think we passed a trooper car back there," said Adam.

"Their car started to follow, but is already out of sight," said Angelina

"I will have to stop anyway as our car is beginning to vibrate," said Aurelius.

"More than it has been?" said Adam.

"Yes, I believe one of the tires is failing," said Aurelius.

"I can't imagine why," said Angelina.

Now the Camaro slowed and was driven to the near shoulder of the road. A concerned trio exited the car and looked at the tires. An ailing right front tire was heading toward soft.

"I think a rental car only carries a temporary spare," said Adam.

Adam grabbed the thin tire from the trunk. Angelina carried the jack and the lug wrench. But an astounded couple saw that the lug nuts were already loosened. They hung near an end of each lug stud like waiting watchers.

"I thought such a change should be hurried along," said Aurelius.

"How could you possibly have…," started Adam.

"Look!" finished Angelina.

Suddenly the Arizona trooper car appeared upon a sandy knoll a half of a mile behind them. Stunned pursuers had almost given up their chase as an impossible pursuit. They had radioed ahead for assistance. Nobody down the road seemed to be immediately available.

Larry probably should have reported a speed of the vehicle at less than two-hundred-twenty-seven miles per hour. He swore there was raucous laughter bouncing around in the background while speaking with the California Highway Patrol dispatcher. Jokes were on the troopers.

"We've got them now," said Joe.

"Looks like they broke down," said Larry.

The Ford Interceptor began to be driven down the low knoll.

Adam had started jacking up the Camaro. But not enough minutes would be available to change a tire. Temporarily he stopped his work and awaited their fate.

Aurelius quickly handed a small disc to Angelina. Its gleaming, glowing exterior looked like a brilliant bar of elliptical soap. She stared at the disc with more than mild confusion.

"It's a Time distorter, just point the clear end at the approaching trooper car and press the indentation in the center," said Aurelius. "Anything touched by its ripple of light will go back in Time for a dozen of your seconds. They will never be able to reach us."

Angelina held the disc and looked at Adam. She did not think anything could surprise her at this point in an ever more bizarre odyssey. Now she pointed the clear end of the disc and pushed the only indentation. Its pale ripple of light engulfed the oncoming car.

The once approaching Interceptor was returned to a position about three hundred yards back down the interstate. Such a road reset was not completed with a blurring backward motion. An immediate reset was instead accomplished. Instant materialization of the car occurred to where it had been twelve seconds earlier. This trooper car would have been back even further if the vehicle had not already slowed to fifty miles an hour. Joe and Larry had been preparing to make a U-turn as a sullen surrender. Few chases were worth a retirement risk.

"We've got them now," said Joe.

"Looks like they broke down," said Larry.

The Ford Interceptor began to be driven down the low knoll.

Already a raised Camaro had been completely jacked up by Aurelius. Adam was quickly taking off the damaged tire. He looked at Angelina and she could only return his gaze with her own confusion. She again pointed the disc at the oncoming car. The once approaching Interceptor was again returned to a position about three hundred yards back down the interstate.

"We've got them now," said Joe.

"Looks like they broke down," said Larry.

The Ford Interceptor began to be driven down the low knoll, but faster than before.

There was futile frustration in the approach of the officers. Here was a sense of déjà vu all over again for this chase. These men had a sudden feeling that something strange had happened to them. How they did struggle to understand what exactly such a happening had been.

Adam had placed the thin spare on the lug studs. Aurelius began to quickly spin the lug nuts into a firm tightness. Just a whir of repetitive motions was completed with white-robed hands. Usually tiring tasks were easily and swiftly finished.

"Adam, please put everything back in the trunk," said Aurelius.

The jack and the lug wrench and the flat tire were quickly packed. Adam was still shaking his head as he did so. He had seen the fastest change of a tire outside of a NASCAR race.

"Let's go, we've changed the tire," said Adam.

"Already?" said Angelina.

"Tell me about it," shrugged Adam.

Angelina looked at the police car now speeding toward them.

"Oh, what the hell!" she said, yet again pointing the disc at the oncoming car. The once approaching Ford Interceptor yet again went back down the interstate, even more than three hundred yards. This trooper car was a greater distance down the highway as it had been driven faster for this last repetition. Now it was on the other side of the knoll. Both troopers had not even seen a red Camaro pulled over to a shoulder of the road. Finally they surrendered to a sense of surreal safety.

The men stared through the windshield of their patrol car like deer that had been caught in starry headlights.

"Let's get us a breakfast," said Joe. "My blood sugar must be low."

"Yeah, I know what you mean," said Larry. "We can let California worry about those crazies."

* * *

Rachel Herr sat in her favorite reclining chair with a continuing apprehension. She had accepted the fate of her oncoming death as a normal ending to a human being. Most other people would probably see death by a rare form of leukemia as not such a normal ending. But east Texans had always known their God often worked upon His children in mysterious ways.

Until recently she had believed in the eternal benevolence of that God. Her own earthly blood river of life had been given by Him. Her own earthly blood river of life would be taken by Him. Simple fairness had seemed to be a significant part of such a process. Even the strongest rocks were eventually worn away.

Such a straightforward philosophy had become somehow confused. The cross of her faith had become somewhat double-crossed. She traced such a change to her exposure to another symbol. A strange dark symbol from that green choker had touched her face. An eerie symbol had only grazed a cheekbone, but even a slight touch had left her terrified.

Suddenly an image of an immense spider had appeared before her. A hairy spider must have been ten feet across. An adhesive matrix of its web had temporarily trapped her. Clutching spokes were as wide as thick ropes. Sensitive strands slightly vibrated as she struggled. The huge insect seemed to be waiting for most of her struggles to stop.

Then this spider began to move toward her. Sharp savage fangs were reaching out for her in a horrific embrace. She could not completely rid herself of its horrifying dripping maw. Such a horrendous image had become fixated in her brain.

Rachel had always feared spiders. She was not certain why her fear was so near and dear. Such tiny creatures had never harmed her in any way. They were really very useful beasts which helped to keep other insect populations under control. But human logic could never seem to completely still human fear.

She had tried to treat her fear in college. Psychology class workshops about persistent phobias had been attended. Rachel talked about spiders and looked at pictures of spiders. Finally she let a tiny spider rest on a palm of her hand. Yet many past preparations were no cure for a single present image of an immense stalking spider. Somehow an expansive web still held her tightly to slimy spokes. Her futile fight was becoming ever weaker.

"Senora, you are burning up," said Consuela. The sturdy Mexican woman had touched a work-worn hand to the forehead of Rachel. An internal inferno was destroying a life.

Her employer and friend had been mumbling about the fangs of a giant spider. Both of the women had long ago realized that many huge spiders were living upon this earth. Usually such bloodsucking spiders appeared in a much too human form. Consuela only had to look at the construction boss where her husband worked to clearly see just such an insatiable insect.

Then Rachel completely revived to a complete reality. She did feel more than warm. Her disease and her imagination were getting the better of her.

"Consuela, please bring me a couple of the painkillers the pharmacy sent over and a glass of ice water."

"Yes, senora, but I think we should call your daughter."

"No, she has her own life to live. Nothing can be done for me anyway."

"I still think we should call her."

But Rachel waved Consuela from the living room. She glanced at a nearby picture of her long-ago family. A husband and a wife stayed smiling with a very young Angelina between them. All three of them had been a devoted group of voyagers through much too human lives. Once they had been together as a tried-and-true trio. One day they would be together again.

Now she pressed the control button to tilt the footrest of her chair. Then the low murmur from its electric motor whirred in her head. When a proper position of the footrest was reached, the monotonous murmur faded away.

Rachel hoped the immense spider would do the same.

UNIVERSES

Needles, California, stayed at the border with Arizona like the best little town that Adam and Angelina had ever seen. Their rented red Camaro limped into the town like the car needed more than a brief rest. Its temporary tire had turned steadily for only a last thirty-something miles. Yet such a pace had been many miles too slow. Another replacement tire had to be found or this town was the temporary end of a road.

The struggling car was driven to a corner service station. An attendant almost as red faced as the color of the Camaro walked toward a quartet of gas pumps. “Fill her up?”

“Yes, with premium, we’re on dead empty,” said Adam. He had been driving since the temporary tire had been put on. No unnecessary speed had been used after a necessary change. “We also need a new right front tire.”

“Your tire is toast, but most people lose something out in that desert.”

“Have you got the same kind of a tire in stock?”

“I don’t, but Eddie at the truck stop will have one. He’s got about every tire ever made in his warehouse. You’re riding on steel-belted radials, so it won’t be cheap.”

“How long will it take to get a new tire and make the change?”

“Only about an hour, but if you want to get out of the sun, go over to Nick’s. They have a big buffet and you can eat all you want.”

"Where is the restaurant?" said Angelina. She had gotten out of the back seat of the driver side of the car. Her arms were stretched high in a growing heat.

"You're only a few blocks away, just walk down that narrow side street." Then a world-weary attendant saw Aurelius exit the front door of the passenger side. The white robe rippled in a slight breeze.

Angelina saw a sudden tension on the face of the attendant. People always seemed to have a sense of anxiety about someone who looked too much different than themselves. Ways of a world had become ever more wary.

"It's okay, he's from Tibet."

"You can't be too careful these days," said the attendant.

"No, you can't," said Angelina.

Now a together trio walked around a corner of the service station to the side street. An alcoholic man was sitting with his shoulders propped against a building in morning shade, a bottle of cheap wine mostly hidden in a paper bag. The man looked to be about seventy as another more than middling gulp of wine was taken. Pop cans and ragged clothes and other remnants of a life were piled in a nearby shopping cart. His otherwise empty cart seemed to hold his entire existence.

Aurelius glided across the street. The white robe stood next to the nearly motionless man. This spot of darkness awaited an enlightenment.

"Good morning, sir."

The unkempt man looked at Aurelius, startled to have somebody stop to speak to him. Ordinarily his days were spent within the isolated universe of a tormented transient. But something was extraordinary about this voice which readily reached him. It was a unique sound which rang pure and clear, much like a distant bell in a green and quiet valley.

"If you say so."

"What is your full name?"

Then this distrustful man hesitated for a moment. Usually the only people who asked him any questions were a variety of police. Yet this white-robed individual certainly did not look like a policeman.

"Audie William Richards."

Aurelius stayed motionless for several seconds in the shade. "Your parents named you after Audie Murphy, a hero of the Second World War."

"I was sure no Audie Murphy," said the morose man, drinking another gulp of cheap wine. Similar bottles had become his always loyal companions. How he did cling to them.

"You were a soldier in Vietnam, a brave soldier who always did as he was ordered. No shame is in such service," started Aurelius.

The lost and lonely man held the paper bag with the bottle of wine in his lap.

"You must accept what was seen at Quang Nam," continued Aurelius. "You must see it as a failure of humanity and not as a failure of self."

"I can't."

"Why?"

"Look at me. I *am* a failure. I'm almost nothing."

"No, look at *me*."

Slowly an invigorated man stood. Ageless eyes of Aurelius had captivated him. Grey ellipses were drawn together to form a forever symbol. It was as if someone wondrous was watching him, as if some place wonderful was waiting for him.

"You can see a light. You can feel the benevolence. It reaches out for you."

"Yes, yes, I can feel it."

"Your son and his wife are waiting for you. They have a new granddaughter for you to visit."

"Yes, I see them now."

"Fullerton is not so far away."

"No, no, it isn't. Fullerton is not so far away."

"You should go to them. It is not such a long train ride."

"I should go to them."

Now a hopeful man briefly held onto the shopping cart next to him. His wine bottle in a paper bag was dropped into the cart. Pop cans rattled against thin metal bars. Otherwise noiseless bars were somehow broken. Finally he saw the thrown away junk which had been accumulated.

"I don't need any of this stuff."

"No, but you will need a train ticket." Aurelius held out an opened hand to Adam and Angelina. Their wallet and purse were already being opened. "Fifty dollars should be sufficient. Do you know where the Amtrak station is located?"

"The El Garces Complex," said the man. He took the money and hurriedly walked a short distance down the street. Lastly he turned toward the trio. "Thank you for everything."

Then a reborn man disappeared around the corner to the rest of his life.

"You saved him," said Adam.

"He will save himself," said Aurelius.

* * *

Harriet Sage began to pour a second pitcher of lemonade for Solomon and his three guests and herself. The quintet sat around a low table on the terraced patio under a late afternoon sun with temporarily empty glasses. Two of these guests had drunk a first pitcher of lemonade like severely dehydrated camels. All three of those guests did not speak much about their lengthy trip across the arid southwest. Thirst for a cool beverage seemed only exceeded by a search for answers to things wondrous and taboo.

Harriet as hostess had been the quietest of differing questioners. Adam and Angelina also quickly headed for a sideline of the main discussion. Aurelius and Solomon carried their conversation with a clarity only completely understood by Aurelius. But Solomon was a fast learner. He was a man ready to understand what could not be readily understood.

"Human beings generally view distance as the product of speed multiplied by Time. To increase an amount of distance traveled, a rate of speed must be increased to maintain the same unit of Time," said Aurelius. "Such a formula works just fine upon a surface of a planet, but does not accomplish much within a vastness of interstellar or interuniverse space. Any distances involved are too great at any rate of speed, even the speed of light, to travel much of anywhere without consuming a very extensive amount of Time."

"This is a problem we have as yet been unable to resolve," said Solomon. He was a highly educated astrophysicist more than impressed by the astronomical knowledge of a very old man. Also he was a scientist more than interested as to the source of such knowledge.

"But what if Time could be compressed?" said Aurelius.

"You mean, move faster than the speed of light in a unit of time?" said Solomon.

"No, I mean actually compressing a larger unit of Time into a smaller unit of Time. A larger unit, say a month or a year or a million years, could become a much smaller unit, say a second or a minute or an hour. You could then travel vast distances in a fraction of a second if a circumstance required."

"I can't grasp the theory."

"This is no theory, just think of Time as a sphere, expanding and contracting a universe forever. As a rough analogy, think of a human heart, diastolic and systolic functions causing repetitive expansion and contraction, a natural beat of an existence."

"How can this be a fair analogy when the human heart will not beat forever? At least not on this earth."

"Please bear with me for a moment. Such a comparison is not a perfect analogy, but it will serve our purposes for this discussion. Time can develop an arrhythmia, similar to a human heart. Then Time can contract much too quickly, and a natural order of things becomes unnatural. Such an unnatural order is fine if it is controlled on a tiny scale, as in our discussion of an interstellar or interuniverse traveler. But if such a contraction occurs on a massive scale, a universe can perish, much like a person."

"If a universe contracts, all of its galaxies moving extremely quickly to a singularity again, would there not be, under your proposal of time, a subsequent expansion again?"

"No, because such a singularity is crushed at too fast a rate, and Time and physics cannot function anymore. Such a singularity is basically crunched into its own individual oblivion, a failure on an almost unimaginable scale."

"What could cause such a swift contraction to something as vast as a universe?"

"Such a hyper-speed contraction is the curse of the conflict between matter and dark matter, energy and dark energy. Any sphere of Time expands and contracts normally when the forces are in a controlled equilibrium. But when such an equilibrium is broken, anything can happen."

"What could break such an equilibrium?"

"Do you see yourself as a philosophical man, a religious man?"

"I suppose that I do. My wife and I have certainly tried to live such lives." Solomon looked at Harriet and she nodded a silent agreement. The couple was a bonded pair in many ways.

"Then think of it as a conflict between the forces of forever light and the forces of endless dark, a struggle between harmony and entropy, a battle between good and evil...an eternal Armageddon between life and death."

"I still cannot completely absorb what you are telling us. I feel like a new college freshman trying to solve my first set of differential equations. Somewhere on the blackboard is a correct answer, but I just cannot seem to find it."

"You can include me for the first sentence of Solomon's last statement," said Adam.

"You can also include me," said Angelina.

"Ditto," said Harriet.

"Okay, let me try to explain this confusion in another way. Solomon, let us assume you were born only one hundred years earlier than your actual birth date, say 1861, the year in which your Civil War began. Let us also assume that you became a physicist in 1890, the year in which the first electric tabulating machine was invented. What would have been your concept of Time?"

"I would have thought that time was an ever-forward event not really slowed or stopped by anything. The ever-pure Arrow of Time."

"Yet only twenty years later, when Einstein finished publishing his 1905 and 1910 theories on relativity, you would have thought that Time could be affected by speed. You would have believed that the faster anything could travel, the more that Time would slow for the traveler."

"That's true."

"What would have been your conception of the universe?"

"I would have thought that the universe was composed of only a single galaxy, our own Milky Way."

"Yet less than another twenty years later, after the work of Edwin Hubble in 1929, you would have thought that other galaxies were beyond your own. You would have also thought all of these galaxies were moving away from each other."

"That's also true."

"What if somebody told you then that the Milky Way Galaxy would collide with the Andromeda Galaxy, your closest large galactic neighbor?"

"I probably wouldn't have believed it."

"Yet you now know that these two galaxies will collide and form an even greater galaxy."

"What you say is all very correct, but you still have not explained away the problem of entropy, a continuing lack of order and loss of energy in an entire system. I do not see how all of the galaxies of any universe can come back together after they have been in such a continuing and growing disorder."

"*Your* universe will. It is doing so now."

"I still don't see how it can be happening. If I drop my empty glass on the stone of the patio, it will break into dozens of pieces. No matter how long I look at those pieces, they will never come back together again. The system of the glass is too disordered, and there is not sufficient energy remaining in the system to reverse the process to again make this a whole glass. In other words, once broken, forever broken."

"But a forever can be much more forgiving. Suppose you could watch those pieces of glass for a million years or even a billion years. Would you still be as certain of the outcome?"

"Such a wait would be meaningless. Those pieces of glass would be gone, long eroded by wind and rain and who knows what other activities."

"Yes…but glasses and galaxies are not the same."

"I still can't wrap my mind around many of the concepts you have described."

"Then think of these concepts in a different way. Let us assume that you will be born a hundred years later than your actual birth date, say 2061, and that you become a physicist in 2090. Now what would be your concept of Time, your conception of a universe, your beliefs about contracting galaxies and entropy."

"I have absolutely no idea."

"Now you do."

Their conversation became temporarily quiet. Aurelius and Solomon waited for the other to say something more. Adam and Angelina and Harriet tried to completely grasp the enormity of the discussion. Probably the latter was most lost by their conversation.

Harriet was as educated as Solomon, but in a different arena of academia. This wife had never been as enthralled with the sciences as this husband. She was a woman who had more than majored in English literature, familiar with gifted writers and poets from Shakespeare to Shelley. Her serious scholarship had seen the vaporous ghost in Hamlet and felt the devouring sands of Ozymandias. Harriet understood that even kings of every kind must eventually fail. Yet this latest regal dialogue with Aurelius had left her ever more lost, yet ever more intrigued.

"I'll get us more lemonade," she finally said.

* * *

The guarded military morgue was dimly lit with only several overhead lights spreading their restricted gloomy glow. An opened stainless-steel door stayed within an expanse of an otherwise closed stainless steel wall. Any remaining steel doors looked like identical opaque windows which had been shuttered against their weakened will. Silent screams still seemed to shudder throughout a nearly empty mortuary.

Already the night janitor had briefly viewed the lone figure of Herbert T. Ross lying upon a sliding drawer. The janitor had been told not to open the small steel door for national security reasons. But a thing that looked like a man was too much of a temptation. And Washington authorities had often exaggerated situations for their own public or private gain.

Not too much of a desire remained to even look anymore at the remains of Herbert T. Ross, a cold and hard manikin of a man. Dozens of bullet holes peppered a pale faux skin, but not a hint of red blood was around these holes. Only a tiny tinge of black stuff remained about any ragged wounds. A machine man had been almost cleansed.

Then a sense of a sudden shadow of something seemed to slink behind the janitor. He was almost sure someone had slithered down a near basement stairs. But such an unannounced entrance was temporarily impossible. Four heavily armed guards were at the top of each long stairwell. Usually bumbling bureaucrats were taking unusual precautions to protect their prize from disappearing into an unknown sky.

"Hello, I am Thax," said a strange voice.

"You're not supposed to be in the building," said the night janitor. He began to reach into a pocket for his cellphone. His reflexes were far too slow.

Thax pounced upon the man like a jaguar on a peccary. He grabbed the cellphone and threw it against the stainless-steel wall. Dull clatters echoed in the underground room as the plastic phone shattered.

"Those guards will be on you quicker than a cat on a mouse," said the janitor.

"You're a *comedian*!" said Thax. "I do enjoy a little comic repartee now and then. Let me see what I can put together on such a rude notice." He thought for a few seconds and then began a brief chant. "One, two, three, four, the guards won't be here anymore. Five, six, seven, eight, don't wait up, they're more than late."

"Very funny, but you still owe me a cellphone."

"And what is your name?" Thax grabbed the back of the neck of the janitor. He quickly increased the pressure.

"Arthur Parrish." Now a heavy hand on his neck was much like a steel vise. Here was an overpowering grip. There was almost the sound of a vertebrae cracking.

"Arthur Parrish…it sounds much like *martyr perish*," said Thax. He looked down at the figure of Herbert T. Ross with sadness. Then he stared at the janitor with a sneer. "Have you no respect for the dearly deceased."

"I don't understand, it's not even a real man," stammered the janitor. He thought there was a very strange lilt to the voice of this stranger. His words flowed like sweetened venom.

"Don't *ever* say such a thing again. *Sticks and stones can't break my bones, but words can ever hurt me.*"

"I don't understand," whimpered the janitor.

"I know you don't, but let me tell you the start of a story about a trio of friends who became martyrs for a cause. Would such a telling be acceptable to you?" said Thax in an ever more eerie voice. His sentences were still being smiled like taunts of a more than angry man.

"Sure, go ahead," again whimpered the janitor.

"These three friends met each other a very, very, *very* long time ago, in a galaxy so very, very, *very* far away. They lived on a planet in a binary star system. I know that your scientists think such a life is impossible. Academics believe the centripetal forces of the two stars would rip any living being to shreds, but this is not always so. There can be an equilibrium found in almost everything. Oh, yes, there most certainly can. What do you think about my sad story?"

"I don't know." Pain in Arthur's neck was becoming unbearable. An impossible grip held no possible escape. A true man almost began to cry.

"These friends were called Thax and Theodosis and Rigel. Astronomers call a certain star in your galaxy by the name of Rigel. This star is a blue supergiant sun in the Orion constellation, but I do not think it was named after the Rigel who I once knew. What do you think?"

"I don't know. I really don't." Not much else should be said. Nothing else could be done. A known man was ever more afraid of an unknown man.

"I know you don't, but let me tell you more of my story. Rigel perished in a place called the White Mountains and was later taken apart in pieces, like a used car. Rigel was alone when he passed on to whatever is waiting for each of us. Now Theodosis has also perished in your not-so-fair city of Washington, DC, and now Thax is all alone. Have you ever been alone?"

"No, not really." The frightened janitor realized he had to give any kind of an explanation. His entire spine had become completely numb. He was thankful that the pain had stopped. "I had to quit high school at seventeen to marry my girlfriend."

"And have you two little playmates stayed together?"

"Twenty-five years, twenty-five years this November."

"It will be a silver Thanksgiving for turkeys, how appropriate. You have already told me too much about yourself. Your lack of education and less than menial work experience, your almost complete ignorance about everything. How much do they pay you to be a night janitor?"

"I get $20 an hour, plus overtime if I work weekends."

"*Overtime*! There is no such thing. There is *only* Time."

Arthur shook his head in agreement. Now a terrified janitor knew he was dealing with a madman. Maybe such a madman was also not a real man. An alien coldness seemed to be around him like stainless steel walls.

"Whatever you say."

"It is not only what I say. It is also what we will do."

"Fine, what do you want?"

"I want to know where the personal effects of the bodies brought to this morgue are kept, and I would like to know *now*."

"Personal effects?"

"You are certainly a *genius* of an individual. Yes, their *personal effects*, bling and rings and other things."

"Oh, you mean their clothes and stuff."

"You finally got something correct. Your teachers would be so very proud of you. Let us stop our talking and do our walking."

The compliant janitor pointed toward a far corner of the morgue. An isolated area had back and side walls of poured concrete. A front wall was an extremely heavy mesh of screen as thick as a little finger. Its padlocked door was made of the same screen welded upon a sturdy steel frame.

"I don't have a key."

Thax ignored the comment and released the neck of the janitor. He began to evaluate the mesh and padlock of the screened door. "Don't you try to run away, because I am the fastest runner you will ever see in the very brief remainder of your life."

"I won't," said a completely subdued man.

"Arthur, my lad, what do you know about the comparative shear strength of metals?"

But Arthur could only give a horizontal shake of his head. He wondered when this nightmare would end. His quiet night had more than quickly crumbled.

"You never cease to not amaze me. The shear strength of a metal is the maximum load which can be placed upon it before failure, usually measured in pounds per square inch. Would you say in our current circumstance that we want the metal with the higher shear strength or the lower shear strength?"

"The *lower*?" Arthur had just blurted out an answer. He did not have a clue about what this lunatic was trying to tell him.

"You're dead center on the money, but I know it was only a guess. Let's face a simple truth, you *did* have a fifty-percent probability of picking a correct answer. These are excellent odds in any number of lifetimes. I would also add that the thick mesh of the screen has a lower shear strength than the heavy padlock on the door. Do you agree?"

"It sounds okay to me."

"You *are* an agreeable little genius for such a dark and lonely night. Now what would you say was the shear strength of that mesh, and don't forget to give your answer in pounds per square inch."

"I don't know…a million pounds?"

Now Thax smiled a sickeningly broad smile. Then a deep and ghastly laugh came from his hardened lips. "I certainly hope not, even I am not *that* strong."

He again began to laugh as the top of the thick mesh of the door was grabbed with both hands. The very heavy screen was ripped like a rectangular piece of latticed tissue paper. This wrecked screen was pulled in pieces to the floor like a thick but flimsy web. It lay on the floor as a mashed matrix.

"*What are you*?" said Arthur in a trembling voice. He began to think this night might include his very last hour on the earth. A faltering man awaited a failing future.

"Your inquiry, my lad, is a very, very, *very* good question." Thax looked to the high ceiling of the morgue like the rippled plaster was a star-filled celestial canopy. "I am least of what I once was…but I am most of what I have now become."

Thax motioned for the janitor to precede him into the storage area. Arthur reluctantly began to walk between the dual rows of oversized file cabinets. He looked over his freed shoulder, continuing his walk. But he knew nothing could be done about his present predicament.

"I know, you also don't have a key to any of these cabinets."

"They won't give—"

"Your story grows incredibly boring. You should take one of those courses, *How to win interstellar friends and influence so very many kinds of planet people.* But I guess you are just the stay-at-home type, am I correct?"

Arthur could only give a vertical nod of his head.

"Well, Mr. Stay-at-Home, here is a riddle for you: *Railroad crossing look out for the cars, can you spell it without any R's*?"

Arthur could only give a blank look on his ever more terrified face.

"No answer is an excellent answer in our situation because we need an *R*, a real big one." Thax pointed to one of the oversized file cabinets. There was a very large typed *R* on the front label of one of the wide drawers.

"And here it is!" Thax punched a hole in the thin metal of the high front of the drawer. Then he reached into the jagged opening with a firm grip and gave a hard yank. The once-locked drawer pulled out and away from now warped runners. Its tubular lock popped out with the harsh force, hanging like a broken cylindrical eye.

"Now we have the personal effects of the late Herbert Theodosis Ross," said Thax.

A thick plastic bag was pulled out of the drawer. All of the contents of the bag were dumped on top of several of the nearest filing cabinets. Any residue of a very ancient existence was readied for review.

Mostly clothes with a pair of steel-toed shoes were in the bag; a black wallet was filled with many forms of past identification; a green choker with a dark symbol was full of future promises—absolutely nothing else could be found.

"There is no Traveler, but the photograph in the *Inquirer* clearly showed Theodosis with the Intergalactic Traveler in his hand," said Thax. "'Terrorist Falls to Terrible Death' was certainly a pathetic headline for such a wondrous and taboo life. Hanson must have taken the star map. He *knows* how important it is to us."

"I don't know about any of this," said Arthur.

"I know you don't, an Intergalactic Traveler is something nobody on this earth has yet seen, except for a few very disloyal people. Now we have no alternative but a false trade. Such a transaction is the only equitable option which remains, a pretended barter between reluctant but reasonable individuals."

"I don't know about any of this," again said Arthur. He did not know what else to say. Something very horrible was heading very quickly in his direction.

"You do not know very much, but ways await for a teacher to inform a student." Thax grabbed the green choker from the top of a cabinet. He turned and backed Arthur against a narrow empty side wall of the storage area. "Let this choker be a remembrance of our only night together," said Thax. He quickly pressed the dark symbol against the throat of the janitor.

Arthur began to tremble violently and uncontrollably. Deep darkness seemed to flow through his head like it would never end. He was falling into a pit of dark emptiness.

"What do you fear? Tell me, I will not tell anyone else. Your secret will be my secret."

Arthur was on the verge of passing out. He clung to that thick concrete like it was his only remaining source of strength. "Claustrophobia…I'm afraid of closed-in places."

Then a brief moment of silence stayed as Thax pulled the choker from the throat of the janitor. Slowly a more than horrific smile spread across his usually emotionless face. He glanced at the opened small stainless-steel door on the large mortuary wall.

"Perfect!" smiled Thax.

Death and Taxation

"You gave us quite a scare, sir," said Adam.

"I gave myself more than quite a scare. Two weeks in and out of a coma is something I don't ever want to repeat," said Director Mitchell. His words were still stable and ever steady. "My last clear memory before yesterday was shooting it out with that thing on the rooftop. What the hell happened?"

Adam was amazed at how firm the voice of the director had remained. Any will of the man was strong even though a body had been willfully weakened. Now Adam quickly looked around the large hospital suite for both of them. Nobody else was in sight, but any walls could have many hidden ears.

"Sir, are we secure?"

Director Mitchell nodded from his wheelchair. "Everything is fine for the moment. I had Harold sweep the rooms an hour ago. Only a pair of cockroaches were found, one in the telephone and one behind the headboard. He thinks John Axt had them installed to curry favor with the congressional committee still finalizing the bureau budget. Now that the bugs are gone, you can go ahead and give me the straight stuff."

"The thing that shot you went by the name of Herbert Theodosis Ross. He worked at the Jet Propulsion Laboratory for the past thirty years, but we could not find out anything else about him. All of the rest of his supposed past was a fraud, a very elaborate and detailed fraud.

"We put out a quick cover story about an isolated terrorist attacking a government building. Unfortunately a local businessman across the street happened to get a cellphone video of Ross falling to the sidewalk. He sold the video to the *Inquirer* and then it went beyond viral."

"Harold told me the bastard killed eleven of our people."

"Twelve, sir, I was told this morning that Special Agent Scully died late last night," started Adam.

Director Mitchell had a few tears in his eyes. He had not cried since his wife had died in a car accident a decade earlier. A little lever on his electric wheelchair was pushed. An arduous journey was completed as the wheelchair moved slowly to a dual draped window. Narrow glass showed where a tan drape was partly opened.

"I also have to inform you that we lost eight military police at a secured mortuary near Arlington," continued Adam. "We had hidden the remains of Ross in the basement, but something must have gone looking for him. I think he had a concealed locater."

"I suppose we don't have any witnesses."

"The civilian night janitor might have seen something, but his mind has temporarily snapped. He just babbles about binary stars and the shear strength of metals."

"What about that other thing, the one found in the White Mountains?"

"I had to put his face on the internet. We couldn't find anything on our own."

"What did any internet tweeters and bloggers have to say about him?"

"We had quite a few hits from hotels and motels and a computer shop in Staten Island. He went by the name of Rigel Norton Reynolds and was supposedly a traveling salesman, but no such person exists."

"What about the star map and the laser gun?"

"They are both safely in my possession, sir. I was certain you would not want the press to even get a hint of these devices."

"Then warehouse them with the other lost items if the heat gets too hot."

"I will."

"Where does what we've got lead us?"

"I'm pursuing an angle with Lanicrim Industries. Reynolds was probably driving that Chrysler owned by Lanicrim, and the computer shop in Staten Island gave us the name of the corporation which paid for his equipment. This company also turned out to be owned by Lanicrim, which is way more than a coincidence. I also was no fan of their head of security."

"Oh, yes, a Mr. Erik Thax if my memory is still in one piece. What's your professional opinion of him?"

"My opinion is that he cannot be trusted. He gave me a run-around for almost two hours during my interview in Manhattan. But never really told me anything of consequence about the stolen car or Lanicrim Industries or anything else. I would have to say he is about the most proficient liar ever heard in my career."

"We don't need that particular apple right now. Didn't Charlie and his group put a report together on Lanicrim Industries?"

"Their report isn't finished yet. They're still having quite a struggle finding out many specifics. I saw him the other day and he told me the project will be the death of all of them."

"Meet with Charlie and put a report together as quick as you can. I'm supposed to be released by Labor Day to give my monthly briefing to the president. I just hope I'm up to it."

"I have to tell you, sir"—Adam leaned ever closer to his boss, lowering his voice to almost a whisper—"rumors are circulating that a group of Republicans and Blue Dog Democrats are putting pressure on the president to get rid of you as quickly as possible. They say that you aren't fit for the job anymore."

"Now there is a real joke in progress. Most of our representatives are political hacks or self-serving idiots. They make a congress which will be remembered as the Wiley Coyote of political history. They keep trying to catch the Road Runner of reality, but aren't really up to the task. Those ACME iron anvils and electric fans just keep turning against them. Good Lord, how did a country as magnificent as ours get mixed up with so many incompetents? Who do they have waiting in the wings to replace me?"

"Hugo Buhner...and he is supposedly complaining about any delay."

"They must be out of their minds. It will be a second coming of the Wehrmacht."

"I just thought you would want to know what you're running against."

"Thanks for the info, but I only have to please one person. I have served four presidents for more than twenty years and neither party has given any personal indication of tossing me to the curb. I will therefore keep plodding ahead in my usual way for at least the near future. But let's be realistic, not much real loyalty resides in this city of stone."

Adam shook his head in a ready agreement. Most people in Washington arrived and departed like longer lived mayflies. More than a few carcasses had been left within these city limits. Many people completely disappeared in such a vicious political wasteland.

"I have a very urgent request of my own, sir. I would like permission to set up a completely false identity for a confidential informant. He would otherwise, shall we say, have trouble traveling around."

"Do you trust this person?"

"Completely."

"I'll speak to Documents. Do you have a name in mind?"

"How about...Aurelius Marcus."

"I know your middle name is Hadrian, but aren't we pushing the Roman philosopher kings a bit too much."

"No, sir, it is a perfect name for this individual. I will let you know if we discover anything else of consequence."

"Okay, now I have to tell you something else of consequence."

"Go ahead, sir."

"I've been pushing your brother's name to the bottom of the termination list over these past months. I won't be able to do that anymore if Buhner replaces me in the near future."

"I understand."

"We could attempt to reach your brother one last try through our contact in Cairo. It will probably be a final invitation to return home."

"I don't know if such a contact will matter anymore, but I think we should take a chance."

"You could go yourself."

"It probably wouldn't be any benefit for either of us. We had a bad falling-out."

"I'll get the ball rolling. You can let me know."

"Thanks for trying to save him."

"And a last something else of consequence."

"Yes, sir."

"Don't forget to marry that girl down in San Antonio."

"Quite a lot is going on right now."

"Do it anyway. No perfect moment awaits anything in this life."

* * *

Charles Delon was a very thin man with a very wide head. Charlie had been the leader of the Financial Forensics Department for fifteen years. He had an MBA from Harvard and a PhD in mathematics from the Massachusetts Institute of Technology. Countless numbers from balance sheets, profit and loss summaries, general ledgers, check registers, SEC filings, and statements of retained earnings with sources and uses of funds usually flowed through his cerebrum with a usually unhindered ease.

The man could pick out any phony figures through a combination of quantitative deduction, experience with anomalous variables and an uncanny intuition. His fellows in the department called him an unequaled financial genius. He was incredibly proficient in the art of sifting through an immense number of available barrels to locate any hidden rotten apples. But if a man could not find many of the barrels, a rot could stay unnoticed for more than many years.

"Lanicrim Industries is the craziest case I have ever investigated in my life," said Charlie. "Nothing else is even a close second."

"I was convinced of that craziness weeks ago," said Adam.

"I haven't been able to write a formal report yet. It's become more than an aggravation to find out much of anything significant about the conglomerate."

"Just tell me what you've discovered, because I've got almost nothing on the group."

"Okay, I've got bits and pieces of it. I'll let you know if we uncover anything else of real importance." Charlie pulled a dozen pages of rough notes from a manila folder. He also held a single type-written sheet at the bottom of those notes. It was an organized beacon of print at the end of a disorganized fog of scribbles.

"Lanicrim Industries is owned lock, stock, and barrel by a Mr. Levid Lanicrim. His conglomerate is composed of at least a hundred separate corporations spread around the world. More than half of these known corporations are shells, primarily for tax avoidance and asset transfer purposes. Any remainder of these corporations actually manufacture something, although I'm not really certain what they're trying to ultimately make."

"The conglomerate has got to sell something. How else could it stay in business?"

"Our patent office has records which show that Mr. Lanicrim has more than six hundred personal patents, from biotechnology to metallurgy to software to supercomputers. These patents provide about five billion dollars of reported annual royalty revenue. He is a kind of technological Renaissance man, a person far ahead of his time. His royalties are the source of the legal money, but there don't seem to be any actual sales of any regular products."

"What about *irregular* products?"

"More than a few allegations have been made over the years that parts of the conglomerate are involved with a variety of such products: synthetic street drugs, phony pharmaceuticals, fake branded cigars and cigarettes, knockoff designer clothes and accessories, stolen intellectual property, and so forth. But any people who make these accusations are never heard from again."

"Do they get paid off?"

"One way or the other. In any event, these are the sources of the illegal money, and it is probably a lot more than the legal part of the business."

"Have you been able to put a total figure on his worldwide revenues?"

"All I've really got is a conclusion based on a series of educated guesses. Since the group is privately owned, it's not subject to a lot of filing requirements mandated for publicly owned companies. As a consequence, no specific worldwide financial numbers are available to review. It's difficult to even get a handle on his legal income, let alone his illegal income. Lanicrim doesn't even file *anything* in many of the countries where he has operations, so it becomes an impossible task to get a completely accurate picture of these operations."

"Give me your best shot."

"I'd say his conglomerate generates about thirty billion dollars of annual revenue. Such a number is based on a projection that only half of his royalty income is claimed, which means his legal income is really about ten billion dollars. I also estimated the yearly fixed costs needed to operate his twenty-six primary worldwide facilities, including the headquarters building in Manhattan, which add to just about that ten-billion-dollar figure."

"But what about his variable costs and maybe a hefty profit?"

"Please, just give me a minor minute. The total thirty billion dollars of annual revenue is extrapolated from an assumption that these fixed costs chew up a third of those worldwide revenues. This leaves a remaining two-thirds, or twenty billion dollars, to cover variable costs incurred and any profits realized from products that are being made, legal and illegal."

"Do you have any idea what is legally being made?"

"It looks like a little of a lot of stuff—specialized metals, advanced electronics, heat-resistant tiles, all very high-tech manufactures."

"To what end?"

"You can't get much information about that not-so-little question from anyone who works in any of the facilities. His group makes every effort to hire career felons, both blue collar and white collar and anyone in between. Most of these people are really hard core—murderers, sadists, scam artists without a hint of a conscience. They're dregs from the four corners of the planet. But a simple truth is that most of them probably only see a tiny piece of the total production pie."

"They don't sound like skilled workers to me."

"They all don't have to be. Lots of grunt work is required in the manufacture of almost anything. Employees with the real brains are probably former Silicon Valley and Wall Street people. Such people can do a lot more harm than any band of common thugs."

"Convince me."

"We're talking about individuals who infringe on technical patents without even an ethical blink of an eye, backdate stock options to maximize personal profits, manipulate energy prices for even more gain, sell junk mortgage bonds with false AAA ratings, market credit default swaps without adequate capital to pay claims, distribute pumped opinions on everything from companies to commodities headed into financial oblivion. These kinds of criminals don't care who starves or what goes bankrupt or how many hardworking stiffs end up carbon monoxide stiff in a garage."

"Maybe a code of silence survives among all kinds of criminals."

"I don't think it is a code of silence as much as a belief in self-preservation. The head of security for the entire conglomerate...," started Charlie.

"Mr. Erik Thax," interrupted Adam.

"That's correct, how did you know?"

"Director Mitchell mentioned his name and then I went to Manhattan to interview him. He seemed like a very practiced liar to me."

"Liar or not, Mr. Thax and his staff keep a tight rein on everyone else in the group. He must be quite a scary guy to keep thousands of people in such a quiet line. We have been unable to get any employees at any of the facilities to talk about anything."

"Do you have a list of the primary facilities?"

"This is the one detailed list of anything that I could find." Charlie retrieved the one typed sheet from otherwise scribbled pages. His hands started to shake as he did so.

Adam quickly looked over the list:

North America	*Los Angeles, New York City, Ottawa*
Latin America	*Mexico City, Panama City*
South America	*Brasilia, Buenos Aires, Lima*
Europe	*London, Moscow, Munich, Paris, Rome*
Middle East	*Kuwait City, Riyadh*
Africa	*Cairo, Johannesburg, Lagos*
Asia	*Hong Kong, Mumbai, Seoul, Shanghai, Singapore, Tokyo*
Australia	*Melbourne, Sydney*

"Ninety percent of the world's gross domestic product must be generated by the countries represented on this list. How did you get it?"

Charlie leaned closer to Adam. Organizational men were going to be conspirators with even more organized secrets. "I got it from a friend of mine at the French DRM. The list was on a flash drive recovered from the property of a Le Monde reporter who was murdered six years ago. All of his script was encrypted, but my buddy finally broke the algorithm."

"It seems like a lot of trouble for a list of cities."

"It's what such a list represented, the first real evidence of a worldwide reach of Lanicrim."

"What happened to the reporter?"

"He was found in the Seine, most of him anyway."

"I'm surprised other papers haven't picked up the ball. Media outlets can get really aggressive, especially when one of their own is killed."

"They did get very aggressive, for a while. The *New York Times* tried to follow the trail, and its lead reporter was soon found hanging from a bridge over the Hudson River. Then both the *Boston Globe* and the *Washington Post* got involved. Several top executives at each firm were more than threatened. Nothing more happened after a lengthy scare, but a message was clearly received. No media outlet wants to touch this story, not even any of the tackiest American or British tabloids."

"Do you have anything else?"

"Only that Levid Lanicrim has recently leased large tracts of land in isolated parts of Asia, Africa, the Middle East, and South America. He has a lot of pull in criminal communities."

"For what purpose?"

"That is the thirty-billion-dollar-a-year question. My friend at the DRM believes they will be used for terrorist training camps. I don't know if his theory is correct, but how and when any of this leased land is ultimately used probably won't be a plus for the rest of our world."

Adam nodded an agreement. He already had too much personal experience with what only a few fanatics were capable of destroying. Now he wondered what thousands of similarly minded people with advanced weapons and a constant source of money would be capable of annihilating.

"What about any government investigations? Somebody holding the levers of power in at least a few of these involved countries must be feeling threatened. How can everyone just ignore what is happening, or what is about to happen?"

"Recent discussions in England and France have talked about putting a coordinated effort together. The SIS and the DRM have already had a couple of meetings on the subject. But let's be frank, our earth has become so fragmented that it's difficult to agree on anything if more than one country is involved. I never thought a day would dawn when so many people seemed so dearly divided."

"We definitely could not get everybody on board, but the United States and its allies still have enough pull to get a majority of major countries on the same ship of state."

"Best of luck with such a project. Notice that your last three words are a personal SOS."

"You can help speed up the process. Get your information typed in a coherent report as quickly as possible. Put everything in the pot, including the few facts and the many speculations. Also toss in the remains of those two machine men, although I still don't see how this case fits together. Such stuff would not have played well before the World Trade Center disaster, but it has become a whole new grimy game."

"Who's going to run with it?"

"I'm certain that Albert Chester Mitchell will want to speak to the SIS and the DRM when your report is finished. Then he can carry the ball into the oval office by himself. It will probably be his last hurrah."

* * *

Swarms of peasants on the Manhattan streets far below seemed much less than insects to Levid Lanicrim. His expansive penthouse on the sixty-sixth floor of his headquarters building had become an aristocratic perch. He was in the top floor on a top city building of a generally wretched planet. Too many years upon this earth had drifted much too slowly past.

"We have a most disturbing situation, Mr. Thax," started Lanicrim. "Adam Hanson has become more than a thorn in our side, he has become an entire thorny crown."

Thax smiled at the comparison. He and Levid Lanicrim had become joined at the hip in both thought and action. Nothing was better than being arm in arm with a comrade in arms.

"He keeps reaching for the brass ring of this merry-go-round," continued Lanicrim. "Such a determined man has been going mostly in circles, but his circles have become ever larger and his reach ever longer. Our unresolved issue of the Intergalactic Traveler must be remedied as quickly as possible. No more delays or deliberations can be tolerated. The day is far overdue to cash in our insurance policy for this entire matter."

Thax nodded an agreement.

"We must be aware of a possibility of an abrupt cessation to our activities on this planet. Means toward an end of escape have been proceeding splendidly. I did think for far too many centuries that we would be waiting for a thousand additional generations to progress from an iron sword to a titanium surface. I suppose we must be grateful that these crafty *Cro-Magnons* have not been a bunch of nerdy *Neanderthals*."

Thax again nodded an agreement.

"I am telling you to expedite our angel in San Antonio to this location at your earliest convenience. You may double or triple her regular speaking fee, plus embellish any importance of an expected audience. Most academics more than enjoy having their egos fluffed and dried at an overpriced expense."

The buzzer on his ornate desk sounded.

"Yes, Jezebel, what is so important to disturb my conversation with Mr. Thax?" He listened to a brief and anxious voice on the intercom. "No, you made the correct decision. Send our visitor upstairs promptly."

Levid Lanicrim waited calmly in silence. His private elevator to the penthouse whirred to a brisk stop. Then a stocky but powerfully built Asian man stepped from opened doors like his own separate self. There was a still very visible scar on the right cheekbone of an obviously aggressive man. Here was a ragged and never forgotten wound of a distant youth. His childhood injury had been so deep that even skilled cosmetic surgeons had not been able to completely erase an adult effect. And cause and effect were rarely as clearly demonstrated as in the circumstance of James Chen.

"Jimmy, Jimmy, Jimmy! How courteous of you to arrive on such *short* notice," sneered Lanicrim. His words dripped with a seamy sarcasm.

"You can save your pathetic humor," said Chen. "My people in Macau are not amused."

"I do not expect them to be amused," said Lanicrim. "I expect them to follow orders, or should I say, *commands*."

"You expect too much. Your allocated share of gambling gross revenues will *not* be increased from five percent to ten percent. We have benefitted profitably from your contacts in Hong Kong and Shanghai, but my partners have voted unanimously to maintain your share at the already predetermined rate."

"*Predetermined*! Nothing in any existence is ever predetermined. Results must always be struggled and fought for, very often with the blood of many martyrs. You have not learned much since your father cut you with a kitchen knife for spilling a bowl of chicken broth on him. I must say it was a punishment which you richly deserved."

"My father more than paid for his parental impulsiveness."

"Yes, I would usually say that a patricide is a most commendable crime. The complete rejection of a father is a very worthwhile goal. But your father had been a trusted member of my organization for many years, far more trusted than you have become. An act of murder in his case has made you more than unmanageable. Any fear has been diminished to a point where you believe your own individual way can be made. I want to tell you a simple truth…I am the *only* way!"

"You don't scare me with your tough talk. We have an equitable relationship which will not be changed under any circumstances. Such a denial is my final word on the matter."

"*Your* word! None of your words now have any meaning to me. You have shown yourself to be an unreliable associate in an unreliable world. Certainly a tithe is a reasonable request from any institution. I believe your only remaining relationship with my office will be a very brief confrontation with Mr. Thax."

"I have heard of the reputation of your head thug. But I must remind you of my own skills in similar areas."

"Oh my, Jimmy, are you going to enthrall us with tales of your fourth-degree black belt in Shotokan karate, or your additional training in Aikido and Jujitsu? You must realize such relatively recent arts are nowhere nearly as ancient or refined as Mr. Thax."

"You are babbling in riddles again. My partners and I bid you farewell. No more minutes remain for such a meaningless debate."

"Your last sentence was the first really truthful statement you have made in my presence today. My patience has been worn to nothingness. Mr. Thax will lead you to your proper position in my organization. I bid you a permanent adieu."

Thax grabbed a shoulder of James Chen in a more than firm grasp. Chen whirled around and unleashed a barrage of harsh hand punches to the chest and abdomen of his attempted attacker. But Thax calmly stood and blocked each strike with alternating palms of his hands. He almost looked bored while demonstrating such incredibly quick defenses.

Then Chen made a final swinging back kick at the head of his opponent. Thax grabbed the leg in midair by the ankle. He rested the foot on his chest, firmly holding the leg straight in front of him. Now he intensely stared at his confused victim. For a fleeting moment, Chen saw the face of his grinning father.

"Remember what I told you," said a strangely familiar voice.

James Chen was temporarily mesmerized. He stayed frozen with the sound of the faraway voice. "You told me that I was a clumsy fool of a son."

"And so you are," said Thax. He smiled his own sick grin as the leg was pulled powerfully down above the knee. A folded femur shattered like a rotted branch.

Levid Lanicrim slowly walked over to a screaming Chen. He stood next to the writhing Asian like a man who had just watched a mediocre martial arts movie. "Jimmy, Jimmy, Jimmy! Now *that* was a more than forgettable performance. But I do promise that people will remember your face. Mr. Thax will show you as quickly as possible to your own pathetic spot upon my personal wall of shame."

THE RUINS OF MEN

Remnants of Puma Punku made one of four main sections of the ancient, ruined city of Tiahuanaco: the Akapana Pyramid and Subterranean Terrace and Kalasasaya Platform formed the remainder of a long ago wrecked place. The Bolivian government had years earlier methodically uncovered these remains, but the shattered city stayed as scattered pieces of what once had been. Such ruins of men were silently surrounded by the rugged Andes Mountains.

Adam and Angelina and Aurelius walked among these ruins as searchers within a broken past. Adam was trying to solve an important case with a greater trail of ruins. Angelina was intent on validating a theory about a relationship between the ruins of Puma Punku and the ruins of Chaco Canyon. Now Aurelius was almost certain of such a ruined relationship.

"This city must have been quite a magnificent place centuries ago," said Adam.

"Extraterrestrial theorists believe that aliens landed on the Nazca Plain and then built Puma Punku. Later the rest of Tiahuanaco was constructed as an homage to this effort," said Angelina.

"Perhaps these theorists are correct," said Aurelius.

Then the trio stopped at the Gateway of the Sun. Here was a large stone entranceway to a disappeared temple. There was a figure of Viracocha in the center of a huge stone lintel. Supposedly Viracocha was the bearded Creator God from which all real knowledge had originated. Other repetitive carvings spread out in rows on each side and below the figure.

Aurelius stood in front of the cut stone gateway. The white-robed figure scanned seemingly identical lines of carved figures. Finally this whiteness spoke in a firm and unyielding voice,

"And the Gods deemed Death to be the Evil,
for if this were not so,
why did they all choose to live Forever?"

"Those carvings have never been able to be translated before," said Angelina, glancing again at the huge stone lintel. Suddenly she thought that Viracocha vaguely resembled Levid Lanicrim. Such a thought was quickly pushed from her mind.

"Extremely slight, almost invisible, variations are in these carvings. It is an exceptionally ancient text," said Aurelius. "Sargon has been in this city. I know his tortured tracks too well."

"I believe it was originally a Greek proverb," said Adam. His knowledge of languages had raced to the fore. Yet he could not find any significant variations in those repetitive stone carvings. Each and every one of these carved figures looked exactly the same to him.

"Such a saying was once Greek," said Aurelius. "Earlier, it was Sumerian, and much earlier, Aboriginal. And still much earlier, a lament in the Rift Valley. But none of them are true. They only become truth if people truly believe that death becomes their own personal ending."

"You're saying that an eternal life awaits after death?" said Angelina.

"I'm saying that people become what they believe," said Aurelius.

Sudden silence descended upon the group. Each of them was temporarily lost in a reverie of personal thoughts, companions on separate quests. Their grail had differed even as their search had grown.

They walked further among the spreading ruins. Many immense stone blocks had been battered about as if an angry monster had broken them apart in a fit of vindictive rage. Most of the stones of many tons had been tossed around like bits of chaff in a violent windstorm.

Eventually a wandering trio approached the Kalasasaya Wall of Heads. The ancient sunken temple was surrounded by a high stone enclosure. This enclosure of shaped fieldstones had many carved rocky heads sprinkled within its clutch of stones. These rocky heads appeared to be from many different kinds of the human kind. Now their faces dotted the Wall of Heads without tears, but perhaps with remaining regrets.

Aurelius quickly excused himself. The white-robed figure glided toward an abandoned shore of Lake Titicaca. This whiteness was drawn to an ancient memory. Any waters of a now faraway lake had once been very close. Many waters had receded with the passing years.

Adam and Angelina walked away with different wants. Adam wanted to speak to her in private. Angelina wanted to visit the spot where the earthly life of her father had been ended.

"This enclosure is where my father was killed," said Angelina. She ran her hand against the nearest shaped fieldstones of the Wall of Heads. "He wrote that this archeological site was the only known ancient site in the world which seemed to prosper with the centuries."

"What did he mean?" said Adam.

"My father compared his photographs of the Wall of Heads to the first sketch of the ruins made in 1549. This first sketch of the partially exposed portion of the enclosure had been drawn by a priest who accompanied the conquistador, Pedro Cieza de Leon. Dad wrote that more heads had been added to this enclosure since that early sketch. Most other archeologists believed such a sketch had only been a rough draft by an early European visitor, so no valid comparison could be made between a first sketch and any secondary photographs."

"It sounds like a reasonable assumption."

"My father was an unapologetic contrarian. He searched more than a few monasteries in Spain over the years, from Barcelona to Guadalupe to Madrid. Finally he found the papers of the priest who had accompanied the conquistador on the expedition. I am paraphrasing, but the priest had clearly stated: *Great efforts have been made on my part to include each and every face of the doomed in my poor attempt to reproduce the revealed portion of this grotesque Wall of Heads, for they are all condemned souls in the fires of Hell, and only the benevolence of our glorious Father has any chance of salvaging their damnation."*

"He was a priest who wrote strong stuff."

"Hell and the Devil were much too real to those early missionaries. If they could not save your heavenly life by conversion, they would kill you to end your earthly life."

"I guess there is a strange, twisted logic somewhere here. Such logic seems much like throwing a suspected witch into a deep pond. If a woman floated, she was guilty and probably executed. Yet if a woman sank, she was innocent and possibly drowned. I suppose every area of human settlement has had its own bizarre rituals to protect itself from the unknown."

"I always hoped to find out what really happened to my own father in these remote ruins. I used to wish he could have protected himself from whatever killed him."

Adam and Angelina walked beyond the end of the Wall of Heads. They did not notice a latest rocky head. The stone was an Asian man with a crack on the right cheekbone where a fleshy scar had once been. He could no longer see anything except the worn ruins of a long-ago city. Eyes of ruined men were the only permanent watchers of this desolate space.

Now the meandering couple continued further toward a spot where Aurelius knelt. White-robed arms had again reached toward a thin sky. This whiteness was near a gone away shore of a lake which had gone a dozen miles away. Aurelius waited for a guiding vision.

Then Adam had a sudden vision of his own. He saw himself as an old man without Angelina and children and grandchildren. His sense of future isolation was as strong as a sense of the present isolated landscape. He was a man thirteen thousand feet high in the mountains who had never felt so low. His violent past had begun to patiently claw at him.

Adam suddenly turned and held both of Angelina's hands. He looked into her eyes with the vulnerability of a man in love. "Marry me!" he said.

But Angelina resisted his impulsiveness. She felt cheated in more than a romantic way. "No, this day is not a day to speak of such vows."

"Marry me, marry me before I become as broken as this ruined city."

The young woman stood as an also confused woman. Angelina had loved Adam deeply for almost two years. Her feelings had evolved as their relationship had ripened; romantic love was not enough for any woman or man. Stability had to be in their lives to make a world right for both of them. Their joining had to be consummated at a proper moment for each of them.

Yet an absolute truth was that Angelina had developed deep doubts about such a relationship. Her growing fear was that she could not completely accept a man who had killed other men. Then her cellphone started to ring. She quickly retrieved the phone from her purse.

"Yes, Consuela," she said.

* * *

All wall blackboards in Solomon Sage's office were covered with equations. Many mutual mathematical attempts to explain the unexplainable had continued onward over the passing weeks. Needs remained within men and women to reduce complicated stuff to more simplistic stuff. Yet too many such complexities continued to resist such a conversion.

Solomon had always had a quantitative mind. He had scored a hundred percent on each of his four high school final math exams and a perfect 800 on the mathematical section of the SAT. His only serious limitation strenuously holding him back was a lack of writing skills. A man who was incredibly skilled with numbers was not incredibly skilled without them.

But Solomon had learned to rely on Harriet for the qualitative half of a marital life. His wife could whip off an articulate personal letter or a lengthy literary analysis with a brief flurry of fingers. Her many words flowed marvelously along with an incredible ease. Her formed sentences sounded like new language born again from an eloquent linguistic womb.

There was a similar aptitude in Solomon with symbols as words, equations as sentences. Here was a calculable knowledge for which he had always yearned. His only problem was that this present problem could not be solved by mathematics—integers were not integrating.

Any universe collapsing at a hyper light speed was far beyond his intellect. An elegant brain felt like a ruined organ. A savant mass of snappy synapses had been reduced to a puny morass of plodding pathways. Numerous numbers had finally failed him. Yet he was in excellent company.

He recalled how Einstein had struggled for the last three decades of his life to complete a Grand Unified Field Theory. Mathematical relationships among electromagnetism, strong nuclear force, weak nuclear force, and gravity had been sought with such resolve. Yet even this greatest of modern minds had failed at a task.

Solomon was certainly not comparing himself to Einstein. Now he did think that success had many more friends than failure, but did not yet see himself as a scientific orphan. This husband needed this wife more than ever to express the thoughts which he was really feeling. An aggravating idea of a growing futility of his efforts was gaining on him. A wise way had to be found through such an incomprehensible mathematical maze.

Then Solomon remembered his favorite morning newspaper comic of years earlier. *The Far Side* had once brightened each early day like a rising sun. He recalled a cartoon sketch of an exhausted scientist slumped before a large blackboard full of figures. His blackboard was completely covered with lines of extravagant equations. Complicated computations had steadily reached a final futile conclusion. Their result was a big round zero.

Such a big zero summarized the result of any recent efforts of this Solomon. Another method had to be made to analyze what was happening around and beyond him. Additional spectrographic analyses of a same sample of galaxies should again be completed as quickly as possible. He also believed his journey of faith could be further finished.

Solomon Sage had recently thought about fervent faith more and more. His faithfulness had been ever strong as he had wandered into middle age. Somehow his beliefs should be made stronger. Such will as idea must not be slowly weakened. A universe without a God was unfathomable to him. A God without a universe also made absolutely no sense to him.

He sat down at his desk and stared at his more than many equations.

* * *

A personal portion of the Alleghany Mountains was tucked into the southwest corner of New York State as a nearly forgotten patch of earth. Many years earlier, Adam's parents had bought an old cabin with fifty acres of this dissected plateau. Once these rolling hills and narrow valleys had held an entire Hanson family so very close. Now only Adam was still around to walk any paths of any earlier years.

Angelina had returned to San Antonio to be with her mother. She had taken Aurelius with her. This ancient man had become a consoling force in all of their lives. Consuela had urged a return as quickly as possible as Rachel was burning with a fever. Furious fire in her blood was not yet fatal, but an unrelenting disease was still slowly and surely consuming her.

Adam had decided to take his own separate trip. He could feel Angelina slowly drifting away from him, much as his brother had drifted away. People whom he had loved the most had left or were in the process of leaving. Their departures varied widely in date and location, but any past and present results would be slimly the same.

The old cabin was looked upon with a confusion of mixed emotions. Adam had maintained the cabin with less and less enthusiasm after the deaths of his parents. He had visited the cabin less and less often since his brother had gone over to the other side. But Adam's recent matrimonial rejection by Angelina had seemingly forced a return to a remembrance of his youth. Finally a week of unused vacation was to be spent alone in a hidden hollow of the past.

He was a true middle-aged man with more a feeling of centuries of oldness. He had killed seven other human beings, destroyed key installations, and stolen crucial information during his service. Adam Hanson was trying to find reasons for the continuation of such service. Too few reasons seemed to remain for such a continuance.

Now Adam realized that he had looked to Angelina over these recent years as a way out of his meandering, meaningless life. She was a final exit to any clean and fresh air outside of an inside warehouse of lost existence. His acts of familial revenge had been piled very high on dusty shelves in that sordid warehouse. Too many obscene actions were falling down upon him with an unhindered force. Eventually they would crush him into his own lonely oblivion.

Something strange was slowly happening to him, a changeling strongly changing within himself. His most recent case had shown the man too many things which could not be really understood: machine men running amok anywhere on this earth; Aurelius arriving from somewhere beyond this earth; a star map and a laser gun in his possession, an ownership against his own company rules. Such wonders were difficult for any man to voluntarily relinquish. He was not yet ready to surrender everything.

The star map had been an amazing technical accomplishment. Scientists like Solomon Sage lauded such an achievement. Yet the laser gun was an even more amazing technical accomplishment as far as Adam was concerned. A law enforcement hunk of him which remained was more than enthralled.

This black laser gun looked somewhat like a regular gun except for the lack of a trigger. A telepathic sensor must be in its handle which engaged when a holder wanted the gun to fire. Also a shielded source of energy was in the handle. Slight radioactivity was steadily emitted by that handle, almost completely protected by an unknown element. Same radiation was emitted by the wreckage of the Chevy Cavalier and the wrecks of the two machine men.

The laser gun had a seemingly inexhaustible supply of energy. Adam had fired the laser several hundred shots over this past week. He had target practiced at a group of thick boulders behind the back of the cabin, becoming quite skilled in the use of the weapon. But he had no idea how it actually worked.

Adam had called Solomon Sage about his opinion of the gun. Solomon had speculated a miniscule nuclear reaction was in the handle which produced a laser. Even an extremely tiny mass would provide an essentially limitless supply of searing blasts. Such a weapon could be fired for many lifetimes without running out of any blazing ammunition. Adam still often felt that his own life was running out.

More than a few pressures would probably be ultimately exerted by the bureau to return the star map and the laser gun. Director Mitchell knew about these alien items and would cover for both of them. Yet a dire difficulty was that this director might be replaced in a very few days. The new boss would not be the same as the old boss. Adam tried not to worry too much about any problems of a rapidly approaching future.

Now he was spending the present of his life making every effort to hide from these past problems. He was mostly walking paths among those rolling hills and narrow valleys of his youth to find such a hideaway. Adam took a very long walk each morning and another very long walk each evening. The silence of a deep forest gave him solace. The quiet of an open field beckoned with a possibility of salvation.

Eventually he wandered to the old tree house which had been built during his youth. He and his brother had board covered a sturdy frame made by their father. This frame had been nailed within grouped branches spreading from a huge oak. Once a close father and a pair of close brothers had worked over the weekends of a summer. Once a closer wife-mother had brought them homemade sandwiches and cold well water for a family lunch.

Vibrancy of a midday sun would warm their leafy glade. Four members of a devoted family would eat and drink and talk beneath this nearest star. Benevolent togetherness had prospered for a loving people. But all things must pass. And even the stars perish.

Adam Hanson slumped like a boy again against the trunk of that spreading oak. Now a boy who had become a man sat beneath the aged tree house made so many years ago. He thought about life and death, love and hate. Maybe he wondered about too many mysteries which could never be completely known.

Then a true man stayed until the sun began its slow decline and disappeared beyond an edge of earth.

GRAINS

Medical bills were accumulating for Rachel Herr. Her health insurance had paid a majority of these expenses, but a significant minority had to be borne by the patient. She was a sixty-year-old woman who wanted to die at home in a personal way. There was always a fear of dying in a very impersonal nursing home. Now there was a fear of dying impersonally poorer.

Rachel had become a mostly bedridden patient. She lay upon her once marital bed and recalled a spousal relationship which had been. She still missed her husband very much. Her mattress often seemed too wide and empty. Her sheet had become almost a barren plain.

Angelina had made every effort to keep her mother comfortable both emotionally and financially. Ever more large invoices seemed to give no small respites for either of the women. Neither of them had regularly taught at UTSA since the spring semester had ended in May. Then her mother had received a fatal prognosis. Their final formal classes had ended.

Recently a resolute daughter had received yet another phoned request to speak at Lanicrim Industries in New York City. This evening offer was triple her usual lecture fee plus any travel expenses paid. And an afternoon offer was made to speak at an archeological convention near Baltimore's Inner Harbor. Both speeches could be completed on the same day.

Now she could leave on an early morning flight and return on a late evening flight. She might be gone no more than a little over a day. Her plans should be finalized as quickly as possible. More money would be more than helpful. Too many prospering obligations must be promptly paid.

"Consuela, I'm going to stop at my office on campus to finalize a pair of appointments," said Angelina. "Make sure my mother gets two of those new pills about eight o'clock tonight. The vial is next to the bowl in the kitchen. I will probably also finish the grocery shopping, so I won't return until late tonight."

"You do whatever needs to be done," said Consuela. "Mr. Aurelius and me will take more than kind care of your mother."

Then Angelina walked into the master bedroom. She kissed her mother on the forehead. "I just have to run a few evening errands, but I'll see you tomorrow morning."

"Our Lord knows more than enough needs to be done," said Rachel. "I just regret not being able to help out anymore."

"Don't worry about it."

"Fine."

But Rachel did not really feel fine about much of anything anymore. Only a nearly vacuous void seemed to be spreading around her. Such a near emptiness only held a clutching web of sticky spokes upon which she continued her struggles. The immense spider was occasionally watching her exertions. Eventually the monstrous insect would engorge itself upon herself.

Angelina and Consuela had done more than enough in their attempts to care for Rachel. Two younger women had waited on one older woman hand or foot, day by night. Aurelius had also become almost a part of the family over a last week and a half. Created comfort given by this elderly man was difficult to explain.

Now Rachel noticed that the immense spider quickly fled from her life when Aurelius was near. Then a greedy insect would immediately depart from her needy thoughts. Her personal web of torment disintegrated into nothingness. Sticky spokes evaporated like they had never even really existed.

"Consuela, please bring me a glass of ice water when you get a chance," said Rachel.

"Senora, just let me separate this last batch of wash and I will bring you a big pitcher of ice water with a glass." Consuela had been walking past the bedroom doorway with a basket of dirty clothes. She had briefly stopped while headed toward the mudroom.

"I already have the water," said Aurelius to Consuela.

White-robed hands held a pitcher of ice water and an empty glass. Such whiteness seemed to materialize next to the woman. She shook her head in a grateful but confused nod.

Aurelius sat in a waiting chair next to the far side of the bed. He filled the glass nearly to its brim with cooling stuff. The glass of water was handed to Rachel like an exquisite gem of a gift. Its ring of clear fluid rippled with secrets.

"I always wondered why people said that bread is the staff of life," said Rachel. "I always thought it was water." She took a long drink from the brimming glass.

"I think you are more than correct," said Aurelius, taking the partially empty glass from her when she was finished. It was set on the nearby nightstand next to the pitcher as a partial treasure. "There was a Time on this planet without water, but that was so very long ago."

Rachel thought this last comment was a very strange statement for anyone to say. She looked at the man and suddenly believed he was far further than old. Somehow she felt that he might even be past her conception of such a word. Her geologist eye sensed something which others could not sense.

"May I ask a very personal question?"

"You may."

Then Rachel stared into those bottomless grey eyes. Something within these eyes was beyond unfathomable. Dappled deepness went on and on like an eternal well. She waited and waited for her seeking stone to hit bottom. Yet there was no such emotional sound.

"How old are you?"

"What is the oldest piece of this planet which you have ever held in your hands?"

"Oh, it was probably a mineral grain of zircon when I was in Australia."

"And how old was a grain of this earth?"

"It was dated at four billion years."

"I am much, much older."

"It's not possible…it *can't* be possible." Rachel was beyond stunned. She stared at this white-robed figure in disbelief.

"Look into these ageless eyes."

She again looked into those grey eyes. The dying woman was drawn deep within a pair of forever orbs. Suddenly vibrant currents of things wondrous and taboo were seen. Steady streams of pictures formed in these eyes. This immense flowing river of intense images was much like a very lengthy film played at a very fast speed.

Someway she could see an extremely dense, bright singularity exploding and spreading outward. Stars furiously formed before her in limitless abundance. Massive supernovae exploded with a magnificent dispersing strength. Swirling clouds of dust became asteroids which began to form circling planets. An earth was becoming ever more whole.

Then a barrage of uncounted asteroids and comets pelted a growing sphere. A very large asteroid collided with that larger sphere in a brilliant collision. A moon was held close to an earth after such a monumental crash. They remained together as celestial companions.

Lava spewed from smoking volcanos and made vast, burning plains. Rains plummeted from billowing clouds and made vast, cooling oceans. Continents drifted together and drifted apart again and again. This earth was roasted and frozen and warmed.

She was mesmerized as the vitality of life began. Silent seas of a world finally swam with a million different living creatures. Vibrant breathing being was swimming and diving and reaching for the shores of those waters. It crawled across secluded sands to extend a new vibrancy to a wanting land. Plants and trees, animals and birds, prospered in varied plenty. Man and woman walked into a waiting Eden.

She could see these early men and women hunting and gathering by day. Puerile people lit fires and looked to an unknown star filled sky at night. They painted in caves and on cliffs with a simple, hopeful beauty. They plowed fields and tended orchards and mastered many skills. Small villages and towns formed and faded. Settlements temporarily clung to rivers and lakes and seas like more than grateful children.

Then great civilizations rose and fell before her vision: massive cities were constructed and destroyed; exquisite monuments were made and turned to dust; huge battles with horrible slaughters unfolded; masters fought masters for dominance, slaves fought masters for freedom. Humanity built and devastated, prospered and failed, wondered and wandered, laughed and wept, prayed and cursed. Reason and a lack of reason struggled for supremacy.

Finally those grey eyes only held a single expansive sun. This star steadily grew into a red giant which covered everything else. Rachel fainted with such an overwhelming redness.

* * *

Consuela had sorted through the basket of laundry. Her waiting washer was started with a large load. She glanced at her watch. A time was seven minutes before eight o'clock.

The devoted woman went to the bowl filled with vials and bottles in the kitchen. Several newly prescribed pills were taken from a vial next to the bowl. She walked toward Rachel's bedroom just as Aurelius grasped the right hand of the unconscious woman.

Aurelius began a reverent ritual, "My blood for yours, my flesh for you…" He repeated the words over and over again. "My blood for yours, my flesh for you…"

Now Consuela stood quietly near the partly open doorway with more than a small share of disbelief. Tiny specks of something were streaming from Rachel's motionless hand. Dark drops started to flow into the hand of Aurelius like erratic black blobs. These black droplets seemed to be trying to resist the pull of worshipful words. Yet Aurelius maintained an intense strength and composure as dark rivulets continued to flow. Finally they were finished.

Consuela thought she had witnessed an ancient communion rite. She turned from the doorway with a pair of pills still clutched in her fingers. How she could not wait to tell her husband about such a marvelous miracle.

"*El es un Dios*," she whispered to herself.

* * *

Now Adam waited in temporary isolation at the far end of a snack bar in the Cairo airport. He ate a few dried dates and drank a glass of bottled water as a parade of humanity moved along the broad aisle. This sprawling metropolis teemed with the strengths and the struggles of his humankind. The lower Nile City held the sixth largest urban area of human settlement in the world. Other more personal settlements also awaited completion.

Adam saw his latest contact walking steadily toward him. The pretentious code name of the man was Suleiman. But not very much magnificence remained within him. He was a manipulator who worked all sides of a political rectangle: the West and the Middle East, the Christian and the Muslim worlds. Always his greatest loyalty was to himself.

Suleiman had also been a trained assassin. He had surrendered such a trade for a trading of information. His latter profession was much safer than his former profession. This latter profession was also a much more profitable job. Such newly found wealth was wallowed within like a hog voluntarily trapped in madding mud.

"I was sorry to hear about Director Mitchell," said Suleiman.

"Yes, he was injured quite badly, but is thankfully on the mend," said Adam.

"You have apparently not yet heard of his death during your recent travel. He had a pulmonary embolus after his monthly briefing of your president."

Then Adam could feel something giving way within himself. His mentor and friend had died with his boots on. He was a man who would be more than missed.

"His loss is a terrible loss," said Suleiman. "Director Mitchell was a fair man in our usually unfair business. I am certain his successor will not be as reasonable."

Still beyond stunned, Adam could only nod an agreement. Hugo Buhner would be an immediate replacement. He was a neo-con Nazi who would not be very benevolent to almost everyone else.

"Who do you think will replace Director Mitchell?" said Suleiman.

"I'm not really certain," said Adam. He stayed depressingly dazed. It did not seem really possible that Albert Chester Mitchell was really dead.

"Do not be sly with me. I am not ignorant enough to believe that the right eye of such a respected director does not know what the left eye could see racing down the road at him."

"Okay, you're correct, I do know who will probably be his replacement. But I still can't tell you until a replacement is officially announced."

"You Americans are too arrogant. One day your arrogance will be more than repaid. Your country will righteously regret its insolence of the last century."

Hostility of this current contact had bubbled to the surface early in a conversation. His angry response was not such an unusual circumstance. Most people could very clearly see a monster in others. But most people could rarely see a similar monster which existed within themselves. How a lengthy lecture to a seen monster was racing down a road so very fast.

"America could often make a pig sick. The United States spends more each year on its defense budget than the next ten countries combined. Your army and air force have eight hundred military bases spread throughout the lands of this earth. Your navy has eleven aircraft carrier battle groups and fifty-three nuclear attack submarines available to cruise the oceans of this earth. Your dozens of drones sweep through the skies, killing the guilty and the innocent alike… and *still* you do not feel safe enough to be honest."

Then Suleiman suddenly stopped his rant.

More than a few other people in the snack bar were looking in his direction. He had been foolish to bring attention to himself in such a public area. His bad temperament had often gotten the best of him. Such a temperament had been an asset in his previous profession. Such a temper would be too much of a liability in his present job.

"I do not want to pursue a discussion about the evils of empire. I only want to find out about my brother," said Adam in a low voice.

"I want you to have no illusions about me. My loyalty is a paid commodity," said Suleiman in an equally low voice.

Adam and Suleiman had reached a minimum of understanding with each other. Their brief relationship was to be a trade of money for information. Any transaction would be a barter of coin for blood. A world had become a big ugly marketplace. You put down your cash and waited to see what could be carried away. No refunds would be given for such transactions.

"I more than understand, but I would still like to know about my brother."

"I have already informed my informants, but we must travel to Giza to have a most current view of the subject. The last I knew, your brother was in western Pakistan, but that is only old information."

"Then let us get new information."

"My car is in the parking lot. We must go to the Mecure Cairo Le Sphinx."

The tab was paid by Adam. Suleiman led the lengthy walk to a new Cadillac. His luxury sedan was parked in a reserved area near the exit.

Their air-conditioned ride to Giza was only twenty miles, but miles traveled became even dustier. The three pyramids and their sphinx guardian on the Giza plateau grew ever more visible even as the road became ever more invisible. Once there were magnificent stony wonders constructed here. Now these wonders had stayed for more than forty-five centuries.

Adam wondered if a people of thousands of years in the future would gaze at the past wonders of America. Traveling tourists would take holographic images of four presidents carved into Mount

Rushmore. Or view three Confederates etched upon Stone Mountain. Or stand on tree-covered hills of rubble which had been Manhattan. Maybe they would think a god had created such constructions.

Two silent men approached the five-star hotel. Their ride had been completely quiet except for a constant whir of the air conditioner. Suleiman quickly parked his car. Then he pointed to the top of the hotel under an early evening sun.

"We must go to the roof restaurant."

Mutually suspicious men took an elevator to the restaurant in shared contempt. Their rooftop vantage point held a sweeping view of the trio of pyramids and solitary sphinx. Suleiman quickly ordered grilled lamb and bottled water. Adam ordered only bottled water. Nothing more was spoken until the lamb had been served and eaten.

"Here is the end of empire, Mr. Hanson. All of you Americans will only be grains of sand in an immense desert," started Suleiman. He pointed to the vast emptiness radiating west from the pyramids and sphinx.

The Sahara stretched to a far horizon and thousands of miles beyond.

"Your United States will go the way of Rome and Macedonia and Persia and Assyria and the others of its kind," continued Suleiman. He had forgotten to include the empire of Ancient Egypt. Almost everyone had such a very narrow view of human history.

Adam looked at the Great Pyramid of Khufu in the near distance. Once this greatest of pyramids had been covered in polished white limestone with a polished gold peak. Now only an eroded man-made mountain stood at the start of boundless sands reaching westward.

But Adam remembered something extraordinary that Solomon Sage had told him: *There were more stars than the number of grains of sand on every desert and beach on the earth.*

Suddenly everything on this particular planet seemed very, very tiny.

"Ah, here is our man," said Suleiman after an additional unspoken hour. "Stay at the table, I must speak to him alone."

Then Adam watched as an immaculately groomed man guided several dozen European tourists to various tables. Adam could see Suleiman pull a map from his pocket as the man was approached. Both men jabbered back and forth with excellent and practiced skill. A helpful guide pointed to a held map as if explaining a few needed directions. A smiling Suleiman thanked the guide and returned to the table.

Suleiman waited while Adam paid the waiter. Somber men returned to the searing Cadillac. Soothing air-conditioning was quickly turned on. Swiftly a cooling car exited the parking lot as an ancient era receded from view. The Cadillac was halfway to the airport before any more words were spoken.

"Your brother is in Badera, Somalia."

* * *

The square clock on the low dresser showed 6:17 a.m. Such an hour was almost a half of an hour earlier than the alarm set by Angelina the night before. Angelina briefly wondered why a late morning sleep was much too elusive on days when she did not have to go to work. Often a late sleep seemed much too wanted on days when she had to go to work.

Then she stretched and began her usual early morning rituals, showering and dressing and eating a light breakfast. Finally she sorted pills for a daily regimen of her mother. Broad assortments of pharmaceuticals were available, so many grains of this medicine and so many grains of that medicine. First daily doses had to be taken at seven o'clock each and every morning. They had become rituals before a final sacrifice.

Soon Angelina finished organizing a variety of pills when she heard noises in front of the house. Then she walked to a living room window and pulled aside the curtains. Two dozen people were on and near the sidewalk. A dozen of these individuals were standing on the sidewalk near the low wrought-iron fence which bordered the front yard. Another dozen individuals were kneeling on the strip of lawn between the sidewalk and the street.

They had hung wreaths and strings of beads from the top of the low fence. Flowers and other gifts had been set against the bottom of the fence. People standing on the sidewalk spoke in whispers. People kneeling on the lawn prayed silently.

Angelina recognized a few people within this small crowd. Several of the couples were fast friends of Consuela and her husband. Evidently they had heard how ill Rachel Herr had become. They had arrived as pilgrims to soothe her suffering. Such kindnesses should always be more than readily welcomed.

Now an elated daughter grasped a handful of pills for a sleeping mother. Her angst was temporarily gone. She walked into Rachel's bedroom and saw Aurelius kneeling at the far side of the bed. Rachel was as motionless as the surrounding sheet. Both eyes of the older woman were calmly closed. She seemed to be completely at peace. Elation quickly faded to fear.

Then Angelina forgot about any pretended carried cures. Her handful of pills fell from her grasp like very heavy tears. They made muted sounds falling upon a carpeted floor.

She raced to the near side of the bed. Her mother did not seem to be even weakly breathing. Angelina pressed an ear to the chest of Rachel. She could only hear a deafening silence. Not even a slight hint of a heartbeat remained.

Angelina began to sob at the bedside of her mother. She clutched at the cool flesh as her weeping continued. Nothing could seem to console her.

"Why didn't you get me?" cried out Angelina.

"For what purpose?" calmly stated Aurelius.

"I wanted to be with her… I needed us to be together when she died."

"My child…Death would not dare to be in the same room as me."

Tests

Workmen had labored for almost two weeks to gut the former office of Albert Chester Mitchell. They had knocked out an opposite pair of walls bordering adjacent offices, plastering and painting any remaining walls. Expensive furniture and a costly carpet had been added as last touches to a very heavy hand. The new office would not be the same as the old office. Few mercies would be dispensed to the masses from such a room.

Hugo Buhner had once been described as a gorilla in a suit. Such a comparison was seen by many people as an insult to the large African highland anthropoids which ate leaves and other vegetation. Buhner was quite simply an insatiable carnivore, devouring people much like gorillas ate leaves. He was also a lowlife who had spent too many years in the lowland of the Washington political establishment. No morass was too messy to keep him from wading into its middle with both body and soul.

Now Adam had waited in the foyer of that new office for almost two hours. Director Mitchell would have never been as rude to anybody inside or outside of the bureau. Finally a closed door opened and John Axt exited with a wide grin. More than a few exchanges of information had been exchanged over these past one hundred minutes.

Director Buhner stood in an enlarged office like a king of a nearly remodeled castle. But a few of the more familiar turrets had to be torn down and the moat made wider. No interloper was gaining entrance without a spear through his heart.

"You wanted to see me," said Adam.

"Yes, it has been brought to my attention that Documents recently gave you a set of false identification papers for a confidential informant…a somebody named Aurelius Marcus," said Buhner.

"That's correct."

"I can find no formal file on any such informant. What can you tell me about this Aurelius Marcus character?"

"I can't tell you very much, except to say he is an extremely helpful individual."

"In that case, I am going to put him on the airline watch list. He can stay on that list until you *can* tell me something significant about him. Your informant won't be going much of anywhere unless your memory becomes refreshed."

"Is that really necessary?"

"It is if I say so."

"I don't think such a restriction is warranted."

"Listen, Hanson, you have to get it through your thick head that Mitchell is dead and I am here now. There is not a test of wills between us. This is my will…*capiche*!"

Adam slightly shook his head in silent but resistant agreement. He would not have a say in anything of consequence anymore. All of any former close allies of Director Mitchell were being shoved to a sideline of the bureau. They would be mostly spectators to a savage sport.

"It has also been brought to my attention that a pair of unauthorized items is still in your possession. One item is believed to be a cellphone and the other item is definitely a weapon."

"They are both at a very safe location." Adam still wanted to possess the star map and the laser gun. Such wandering wonders had been hidden in the basement of his wrecked house.

"I don't care where you have stashed them. They are property of the bureau and should be warehoused as quickly as possible."

"I will see what I can do."

"You will do better than giving me such a vague answer. You will personally bring them to John Axt within the week. He will be my primary assistant on most matters."

How Adam did feel his stomach churn. Johnny Meat Axe, as he was derisively called, seemed to have no scruples when it came to pursuits which would benefit himself. This excuse for a man would sell his daughter to slave dealers if the transaction would benefit him. He was a pathetic lackey who was also a grotesque little political pimp.

"John is an aptly named hatchet man."

"I had been told you had a reputation as a smart mouth."

"Not smart enough, I am still in your office."

"Your presence is easily remedied. You will now always report directly to Axt. You can be of assistance on his upcoming project. He will be coordinating any major operations."

"Yes, *sir.*" More than a hint of sarcasm was within his response. Mutual disdain was growing fast. Both of them would remain adversaries until the end of one of them.

"One last problem, *Hanson*, did you ever contact your brother in Somalia?"

"No, I was unable to get in touch with him."

"I'll take care of it."

"I'm certain you will."

"What did you just say?"

"Nothing, nothing at all… I suppose I'm finished?"

"I'd say so."

Adam turned and walked out of the large office. Yet he was amazed at how a single person or a tiny group of people could change an organization. Now the terrorist task force was run by a pack of haughty hyenas. Such a pack was going to eviscerate everyone and everything it could latch onto. Too many carcasses would be strewn around a weary world.

Adam Hanson felt more than alone.

* * *

The National Cathedral in northwest Washington, DC, was a modern marvel, a magnificent church more than a century in the making. Smooth carved limestone and intricate stained glass of the structure had become the highest point in the city. Stony spires reached three hundred feet into the adversarial atmosphere of the Capitol. Many people believed that any available god had long ago left an increasingly radical city. Prayers were usually murmured only for oneself in such a politicized place.

Adam and Angelina sat quietly in his parked car. Tangled traffic showed no sign of giving any immediate pardon. Steady streams of vehicles slowly continued on any surrounding streets. Quite a throng had turned out for the deceased. Albert Chester Mitchell had been as loved as any man can be who was in a position of immense power.

Democrats and Republicans, liberals and conservatives, progressives and radicals had paid their respects. Eloquent early morning speeches had been spoken with professional skills. Sincerity and hypocrisy had flowed throughout the great cathedral in roughly equal measures. Such equality was not a poor proportion in a requiem for any person. But such equivalency was an extraordinary portion of honesty for such a disingenuous town.

"It was quite a ceremony," said Angelina.

"It was a ceremony mostly for public relations," said Adam. "Director Mitchell was actually buried in Iowa last week at his family plot near Ottumwa. He always wanted to be with his wife and parents and the rest of his relatives."

"It sounds like he was a rural guy made good."

"I guess that is a truthful summary of his life. His family had always been farmers until he broke the mold. He used to tell me stories about running through the corn with his brothers and sisters, always trying to catch each other in the maze. I guess he was part of a big happy group of people, but they're all gone now. He was the youngest and the last to leave this earth."

Their quiet conversation temporarily faded to a soft silence. Wanting words were still strained between them. There was the stress of personal struggles and the death of a close friend for Adam. There was the stress of personal struggles and the near death of a close mother for Angelina. Their relationship was being tested by continuing troubles and a growing distance.

But Angelina had long wanted to hear more about Adam's private thoughts and fears. Adam had little desire to speak about such thoughts and fears. Any past had passed and should be put to a soiled rest. Occasionally a ground was not deep or hard enough to hold these memories. Slowly but surely a bitter freeze of cold regrets could push such stuff to a surface of self.

"I'm glad to have been with you for his service," finally said Angelina.

"I am, too," finally said Adam.

"I'm just sorry to have to leave so quickly."

"Yes, I understand your obligations of a lecture circuit. I also understand your responsibilities of caring for your mother. How is she doing now?"

"The doctors told me they have never even heard of anything like her condition. She went into a kind of human hibernation. Her heartbeat and breathing and everything else have slowed to almost nothing, and nothing more can be done for her. I was going to have her moved to hospice, but Aurelius asked me not to do anything. I have to keep the faith and hope this decision is the best choice to make."

"Faith has become a very unfamiliar word to me. I suppose not much of mine is left."

"You have never talked about religion before, at least not with me."

"I lost a lot of my beliefs after my parents were killed. My brother and I were raised in an inner-city Lutheran Church, but I never attended again after the World Trade Center collapse. I guess it doesn't really matter anymore. Reverend Matthews died and the church closed several years ago. My remaining aunt sent the obituary to me and it stated he had served his church for *sixty* years, just like a modern-day Hosea.

"I don't think too many people now would serve anything for sixty years. I also know that far too many of our inner-city churches have failed. Too few of the faithful are left and too little money is left to give. I suppose all of us lose bits of our faith as the years pass, or maybe I have just become too cynical."

"I don't think so. You have probably become more of a believer than you know. I would wager that you can probably still recite more than a few Bible verses with sincerity. I was raised in the Southern Baptist tradition and tradition stays a permanent part of each of us."

"You should have saved your last sentence for my brother. He doesn't believe in any western traditions anymore."

"Do you want to tell me about your brother? I know something is going on with him, but he is another topic we have never really discussed."

"Not too much is left to tell about him anymore. Abel is four years older and was in the army for twenty years, but he quit after his last tour in Afghanistan. He went over to the other side to make recruiting films for a group in west Pakistan. I hear he recently moved to Somalia, but it doesn't really matter where he goes. Abel won't be alive very much longer."

"Why are you so pessimistic about your own brother?"

"It's become public information, so I can tell you. Most people still don't know there is a termination list of American citizens living abroad and aiding the enemies of the United States. I've tried to contact him, but he won't talk to me. He sent word that I would never understand. I don't seem to know much about anything anymore, so he is probably all too correct."

"I guess people can't keep themselves from changing." Angelina placed her hand on Adam's hand. She held his fingers for a moment. But Adam seemed far from her touch.

"It's strange what you remember about a person who was once an important part of your life. Shared events stay in your mind as crystal-clear memories," started Adam. "I suppose every human being has similar remembrances tucked within his or her brain."

Angelina had never heard Adam speak very much about his past. Maybe their recent mutual emotional distress had made wise words possible to be told. Maybe the death of his mentor and friend had made such sentences available to be spoken. She did not have a factual clue as to an actual cause, but a final effect was a greater feeling of closeness to him.

"My family would go to a Sunday after-church picnic every summer at a big park at one of the Finger Lakes," continued Adam. "Reverend Matthews was always a fan of Charlton Heston. He especially liked the actor as Moses in *The Ten Commandments*. The good reverend would say a brief prayer before each picnic, and sweep an arm toward the blue lake and the green wooded hills and the wide beautiful sky with a few drifting white clouds.

"Then he would say in a firm but gentle voice, '*Behold His mighty hand!*' We would joyfully sit down to a lunch of hot dogs and potato salad and chocolate cake. I look back at an afternoon like that with my parents and my brother, with the reverend and the other people of our congregation, and wonder what happened to such a world. Somehow it just slowly but surely disintegrated, evaporated into a past where we can never be again."

"I guess we all have our day of running through the corn," said Angelina.

"I guess so," said Adam.

* * *

The helicopter from Newark Airport landed firmly upon the roof landing pad at the headquarters building of Lanicrim Industries. Thax set the corporate copter down among the winds of the surrounding Manhattan skyscrapers with a skilled hand. Soon he guided Angelina to a small private elevator. Then he led her to a very large hall.

Now Angelina stood at the lectern in front of an arc of an amphitheater. Rows of rising banked seats seemed to clutch at her. She thought this lecture hall could hold a thousand people. Yet nobody else was about except for the seemingly always present Mr. Thax.

She glanced at her wristwatch, knowing a very tight schedule had to be kept. Her flight from Baltimore to Newark had arrived fifteen minutes ahead of schedule. Obviously a gain of a quarter of an hour was going to be lost. An early evening audience had best begin filing into this amphitheater very quickly. A night flight home would not be missed for even a triple lecture fee. How she did not want to surrender a straightaway return to the bedside of her mother.

"Hello, Angelina," said Levid Lanicrim. "Excellent work, Mr. Thax." Lanicrim seemed to just materialize at the far end of the stage. "I can see that you have safely brought our insurance policy to this little lair."

"Where is everyone?" said Angelina. She pretended not to hear the recent reference to insurance. Such a statement seemed to be completely foreign to her situation. Nobody understood the many ways of any world.

"I must inform you of my deception," said Lanicrim. "Usually this great hall is used for the quarterly meetings of my most trusted employees, a managerial elite so to speak. Not tonight though, as an entire evening has been reserved solely for you."

"What do you mean?"

"I mean, my dear, that your talk today will be a very private affair. I will be an audience, and Mr. Thax will stay as a less than innocent bystander."

"I'm lost."

"Oh no, not yet, my dear. I would like very much for us to have a bit of a chat, a kind of final payment of a premium."

"I'm still lost."

"You have the face of an angel, but I am starting to wonder about the quality of your mind."

"I did not travel here to be insulted."

"Nobody ever does, yet I will give you a more than fair chance to redeem yourself."

"This is nothing but complete nonsense." Angelina reached for her purse and valise, but Thax more than menacingly stood in her way. Miracles would be needed to move him.

"My advice at this point in your circumstance would be not to do anything which could be considered rash. Mr. Thax's reflexes are incredibly quick, and he often reacts far too impulsively. You would think something as ancient as he has become would have slowed much more with the passing years."

"What do you want?"

"I only need a little intellectual sparring."

"To what end?"

"To whatever end we reach, probably your lack of freedom."

"You're beyond insane. You see yourself as a master of this planet, much like too many wealthy people."

"Now you insult *me.* I have been a master of far more than a single planet."

Angelina believed she was dealing with a complete psychotic. She would have to play his demented mind game to win a chance of survival. Other possible ways to escape such an overpaid trap were not available.

"Okay, I propose to give you a list of historical events and you will give me the year in which they occurred," said Angelina.

"Excellent, you might still save yourself," said Lanicrim. "Would you also want a specific day and hour of these occurrences?"

"You know that many historical events cannot be narrowed with such precision."

"Really…and who told you such nonsense?"

"Shall we begin?" Angelina would not take his bait. She would not be detoured from her present task. An impressive woman would make more than a fool of an imperious man.

"Please allow me a moment to become seated." Lanicrim briskly walked to the middle of the first row of seats. Then he quickly sat down with his left arm draped over an adjoining chair. He looked like a man casually waiting for a movie to start. "Begin as you shall… and may I suggest that we speak of nothing after the fall of the Western Roman Empire. These last fifteen or sixteen centuries hold such recent histories."

"I agree."

"Then proceed."

"Rome sacked by Visigoths?"

"410 AD."

"Edict of Caracala?"

"212 AD."

"Flavian Amphitheatre completed?"

"82 AD."

"Decree of Milan?"

"313 AD."

"Treaty of—"

"Perhaps we should regroup," interrupted Lanicrim. "You are an archeologist, why don't we at the very least restrict your questions to events before the common era?"

"Agreed," said Angelina. She was determined to trap him. Her intellect would show how wrong he could be. Her will would overwhelm him.

"Let us make our little quiz show even a bit more interesting than it appears to be. Why don't you ask me questions in descending chronological order? I need my amusements, and Mr. Thax also often needs the same. Although I must tell you in all honesty, his amusements can be incredibly unique."

"Whatever," said Angelina.

"Then ever onward," said Lanicrim.

Now Angelina hesitated for a moment. Memorable historical events were quickly pulled from scholarly memories. Her academic dig was not very far down. Such layers of knowledge were just beneath a surface.

"Battle of Actium?"

"31 BC."

"Caesar invades Britain?"

"55 BC."

"First Servile War?"

"135 BC."

"Destruction of Carthage?"

"146 BC."

"Macedonian Wars end?"

"148 BC."

"First Punic War ends?"

"201 BC."

"Alexander the Great dies?"

"323 BC."

"Battle of Issus?"

"333 BC."

"Battle of Granicus?"

"334 BC."

"Peace of Philocrates?"

"346 BC."

"Cyrus the Younger killed at Cunaxa?"

"401 BC."

"Battle of Plataea?"

"479 BC."

"Thermopylae?"

"480 BC."

"Marathon?"

"490 BC."

"Greek city states revolt against Persia?"

"499 BC."

"Cleisthenes establishes Athenian democracy?"

"508 BC."

"Solon becomes Athenian Archon?"

"594 BC."

"Assyrian Empire ends?"

"612 BC."

"Destruction of—"

"*Please* stop your list of petty human nonsense," again interrupted Lanicrim. "You must realize that I know *everything* about this puny planet which is almost worth such a knowing."

Now he looked at Angelina as a readily available prize. He would crush his prize down to an acceptable size. Angelina must realize her situation was hopeless. But a hopeless person can also become senseless. And Lanicrim did want her senses to eventually be extremely receptive.

"I am going to give you one last chance to baffle me, a solitary test of the wheel to completely save yourself from myself. If you do not succeed, you will be more than mine."

Thax was gratefully smiling. Passing centuries had boiled down his past to a very harsh present. What once had been had almost been forgotten.

Angelina's mind was racing. Some bit of something must be known that this messianic maniac did not know. She tried desperately to think of anything which might confuse him. Then she thought of the Boy King of Ancient Egypt.

"What year did the meteorite fall to earth in an area of the Sahara later named the Great Sand Sea?"

Now Lanicrim gave out a booming laugh. His bellowing chuckle filled the amphitheater. It was a deep and ugly expression of intellectual contempt.

"Which one?" he finally snickered.

But Angelina was not taken aback. She had foreseen a possibility of multiple meteorites and would make a final attempt to win a contest. No other choice was chosen to try to escape her cloistered prison.

"The meteorite that formed the green glass from which the sacred Scarab Beetle of Pharaoh Tutankhamen's burial necklace was carved."

Lanicrim looked at Angelina like she was a little child. He shook his head back and forth in mild amusement. "Do you really want to know about such an ancient Armageddon?"

"Yes, I really want to know."

"28,176,983 BC."

Angelina slumped within herself. She had begun to believe that Levid Lanicrim might really be Viracocha, the creator god of knowledge carved at Puma Punku. She had no way of knowing if he had just stated the correct year. But her mother had told her that the meteorite had fallen to earth about twenty-eight million years ago. Probably the given year was all too right. Suddenly she felt all too wrong. Her failure had made her fate.

Then Thax moved quickly behind Angelina. He fastened the waiting green choker firmly around her neck, its dark symbol clutching at her throat. She gasped and fell to her knees.

"This choker was once worn by my loyal Theodosis," said Lanicrim. "He and Rigel will be missed, but now we have a different miss." Lanicrim nodded to Thax. "Take her upstairs and bring her purse and valise. We do not want to leave any evidence that our beautiful angel has ever landed here."

Angelina was covered with a hooded black robe. Her eyes were wide beneath the holding hood. Now she was held by much more than a thickness of enveloping cloth.

Odysseys of the Soul

Adam looked out of the heavily tinted front window of the black SUV. Three other bureau agents were in the car with him. Their car was one short segment of four long snakes of vehicles slithering along the streets of Manhattan. Official marked and unofficial unmarked vehicles made large meandering caravans traveling from different directions. Such short odysseys would converge at a previously unspecified destination.

Yet Adam was one of the few people who knew the location of this secret destination. Any endpoint of their travels had to be the headquarters of Lanicrim Industries. An early morning raid would involve a hundred bureau and border agents plus five hundred New York City police. Those many words of Agent Axt from several hours earlier were still ringing in his ears. These words sounded like a solitary death knell for Adam's own career.

"Our operation will be completed in coordination with the Canadian and Mexican governments," had stated Axt. "Raids will simultaneously occur in western Europe at cities in England and France. Exact locations of these raids will not be divulged until all law enforcement personnel are transported to such locations. Therefore no outside communication with third parties will be allowed until this operation is completed."

Now Adam felt fortunate that Angelina had left New York City hours earlier on a red-eye to San Antonio. Angelina had not told him where exactly she was speaking in Baltimore and New York. But he realized they had not spoken enough to each other about too many subjects. Maybe most relationships failed in similar ways.

Finally the quartet of caravans converged at a Manhattan skyscraper not far from the East River. The dark building was clad in blackened stone which did not reflect many early rays of light. It seemed strange so many people would be working in supposed offices throughout the day and the night. This present case had become so bizarre that anything seemed possible. No end was in sightless sight for things wondrous and taboo.

Then a corporate logo was visible on a thick rectangle made of the same soulless stone.

LANICRIM INDUSTRIES
Knowledge is freedom

Such a motto sounded to Adam like the slogan over an entrance to a Nazi death camp: *Arbeit Macht Frei*—Work Will Set You Free. He thought not too many freedoms had ever been earned in such places. Murderous masters and struggling slaves had always seemed to have existed. It was a terrible truth that others would always try to enslave others.

Sudden scattered gunfights erupted in the front lobby. Sounds of shots quickly faded as waves of law enforcement swept through the first floor. Elevators and stairs were secured. Exits were completely blocked. All possible routes of escape had been closed. Mobs of people waited to be arrested.

Adam did not yet know that Levid Lanicrim had escaped several hours earlier. His dark limousine, driven by Mr. Thax, had sped toward the JFK Airport with only a pair of passengers. Lanicrim had planned to immediately fly by private jet to his personal wonderland. The young woman in a black robe accompanying him was already trapped within a looking glass world.

* * *

"Such a delay is more than an outrage," said Lanicrim.

He had just begun to board his private jet on the tarmac at the JFK Airport. But a patrol car with a pair of airport security officers had stopped in front of the plane. Both officers exited their car with a complete lack of awareness about what was really being approached. Such a lack would be a final and fatal mistake.

"I'm sorry, but JFK and LaGuardia and even the Newark Airport have just been closed," said the first officer. "No planes are allowed in and no planes are allowed out."

"My flight plan has already been approved," glared Lanicrim.

"It doesn't matter, we're shut down until further notice," said the second officer.

"Who would give such a preposterous command?" asked Lanicrim.

"We only know that the order came direct from Washington," answered the first officer.

"And that is all we need to know," added the second officer.

"Perhaps Mr. Thax could explain my opinion on the matter more clearly," smirked Lanicrim. He made a brief nod to Thax. His companion quickly chopped down the pair of officers with single strikes to the head.

"And Mr. Thax, would you also move their car as quickly as possible. It was incredibly rude of them to park a vehicle directly in my path."

But other airport security officers had seen the altercation. Another pair of officers raced out on the tarmac with guns drawn. Amazed officers watched as a tall and lean man dragged a parked security car to the side of a plane.

"This incident is indeed most unfortunate, Mr. Thax. Please delay any other law enforcement personnel for as long as possible. We will meet in Wonderland at your earliest convenience."

Then Lanicrim briskly boarded the jet with Angelina. He quickly began to taxi the plane to a near runway. And he briefly watched as Thax was finishing his confrontation with the additional pair of officers. Each of the officers had taken a single shot at Thax. Both of the bullets had struck his torso without any immediate effect.

These gunshots had focused everyone nearby to this immediate area of an otherwise quiet airport. Other officers were running toward a source of the gunfire. Thax thought for a few lingering seconds and made his choice. The corporate helicopter on the roof of the Lanicrim Industries headquarters building would be a best chance for an eventual escape.

Now he raced toward the parked limousine. Groups of airport security officers were already chasing him. Thax ran from those pursuers like a young rabbit racing from a pack of old dogs. He could run for days at twenty miles per hour and now reach a temporary top speed of thirty-five miles per hour. How he did flee from flagging followers.

His dark limousine awaited his dark hand. He sped out of a parking lot to the Shore Parkway. Several police cars were not too far behind him anymore. Both patrol cars had begun to gain ground. More police cars would quickly be not too far ahead of him.

The machine man sped recklessly along the Parkway for a dozen weaving miles in westbound lanes. He zigzagged among growing traffic, looking like a skier on a slalom run. Broad trails of wreckage were left in his wake. Other smaller vehicles had been sideswiped by the larger limousine. More than a few of these others had been forced off the Parkway.

Thax reached the Flatbush Avenue cloverleaf in about eight minutes. His ninety-miles-per-hour pace had to be significantly slowed with the slower congestion of the avenue. He still headed to the northwest like a machine man on an immoral mission.

Suddenly a line of stop sticks was tossed in front of the limo on the inside lane of the avenue. But Thax was speeding past a dump truck at that particular moment. No adjacent lane was available for him to swerve for a few fleeting seconds. He brushed the truck on its right side as far as could be done. Fiery sparks flew as the vehicles struggled against each other while an equally fiery truck driver cursed. He stayed on his truck horn even as the right tires of the limousine ran over the sticks. Two tires began to be steadily flattened.

No sense was saved staying with a vehicle which was rapidly losing momentum. Mile markers on the speedometer steadily drifted ever more downward. Thax decided to leave the limo as the meter edged below thirty. His driver side door was opened and out he did leap.

Officers in the immediately following patrol car watched as a man jumped from a moving limousine. Momentarily the running man fled alongside a slowing vehicle. Then he ran to his left across Flatbush Avenue, jumping approaching cars in the opposite lanes like low hurdles. Soon a climbing man scrambled up a bricked corner of a commercial building. Then he disappeared onto an awaiting rooftop sprawl of Brooklyn.

"Holy mother!" said an officer in the no-longer-following patrol car.

Now Thax was running at full speed, a maddened machine man racing along nearly connected rooftops like an angered antelope. Lofty leaps were made over any narrower side streets. But he dropped to a sidewalk and ran across any wider side streets. No obstacle was ahead of him which would not be readily mastered. Nothing could seem to stop him.

Cars and trucks on any wider streets in his way were jumped with ease. Even a stopped city bus was cleared with absolutely no strained effort. Its driver sat at the stop with wide-eyed wonder. Its load of passengers also sat or stood with a similar awe.

Then a running, leaping roof race continued on and on. Half of the entire New York City Police Department seemed to be after him. Dozens of patrol cars were trying to box him into central Brooklyn, but far too many streets were available to survey. And Thax was much too fast for such a strategy to have an immediate success.

Thax ran and ran until he saw a spreading grassy area in front of him. For a moment, such a meadow looked like a green space from his very ancient youth. Actually this area was only the broad and verdant lawn of Prospect Park. Yet Thax had never before been here.

He had always driven only along any main byways of Brooklyn and Queens. Neither borough had ever really been seen in a close and personal way. His car travels were mostly to and from the JFK and LaGuardia Airports. Stays in New York City had otherwise been restricted to wealthier sections of Manhattan.

Now he stood next to a big stone arch and stared at its many statues. But a patrolman quickly appeared around a corner of the arch. Thax grabbed the upraised gun from a hand of the patrolman in a blink of an eye. Then he just held the officer by a shoulder in a firm grip.

"What is it?" said Thax.

"What are you talking about?" said the officer. He looked at the face of a deranged man and could see almost nothing. Only a crazed expression of a hardcore doper was evident.

"What is *it*?"

The streetwise officer thought he might be dealing with a new synthetic drug. Brutal fingers of the man were beyond belief. Eyes of the man were beyond a benevolent earth.

"This stone arch, *what is it*?" again asked Thax. He was becoming ever more annoyed. And his annoyance could never be a positive sign for anything else near him.

"It's the Soldiers and Sailors Monument from our Civil War." The calm officer felt like he should give any kind of a calming answer. Brief longing looks were made at his handgun, held in the hand of a madman.

"Not *our* war, *your* war."

This officer was a hardened veteran of the force. Yet something about his current confrontation seemed much more than unique. He tried to maintain his composure within a growing craziness.

"You're right, it was my war."

"And how many died in this war?"

"I think it was over half a million dead."

"Half of a *single* million. That is a herring in a school of herring."

"I think that's about what it was."

"Don't *think* anymore, just listen and learn. Monuments have been made which you cannot even imagine. The Arch of Mephistoclea, now *there* is a monument to the dead, taller and wider and more magnificent than anything ever built on this planet. You have to remember, of course, that more than ten billion perished in the Six Mephistoclean Conflicts."

The officer nodded compliantly. His share of lunatics had certainly been seen over the years. He hoped at least a few of his fellow officers would surely arrive on the scene.

"You don't *believe* me," said Thax. Pretended politeness in this pathetic patrolman was easily evident. Weakness poured from any true man like water from a broken bucket.

"I do, I do believe you," said an ever more concerned officer.

"Do not play me for an unwise guy. I do not think you really believe *anything*!"

"No, you're wrong."

"Then tell me what you believe, tell me what you hold in your heart of hearts, tell me what you are willing to suffer and bleed and die for…*tell me*!"

"My wife, my children, my fellow officers. I don't know what else you want me to say."

"You are a tiny, tiny, *tiny* man. I can barely see you anymore." Thax looked at the officer with an angered contempt. "Your beliefs are even tinier than yourself."

Then a police car stopped near the arch. Hard screeches of rubber told of the speed which it had been driven. Two officers exited the car with readied handguns.

"I will leave you to the days of your life, little man. But a night will fall when you are old and broken and near death. When such an hour arrives, remember what you could have been, what you would have been, if only you had taken the road least traveled, a trail rarely tread."

Now Thax tossed the officer against the stone of the arch. He quickly turned and ran toward the subway station several blocks distant. Any open stream of streets had to be left as quick as possible. Another pair of newly arrived officers drove their patrol car directly toward an again running machine man. Thax jumped the length of the car and ran to the subway station.

Soon he reached the steps of the already crowded station. Then he raced down the steps into a growing morning mob of commuters. Thax hopped a token gate as the cashier yelled at him. He pushed a dozen people out of his way to be on his way, looking along both stretches of sunken tracks. Approaching trains were not anywhere in sight.

Throngs of waiting commuters watched in disbelief as he jumped from the concrete platform. He ran along a beckoning northwest tunnel toward the East River. His fast three miles were completed in a bit over five minutes, a pace not quite quick enough.

Half a dozen police were waiting for him at the mostly emptied Adams Street Station. He plowed into a scrum of officers more powerfully than the greatest fullback who had ever lived. All of the officers had encircled and attempted to tackle him to the concrete. All of them would regret their efforts.

Thax's flailing forearms and knees cut through the mass of uniforms with ease. He left a sprawling mess of men behind him in a handful of seconds. Then he was up the inside subterranean steps to the outside metropolitan city.

The Brooklyn Bridge was before him. Thax began to race along a pedestrian walkway of the bridge. He was not too far from his helicopter on the landing pad of the Lanicrim headquarters building. Then he saw a group of officers running from Manhattan to greet him. Also a growing group of officers was running from Brooklyn to grab him. Only a single way to travel awaited at a cornered point in his ever more wayward path.

Steel cables strung from the east tower beckoned to him. The nearest cable was climbed upward like a better-than-best acrobat. He suddenly saw Adam Hanson among the group running toward him from Manhattan. The Lanicrim Industries headquarters had been much more than secured by the local authorities. Freed federal officers had joined in a hunt.

"Hanson!" sneered Thax, hanging by a single arm from the cable. His kept police gun was taken from his belt. Three shots were fired by the machine man at the approaching true man. One bullet ricocheted off of the tower in front of Adam, striking the cellphone in his pocket.

Adam fell backward, but was not seriously hurt. Now he pulled out the laser gun for retribution. He had planned to give the laser gun and the star map to John Axt after this raid. But such a weapon seemed more than needed in his present circumstance. Adam shot at Thax, still holding onto the cable with less than a little effort. Several bursts of laser fire zipped past the machine man like tiny comets. Thax neatly leapt to another nearby cable.

"Where in hell did you get that gun?" said Axt, pointing to the laser. Those blazing photons made a bright light sight. It certainly did not look like any weapon he had ever seen.

"It's brand new," said Adam.

"Oh?"

"It's made by ACME."

"I'll have to get one of those babies."

"If you say so."

John Axt did not want to be outdone in any way by Adam Hanson. He would show Hanson and Buhner and everybody else what could be done in such a situation. Axt was going to run past that nearer bridge tower to take a better shot at a wanted individual. Still a pretend person was hanging from a matrix of bridge cables like a demented chimpanzee.

Thax saw Hanson crouched behind the east tower. Such a human being should have lost his being weeks earlier. He was a true man who had truly become far more than a nuisance.

The machine man again tried to steady himself on a steady cable. He aimed at Hanson's head and fired the handgun just as John Axt popped up in front like a jack-in-the-box. And the bullet tore into Axt's chest like a final farewell to his life. He clutched at his bleeding body for several seconds and collapsed. Not even a moan escaped his lips as he slipped into oblivion.

Then Thax climbed along ever more cables to a reach of the east bridge tower. A stony tower looked to him like a steady stairway. An ascent upon its limestone facing was started with steeled fingers. Up and up and up, he did go, glancing at the angry mob on the bridge.

Crowds of onlookers watched in disbelief at the amazing actions of the machine man. Adam had a last attempt for a kill shot at the fleeing figure. Another laser burst ripped off Thax's right ear. A hunk of artificial flesh drifted to the East River below like a very heavy butterfly.

Throngs gazed with absolute astonishment at an ever more astounding figure. Thax easily scrambled up the remainder of the vertical rocky tower with an incredible strength and agility. He might have been on a wide and sturdy ladder instead of a near and sheer man-made cliff. Thin crevices or tiny unevenness in the limestone blocks were like thick rungs to him.

He reached the flat top of the east tower and looked down. Longing looks were also made at the Manhattan side of the river. Thax knew he was almost trapped. His only remaining way of escape was the filthy water far, far below. But he still walked toward the south side of the tower.

"He's going to jump, that's about two hundred and forty feet to the river," said an officer.

"We won't have to worry about that thing anymore," said another officer.

"Don't be too sure," said Adam to himself.

Then a growing crowd watched as the figure of a man went to the narrow edge of the tower. Onlookers gasped as a perfect arch of a dive reached for the river. Down and down and down, he did go. Thax made a very tight splash for such a tall dive.

His urban odyssey was finally finished.

* * *

Solomon Sage had become very comfortable on the leather couch. His brown hide hideaway waited for thoughtful early evening hours. Later evening hours would be spent waiting for his wife. Harriet had left for a seminar on the life of Chaucer. Many early writers still spoke to her in complete ways. Yet too many books and blogs of human thought waited to be completed.

Solomon wanted to know the end of such an intellectual odyssey. He wished to understand the point when his species would really grasp a place and a peace of its existence. The long and arduous journey to such a point had only just barely begun.

Solomon recalled several dozen of those most memorable steps upon this beginning path. His scientific mind sorted through the passing centuries for the most memorable astronomical moments. Any final destination was far beyond his knowledge, far beyond his earthly being. But there would be a distant day when men and women would even understand the dust of dreams.

More than two thousand years had passed since Euclid had devised the principles of geometry; Aristarchus accurately computed the distance from the earth to the moon; Eratosthenes calculated the circumference of the earth and the distance from the earth to the sun; Hipparchus developed trigonometry, predicted solar eclipses, and completed the first celestial map.

The past thousand years had been witness as Copernicus presented a sun-centered solar system; Tycho Brahe advanced celestial observations and discovered supernovae; Lippershey invented the telescope; Galileo refined the telescope and viewed the moons of other planets; Leibniz and Newton developed calculus; Newton published his thesis on gravitation; Kepler determined the elliptical orbits of planets; Roemer measured the speed of light; Herschel cataloged nebulae and clusters; Piazzi discovered asteroids, and Huggins began the spectral analysis of stars.

The last century or so had seen discoveries of special and general relativity; a realization that a vast multi-galactic universe spread far beyond our own Milky Way Galaxy; the detection of quasars, pulsars, neutron stars, black holes, and cosmic radio waves; the development of rocketry, advanced telescopes, and interstellar space probes; the refinement of supercomputers and desktop computers, laptop computers and handheld computers. Knowledge of the human species could be grasped in the hollow of a hand.

Yet what did we *really* know about our incredibly vast and complex universe!

Now Solomon had reached a belated belief that he was an ant in a glass-faced box. He was digging within that box with eight billion other ants. They knew an inside box so well, yet could not really comprehend much of what was outside of the box. The rest of a room was somewhat known, but a greater house and neighborhood, a city and a continent, and the real extent of their world of existence were far beyond them.

Then Solomon pulled out a dozen old vinyl records from a nearby cabinet. He had kept more than a few of those singles and albums from his youth. Scatterings of people such as himself had also kept a usable phonograph. Oldies but goodies soothed his older self.

Harriet had always preferred her own set of classics. Rachmaninoff and Debussy and Krieg were still her favorites. Solomon and Harriet filled most of the missing blanks of knowledge for each other. Maybe such a complement was the truest measure of a truly human existence. The couple made a mated pair held by a pull of mutual affections. Life held onto life with an ageless and unknown wisdom.

Solomon was an especially ardent fan of Judy Collins. His favorite of her songs was *Both Sides Now*, written by Joni Mitchell. Musical clouds of life and love wafted through the melodic air of the living room. They clung to him like billowing and wonderful acceptances.

How he did listen to the lilting lyrics of a softly beautiful song again and again. Finally he had to acknowledge that the amount of knowledge known by humanity was much too miniscule. It was an infinitesimal atom of a highly complex creature, a single sensed raindrop in a mighty massive hurricane.

He really did not know very much at all.

KING OF THE JUNGLE

Polluted waters of the East River and Upper New York Bay had been left far behind. Thax had swum several miles underwater down the river toward the equally putrid bay. Finally he had surfaced and free-styled southward until evening. Then he boarded a sleek forty-five-foot sailing yacht passing in the night.

Thax was more than pleased that the yacht had an inboard motor and a sail. His hijacked yacht continued an approximate southerly route for continuing days and nights. Four days earlier it had passed the wide expanse of Chesapeake Bay. Five nights earlier it had also passed a middle-aged couple who had been tossed over a side like unwanted ballast.

This machine man knew enough about sailing to make a respectable moderate speed run toward South America. He had been on a variety of watercraft owned by Lanicrim Industries during an array of entertainments. Thax did not know that the man and the woman tossed over a side of the yacht had accomplished their own more-than-respectable-moderate speed run.

The courageous skipper and his wife were excellent swimmers, somehow staying afloat for seventy hours. They were beyond exhausted when saved by another passing yacht of the same class. Soon their scary story about a one-eared hijacker was told to local authorities. Their scarred hijacker was soon enough identified by federal authorities.

Thax was fleeing along the eastern shore of Florida when he saw a coast guard cutter bearing down upon him. He knew no sense was salvaged arguing with the fifty-caliber gun on the cutter. The pursued slipped over a side of the yacht when the pursuer was still a mile away. An abandoned yacht would be found empty. A search would not be so easily ended.

Continuous motion of rolling ocean waves lapped at Thax for another day. Nothing else seemed to be within a broad expanse of saltwater except himself. Eventually a pod of orcas sped northward past his bobbing head halfway through that day. Kings of a watery jungle passed in a synchronized fast swim. Warm prey was sought in cooler climes.

Now any sky overhead was as empty as a surrounding sea. Not even any gulls were circling him. He was a machine man in a watery desert. Then he saw a speck of something to the north. This speck became ever larger as a hulk of a freighter cruised ever closer.

The Pearl of the Orient was a nearly broken freighter with an already broken cargo. This heavily loaded freighter was slowly struggling from Philadelphia to Djakarta. Tons of various scrap metals were temporarily held in its hold, its current trip a last voyage for the dilapidated ship. A corroded hulk was to be grounded at Alang on the coast of India and ripped apart. An old boat would become as smashed as its shattered cargo.

The international crew of the vessel was almost as varied as that cargo. At least a dozen different nationalities were represented on the floating wreck. None of them seemed to speak much English except several of the officers. The captain and the first mate were from New Delhi and fairly fluent.

Thax had ripped a strip of cloth from the bottom of his shirt to cover his missing ear. He calmly explained how his sailboat had been struck by a rogue wave. And a brave little boat had sunk like a large stone. Nothing had been saved but himself and the clothes on his back.

When asked about the injury to his head, he quickly added that a glint of a tiny cross pierced in his right earlobe must have attracted a predator. The fleeing fish had snatched its flashing prize with his ear. It was indeed a most terrifying experience.

"Probably a barracuda," said the captain. "They are attracted to shiny stuff."

Then Thax was ushered below deck for a shower and medical treatment. He insisted on dressing his wound himself. Adhesive tape and an elliptical gauze patch and hydrogen peroxide were given to him. New clothes and boots were also put on a bunk assigned to him. His other clothes and boots had already begun to rot from a salty sea.

Suddenly he felt a need to take a nap. It was an urge which was an extremely unusual event for him, a need that had abruptly overwhelmed the machine man. He lay down on his bunk and closed his eyes, sleeping the sleep of the nearly dead.

* * *

Now the vacated office of Adam Hanson seemed beyond bleak. His packed cardboard box stayed next to him like a nearly forgotten companion. He had not called or texted Angelina over this past week from his new cellphone. His current cellphone number had been emailed to her home computer in San Antonio. There had yet to be any kind of a response from her. Here was a personal gap becoming ever wider.

But Adam was in no mood to be aggressive in any relationship. He was being transferred out of the Federal Terrorist Task Force at the request of Director Buhner. Supposedly Adam was being bounced because of his failure to surrender possession of both of his unauthorized items.

He had turned in his own mangled cellphone as a substitute for the first item. His phone had been destroyed by the ricochet bullet beyond any reasonable recognition. Adam had given a sworn statement that the unauthorized weapon had fallen into the East River. This weapon had been reported lost during the same confrontation on the Brooklyn Bridge. Buhner had accepted a first lie, but not a second lie. Nothing else was owed to such a petty tyrant.

None of their gamesmanship seemed to really matter anymore. Buhner was having him moved to another section of the bureau in another building. His first new case was going to be investigating government corruption in a suburb of Rochester, New York. The reason given for this assignment was that Adam was a native of upstate New York. He would know the territory so very well. But a real reason was that Adam was being pushed into a far backwater of the bureau. Most people would discover such a territory at the back end of their careers.

He looked at the cardboard box. Photographs and awards for valor were tucked within that single box. Not much else was available to be taken with him. His memos and files and almost everything else were property of the bureaucracy. Final furtive results of many years of ever more wretched work were boxed and ready to go. Even more bad memories would quickly be taken from this building.

Then Ashley Fawne walked down the hallway toward the doorway of his former office. She held a white business envelope in her hand. *Personal and Confidential* was written on the front of the envelope in impersonally scrawled letters.

Ashley was a beautiful blond woman who had suddenly become Buhner's very personal secretary. It was a new position which had been created to avoid very specific education requirements. Somehow this young woman had also been appointed even though she was far down a civil service list. Quite a number of forced waivers must have been required to reach her. She was a nice girl with a heart which bordered on naïve.

"Director Buhner wanted me to give this envelope to you," said Ashley. "He also wanted you to give me your electronic office and garage cards." She seemed to be ashamed about having to do such a dirty deed. Yet she did not seem to realize how many dirty errands remained to be completed. Life could be a hard learning experience for a person with morals.

"Fine with me," said Adam.

"Director Buhner would have brought the envelope to you himself, but he had to meet a group of senators at a charity golf event," said Ashley. She felt like an explanation was needed for such an impersonal visit.

The simple truth was that Hugo Buhner did not want to ever see Adam Hanson again. Such hostility was more than mutual. There was no possible bridging of such varied views.

Adam did not immediately say anything to her. His office and garage cards were retrieved from his suit coat hanging behind the door. Kept electronic cards were cautiously held as the envelope was opened. An enclosed solitary piece of paper showed only a single cold line of dark print:

09/29 E.K.I.A. Badera, Somalia 20:06

Now Adam did not show any extreme reaction. He told Ashley to wait a moment more. His Glock and shoulder holster were calmly placed on the desk. His badge was also put upon that growing pile. Finally his office and garage cards were handed to Ashley.

"I quit," said Adam.

His suit coat and cardboard box were grabbed as he headed toward the row of elevators. He stood in front of an elevator until a down arrow was displayed. Adam had a brief glimpse of Ashley Fawne still standing in his former office doorway. She stood silently with absolutely no real idea of what had just really happened.

An elevator whirred to the lobby as a relieved man stayed quietly within its walled confines. Adam suddenly felt like a partly freed man. Hugo Buhner and the rest of his bureaucratic tangle were being left behind. Men like Buhner saw themselves as kings of such jungles. But even royal reigns are often significantly shortened.

He walked to the parking garage for a final walk from the bureau. It was to be the very last day of his law enforcement career. Adam recalled what Angelina had told him about the ides of every month. Now a chastened man believed that a person should beware of all of the days of all months. Any human life could end within any hour of any day at any spot on the globe.

Adam drove far beyond the clutch of Washington, DC, on secondary roads. Lures of the mainstream had lost their luster. He drove on and on in a traveling trance. Eventually his car was stopped at an isolated lookout a hundred miles into Pennsylvania. Nothing was around him but rolling green hills. Numerous hills went on and on in a very verdant view.

Then he got out of his car and walked to an edge of the lookout. He sat upon the thick stone wall which protected a cliff side perimeter of the turnabout. His brother should have had a similar protection. Abel Trajan Hanson had become an enemy killed in action.

Abel had been executed less than three weeks after Director Mitchell had died. He had been blasted in a remote land at the airy whim of a remote-controlled drone. Probably the distant deed had been done by an RQ-170 Sentinel. His death had been covertly completed on a Sunday evening. Yet Adam quickly remembered a seven-hour difference in time zones.

His hour of death had been just after one o'clock in the Finger Lakes of central New York State. Such a relatively recent hour had been a final farewell to any afternoon church picnics at Cayuga State Park. Any antique philosopher kings had really perished long ago.

Adam burst into tears, weeping for too many lost years. How these passing years did take too much from his human kind. He cried until his droplets of recollection were finally stilled. But he still remained a keeper of memories safely kept within the most secret, sacred part of him. A true man would never, ever relinquish such remembrances.

Then he continued his travel to an old cabin hidden in the ancient Alleghany Mountains.

* * *

More than a week of sunny days had passed quietly for Thax. *The Pearl of the Orient* traveled slowly but surely toward the Panama Canal. It was a Latin American destination which was far more than acceptable to him. He could find assistance at the Lanicrim Industries building in Panama City. Six hundred employees worked at various tasks at this location.

Sudden shouting started on the top deck of the freighter several days before reaching the Canal Zone. Amazed members of the crew pointed to a huge bird circling the freighter. A gliding albatross seemed to circle the ship without any effort. An enormous waved albatross stayed on a local wind for almost half of an hour.

Such a flight was not a very good omen. None of the men had ever seen this cream and brown portent on the Atlantic side of the Isthmus. None of the men had also ever seen this kind of a bird so far north. Such a bird was found on the Pacific side of the Isthmus and further south.

Reasonable crewmen might have once accepted that a night storm had blown an albatross so far to the northeast. Even a very powerful albatross could not have resisted such powerful winds. But any sense of reason evaporated when the huge bird landed on the bow of the ship.

Such species of birds were always continuous flyers over water. None of the men had ever seen any kind of albatross land on any kind of cruising ship. None of the men had also ever seen a waved albatross with a wingspan which must have measured seven feet across. It looked like a feathered demon sent from a waiting hell as a winged warning.

The albatross only stayed on the ship for about five minutes. Preening moments were about five minutes too long as far as the crew was concerned. Patches of feathers were cleaned with a practiced dignity. Then a cleansed albatross took to the air, again circling the freighter after it flew from the bow with a brisk wind. It was an increasingly ominous maritime sign, finally winging ever westward in sweeping arcs.

Most members of the crew began to jabber in half a dozen languages. More than a few words and gestures were directed at Thax. Too many men of the sea still held too many mythical beliefs. Monsters were lurking almost anywhere about the briny deep. Even as an albatross disappeared in the distance, fears of the crew only appeared ever closer.

The entire crew knew this trip was a final voyage for such a worn-out freighter. These men did not want this trip to be a final voyage for themselves. Ships of the earth had become their watery homes. Seas of the world had become their unfathomable estates. None of those men wanted such a fleeting ownership to end for many more years.

Thax never went below any deck after that particular incident. Now a top deck remained his only berth all day and all night. He did not want to become trapped in a thick steel room by a bunch of deranged members of a merchant marine. Their once welcome guest had become their unwelcome pariah.

Finally a shore of the Isthmus of Panama edged into view at dusk of the eleventh day. The superstitious crew was only a mile from the canal when its members decided to take action. Several dozen of the men cornered Thax on the stern of the ship with planned mayhem. Their captain was holding a pair of very heavy shackles. Their first mate was holding a twelve-gauge shotgun. Coast guard messages had recently relayed the description and crimes of Thax.

"You are a wanted man who is unwanted by us," said the captain.

Thax slithered over a railing of the stern faster than a water snake in a swamp. The shotgun was still fired once as the diving figure disappeared into the salty sea. This figure never surfaced until it reached the surf near the Panamanian town of Portobelo.

Then a one-eared merman steadily walked out of low waves on the outskirts of the town. Such an astonishing sight was only witnessed by a retired fisherman. The stunned man crossed himself and mumbled a prayer for his self to a desired deity. Another prayer was mumbled for the town as the merman turned in its direction on the beach. Now a reticent retiree watched in amazement as a very fast swimming merman became a very fast running landman.

This machine man speedily ran across hot sand toward a nearby railroad. The Panama Railroad Line roughly paralleled the south side of the great canal to Panama City. Thax waited only about a half of an hour before a locomotive rumbled down the tracks. He hopped onto a following freight car to travel the next fifty miles with relative ease. Another strip of cloth was ripped from the bottom of his newer shirt during his short trip. An injury from his missing ear must again be hidden. Waterlogged adhesive tape and gauze were gone.

His search for the Lanicrim Industries building was very brief. Thax looked at a dark building from six blocks away. He stood on a street corner with more than a brief disbelief. Yet his journey was about to take another detour, a trip becoming ever more difficult.

American and Panamanian troops had surrounded the perimeter of the building. His supposed sanctuary was being emptied of its employees. Heavily armed soldiers were marching hundreds of handcuffed people to a long line of buses. They were being led to a variety of prisons.

Thax stood for several moments to get his personal bearings. He was almost 1,500 miles from his final destination, a distance computed as a straight line by the flight of a bird. He had quite an array of incredible physical powers, but a power of flight was not included within his physique. It was one attribute which would be sorely missed.

Now he was a more than wanted murderer which was now probably known by much of the Americas. Any journey along the populated west coast of Latin and South America could not be completed without a ready recognition. A clean reach of the Pan-American Highway was also a lure which needed to be avoided. Thax would have to continue to hide from public eyes as much as possible. His missing right ear might as well have been a monstrous neon sign.

He would try to more than repay Hanson for giving him such a scarlet letter. How he secretly fumed for not being able to deal with that true man back at the East River. Still currents of time would often flow together in most unexpected ways. Ripples of existence could again be made right for him.

Then only a single possible private path remained for his very long journey to Wonderland. Waiting jungles of Columbia and Brazil would have to be conquered. He could stay on a mostly unpopulated eastern fringe of the Andes Mountains for much of his travels. Not too many human beings would be encountered on such a route. His only additional problem with such an extended route was that six hundred to seven hundred miles would be added to his total journey.

Probably he could only average about eight or nine miles per hour on such a journey. Such a slow pace would require at least another week and a half to reach the Wonderland. Many slim trails and any slender roads and a thick foliage would take their tolls on him. No other options were available to avoid such a taxing trip.

Soon Thax began to run to the southeast with steady strides. Soon enough he stumbled upon an almost-forgotten dirt road stretching in that direction. A full moon was his only watcher for another hour until a shabby shantytown appeared along a single side of the dwindling dirt. And a surly looking group of men wavered in bright night-light as they started to block the beckoning trail. But Thax was in no mood to be passive anymore.

Open dirt of this remnant of a road was at least a temporary relief from close clutches of trees and shrubs and vines. Many miles could be covered in only a few hours on such a trail. He was not going to make even a temporary additional detour for anyone. His early vow about avoiding human beings had quite quickly been broken.

An overweight man with an equally heavy grin approached him. A king of this hobo jungle sauntered to the lead. Spanish words were spoken in a harsh tone of voice. Yet a lack of understanding must have shown on Thax's ever more taut face.

"Oh, a gringo," finally said the stout man in stunted English. "We are certain you are a very generous gringo...no."

"I am more than certain you will get nothing from me," said Thax.

"We think a toll must be paid by anyone who uses this piece of a road. Even an ignorant gringo must see there is no other choice. Here is but a simple truth of life," spat the king.

"We always have a choice in life. Even an ignorant slob of a clown such as yourself must see such a simple truth," spat a supposed peasant.

This amused leader was not amused anymore by this conversation. His gaping grin faded to a slim purse of lips. Angered disgust was shown by a crude splat of spit. "You are not so generous as we had supposed. Now we have no choice but to take what we want."

Four men from the group began to approach in ready pairs with readily held machetes. Severely sharpened blades showed soft gleams of moonlight. Their tragic task had been regularly relished for too many gory days and nights. But this moonstruck evening would hold a bloody confrontation which none of these hombres would ever forget.

Thax calmly looked to the side of the narrow road opposite the shantytown. Used building materials were accumulated in a lengthy pile. Sheets of corrugated metal and cracked plywood were haphazardly tossed upon each other. Pieces of ragged timber and dozens of concrete blocks helped to form a jumbled heap. Among this dirty mound of thrown away stuff was also a scattering of railroad ties.

Thax reached toward the waiting pile of debris. One of the creosoted railroad ties was picked up in his left hand. The thick wood tie was upraised like a dark baseball bat.

"Take whatever you can," said Thax.

Now he knocked over the first pair of suddenly stopped attackers with a single swipe of the railroad tie. He clubbed the second pair of assailants like wayward rats. A crumpled quartet stayed motionless on the bloodied earth.

Any remainder of the once aggressive group on the road quickly hit the road. An amazed mob of men looked like they had just seen a fifty-ton tank bearing down upon them. They made a hasty retreat from their lifeless comrades. Humbled thugs started to disappear far beyond any near shacks of the shantytown.

Their fat leader waddled away like a terrified duck. Thax disgustedly flung the railroad tie at the fleeing slowpoke. The corpulent man was crushed by the impact of the thick spear. No more vulgar spitting would ever be done at this tawdry town.

Then Thax began to run along the open reach of gained ground. Moonlight dappled dirt of the partly overgrown trail looked very wide indeed. Every effort would be made to avoid other humans during his lengthy journey. But such an effort would soon enough fail him.

THE LABYRINTHS OF LIVING

Steady snowmelt from the Andean Mountains flowed ever eastward with increasing strength. Countless crags and valleys birthed the greatest of earthly rivers as the mighty Amazon was made by many parents. But numerous headwaters of the great river were not settled by many people. Living loneliness prospered within an otherwise vibrant labyrinth of life.

Thax looked to these western mountains with decreasing strength. Occasionally he was becoming tired. Here was a feeling which could not be really remembered. Occasionally he needed to rest. Here were respites which could not be rationally understood.

Yet he thought his physical problems must be due to the unrelenting tropical heat of Columbia and Brazil. Columbia had been hot, but Brazil was hotter. Temperatures never seemed to be anything but searing. Humidity had also never seemed to be anything but extremely high. Elevations of the Andes beckoned with a welcoming coolness.

Now Thax had begun to follow the Ucayali River upriver when he heard a strange and repetitive noise. Intermittent thumps sounded like the largest and slowest of a breed of woodpeckers was working at a wooden task. Its call echoed ahead of him with an erratic beat. Then he encountered a trio of men chopping down a huge mahogany tree.

"Poachers..." said Thax to himself. He knew all about all kinds of illegal activities on this planet. For many years he had been very seriously involved with most of them.

The illegal timber trade had been booming within western Brazil and southeastern Peru. Cedar and big leaf mahogany trees could not hide even in such an isolated forest labyrinth. Magnificent trees were being taken down in the most secluded of spots.

These thieves must have been the poorest of poachers. None of the men had a chain saw, only a single axe. This massive mahogany tree must have been a first attempt at entering an unlawful market. They otherwise would have had much better equipment to hack at a tree which was two hundred feet tall. A woody giant seemed to look far down upon them.

Tired men took turns swinging their axe with unprofessional skills. They had not even built a platform or a springboard to cut the tree at its higher nine-foot-wide diameter. They instead hacked away at waist level at the lower twelve-foot-wide ground diameter. This jungle goliath would not be brought to earth for many hours.

Lately Thax would have avoided such men, shunning humans since his hurried exit from Panama. But his clothes and boots were again ever more tattered. Ready replacements for these disintegrating clothes and boots were readily waiting before him.

The machine man with a missing ear appeared from the dense foliage like a local apparition. Three workers were temporarily stunned. Exhausted men spoke hesitantly back and forth in Portuguese with more than a little anxiety. An unknown dweller of an unexplored part of the rainforest had most definitely been encountered.

"*E uma criatura da selva!*" said the first man.

"*Ele vainos matar!*" said the second man.

Thax had already picked up the largest of their temporarily shed shirts from a furrowed fallen log. He tossed his old shirt to the ground and put on his newest shirt very quickly. These motions were not quick enough to cover the pair of bullet holes in his torso. One of the holes was in his chest and the second hole in his abdomen. His wounds looked like strangely separated eyes. Only a slight black fluid showed where red blood should have been.

Already the first and second of the three workers were on their knees. Apprehensive men prayed to every god and goddess which had ever been known to exist. They had dishonored the secret lair of the creature. Horrible personal prices would probably have to be paid for such a desecration.

But the third man was not as superstitious. Real men had to always defend themselves as there was no other real substitute. No god or goddess he had ever known had ever protected him from anything. A ragged gap on a side of its head and a pair of holes in its torso told that the creature could be injured. Any creature which could be injured could be killed.

Thax had motioned for the first man to take off his pants. He had also motioned for the third man to take off his boots. Quickly the first man complied with these directions. Slowly the third man began to unlace his boots.

Pants were hurriedly exchanged with the first man. Thax had just put on this newest pair of pants when the third man struck him from behind with the axe. There was a powerful blow which entered several inches into the right artificial shoulder. Here a stuck axe stayed firmly in its temporary resting spot near the neck. An amazed man tried to pull out the axe after his first strike. Even ever more straining efforts failed him.

Then Thax turned toward the speechless man who had struck him. He knocked the man over with a single slap of an open hand. His temporarily unconscious victim stayed motionless, face to the ground. Both woodcutting friends remained equally motionless on their knees. They were starkly staring at the creature with more-than-horrified astonishment.

Now an aggravated machine man grabbed the axe still embedded in his shoulder. Its metal head was easily pulled out. Hardened steel exited a synthetic shell with a rough raspy sound. Hardwood of the handle was broken over a knee, its black blade thrown into the jungle with an obvious contempt. The hunk of dark metal arced far above a far treetop.

Thax stood over the now-crawling man with the pair of partly unlaced boots. His pair of once-kneeling friends were on their feet.

They ran as fast as fearful men can run. Their isolated village would solemnly hear about the powers of such an unholy beast. Several screams echoed behind them before silence again filled the jungle.

No trees would be felled anywhere near this lair of the creature for many years.

* * *

San Antonio police had blocked vehicle travel to the street on which Rachel Herr still lived. Limited access seemed like the best solution to prevent the occurrence of even more traffic accidents. Collisions which had recently happened had been very minor. But major laws of transportation probability should not be allowed to be tested any more than necessary.

These accidents had occurred because of rubbernecking at a prospering crowd of people. Growing throngs of watchers now wandered along the street. Still a minority of visitors had stayed as permanent pilgrims. They wanted to stay near the house of the woman where a miracle of life had happened days earlier. Yet a majority of visitors were only temporary gawkers. They wanted to see the house of the woman who should have died days earlier.

Consuela looked past a slightly pulled aside curtain in a front window. She could see Adam Hanson attempting to wade through the labyrinth of a crowd. How she did regret telling her husband and a few neighbors what had been seen in the bedroom of the senora. Her words had slowly but surely spread like a religious wildfire.

Several dozen of the devout had been replaced by hundreds of the flawed faithful. Quiet of a reverent night ceremony had been replaced by noises of a raucous day crowd. All of these people seemed to await a waiting sign. Consuela had learned another life lesson. Nothing more would ever be told about what was witnessed within this house.

She had been trying to contact Adam for more than three weeks since the disappearance of Angelina. Attempts had been made to call and text his cellphone without success. Consuela could not know that his phone had been destroyed by a ricochet bullet. Then she had sought his Washington office phone and email. But she was told he no longer worked at the bureau.

Now this devoted woman had wracked her weary brain as to what to try next. She had already filed a missing person report. Every listed person in the private phone book of Angelina had been contacted. Even the personal laptop of the senorita left at home might have recent emails or other valuable information. But Consuela did not know the password.

Aurelius had found the middle-aged woman weeping in front of this computer several days earlier. She had tried every password which could be assumed to be correct. Names of parents and friends and pets had been tried. Everything else that can be remembered by a stressed brain had been attempted. Every person seemed to have a moment in life when at least a temporary giving up was at hand. Consuela had just such a surrender at her fingertips.

"Perhaps I can help," had said Aurelius.

Whiteness flowed around a waiting chair. Fantastic fingers were only repetitive blurs as every word in the English language seemed to flash past. Words went on and on and on in alphabetical order. Such an exercise was like watching a digital dictionary being listed before Consuela's bewildered eyes. Aurelius worked continuously for hours.

Kalasasaya was a finally reached word. Aurelius seemed to instinctively stop typing. And a large *welcome* sign blinked on the screen.

"What does such a password mean?" had asked Consuela.

"Kalasasaya is the place where Angelina's father was murdered years ago. Still this name has burned itself too deeply into herself," had answered Aurelius. "Morning will come when her mourning finds peace within that self, but it will be a difficult truce for her to make."

Consuela had quickly checked the emails of Angelina. Soon she found a message from Adam with his new phone number. She had soon enough called him, and here he was the very next afternoon. A rejected suitor had become a more than concerned man.

Now Adam walked in the opened front door as if on cue. He discussed with Aurelius and Consuela the circumstances surrounding the disappearance of Angelina. Adam told them that he had not seen Angelina since the morning before a raid on Lanicrim Industries in Manhattan.

The story about the raids in New York City and Los Angeles had become public knowledge. Daily news reports had continued for days as these raids had continued on a worldwide basis. Thousands of wanted felons had been arrested and jailed. Many of these thousands would receive lengthy prison terms.

Then Consuela anxiously added that a Mr. Thax had made numerous phone calls from Lanicrim Industries to the house. He had been calling for a Mr. Levid Lanicrim. They had wanted to speak to Angelina about a lecture in New York City. Angelina had refused their offers more than once. Finally such an offer had been reluctantly accepted.

"Devil criminal," suddenly said Aurelius.

"What did you say?" said Consuela.

"Devil criminal, that is what Levid Lanicrim really means," said Aurelius. "He is the Sargon of my search."

"Yes, of course," said Adam. He could not believe such a simple arrangement of a name had not been recognized earlier. Adam was a man of letters who spoke seven languages and still had missed an artless reorganization of letters.

Adam quickly pulled the new cellphone from his pocket. Several of his remaining friends at the bureau were called. The flight plan of the Lanicrim jet which had fled from the JFK Airport was needed. He was told an F16 had quickly been scrambled from Washington to intercept this private jet. Somehow even a speedy F16 could not catch the jet. But a reason for failure was clear to Adam. He recalled the top speed of that red Camaro much too clearly.

Only deafening silence immediately followed this last phone call. Angelina had probably been spirited away by Levid Lanicrim. He was a being which was actually the Sargon of what knows where. Suddenly Adam thought about the star map. Probably an Intergalactic Traveler was required for a final escape. Possibly a trade had been expected to be completed. Yet a trade could not be made until the location of Angelina was known.

Sargon must have attempted to contact Adam at his former cellphone or office numbers. These numbers were as dead as Angelina might be. Such a thought of such a death brought an immediate depression. Loyal love Adam still felt for this young woman was almost too much to bear.

"May I see Rachel while we wait?" said Adam. "Or perhaps she should not be disturbed?"

"You certainly may see her," said Consuela. "I think she knows we are near, but cannot tell us of her journey."

Adam went to the bedroom of the comatose woman. Rachel lay on the bed with closed eyes like a sightless nomad. She was a woman wandering among things wondrous and taboo. Now he knelt next to her and prayed in a way which had not been done by him for too many years.

* * *

Thax was running again. His alloyed bones took stride after stride, but with more and more rests. He had used any continuing respites to evaluate a surrounding geography. Every effort had been made to avoid any unnecessary travels. His lengthy trek of a journey had to be shortened as much as possible. Something was slowly eating away within himself.

He had continued to hug the Ucayali River for his continuing continental marathon. This wandering river had been followed from Brazil into Peru. Then he could cut across the desert toward the Nazca Plain when an opportunity of topography presented itself.

Cries and calls of many different kinds of birds had continued to follow him for most of his daylight travels. Screams and shrieks of many different kinds of animals had also followed him for much of his nighttime travels. These were the many warnings of the more than wary.

Each and every bird and animal that he had so far encountered had fled before him. They had seemed like local townsfolk fleeing a roaming Frankenstein. The ragged gap on a side of his head and the wide gash in his shoulder were much too visible. Even a monster within had also become much too apparent. Yet even a monster can desire company.

Suddenly he stopped his running.

Slight movement had been seen in a broad clearing ahead of him. Sensitive sensors in his electronic eyes zoomed through a narrow break in the surrounding foliage. Mechanical lenses zeroed in on a magnificent jaguar. Now a bulky beast was lying upon a sandy shore of a wide stream which flowed into the river, haunches remaining in the slow flow of tributary waters.

"Ah, a ruler of an emerald labyrinth," said Thax.

This mature jaguar had pulled a swimming turtle from the stream. Then a caught turtle had been turned over on its rounded back. Head and legs had been completely withdrawn to try to salvage a situation. Many hidden appendages seemed to be waiting for the worst that would happen. Any healthy grown jaguar could easily bite through the thickest of turtle shells with a few chomps of extremely powerful jaws. Only a lavish licking of this strengthened shell would be the only gentle enjoyment of a snack.

The jaguar had also sensed Thax, sitting slowly on its heavy haunches. Something it could barely see, something it could barely hear, was very near. An extremely wary animal raised its nostrils to the slightest of a wind. A scent was confusing and beyond unknown. But warnings clicked in the most primitive part of its animal brain.

Now a powerful jaguar was on its sturdy legs. A brawny beast that could kill in a single leap was ready for almost anything. An ancient human face was smiling through the brush.

"I see you, my beauty," said Thax with a wide grin.

Greedy greetings were snarled by the jaguar. Usually any beast did not want to share any tempting treat. Turtles were no exception to a ruler. Yet primeval wits told the jaguar to be cautious. Several tentative charges were made toward that human face.

"You want to play?" said Thax with an even wider grin.

Thax stepped completely from the verdant foliage, standing in front of the jaguar without any hesitation. But a tentative beast had found too much hesitation, stopping several dozen feet before a supposed prey. The animal began a slow stalking exploration, not crossing an invisible boundary around this quarry.

Thax stood quietly while the jaguar circled him. Again a baffled beast only sniffed the air to a very eerie scent. Finally such an aroma told the animal to be more than afraid. It gave an eerie wail and bared both huge canines at the threat. Then a bewildered jaguar ran along the shore of the stream.

"Let us race!" yelled Thax.

The jaguar looked over a muscled shoulder to see that something was chasing it. This brawny beast had never before been chased by anything else in its life. Its efforts were strenuously increased as ears were firmly laid back and heart furiously pumped for escape. Now a fleeing jaguar reached for a top speed of forty miles an hour.

Eventually Thax slowed as the jaguar ran ever faster along the bank of the stream. Soon he stopped completely on a sandy slope as the beast took ever more distant strides. Then a retreating jaguar disappeared into the jungle and Thax smiled a farewell.

"There was a day, my beauty, when I could have caught you. I want you to know what I could once do. I want *everything* to know what I could once do."

Sudden stabs of deep pain caused him to suddenly crumple forward. Perilous pain was a sensation which had not been felt in many centuries. How could such misery have prospered within him? He ran a palm of a hand over the ragged gap where his right ear had been. He also ran a finger through his shirt over the pair of bullet holes in his torso.

Suddenly he thought about those ocean salts. Residues of a reviled earth had poisoned him. Tiny pieces of this pathetic planet were slowly corroding parts of his metallic self. A thing which could once almost move a mountain was being devoured alive by growing salty sores.

He must reach the Wonderland to be repaired.

Thax arose and walked slowly toward the clearing. And the turtle was still on its rounded back. Turtle eyes did a limited looking for a way of escape, four legs clawing at only emptiness. No footholds were to be found in the humid air.

Now he looked at the turtle for a moment, watching its useless struggles with a sudden interest. But a terrified turtle must have seen this new watcher, again tucking head and legs into a protective shell. Appendages waited to be devoured.

Thax only turned the turtle upright. The turtle did nothing but remain motionless, head and legs stored within a hardened exterior. Then a very strange personal enlightenment did happen.

Thax began to rest his right hand upon the turtle shell. He started with the thumb of that hand, giving a slight touch to the shell. His other four fingers caressed the surface ever so softly.

"You remind me of something…so very, very, *very* long ago."

Long lost emotions almost overcame the machine man. He tenderly rubbed that shell with the gentlest of caresses. There was a secret something more than soothing within a smoothness. Here was a sacred someone not quite gone from a memory. Yet it was a nearly failed remembrance, flickering even as Thax also started to flicker away.

"We are all struggling, aren't we! Choices we make and promises we break. Oh, to have another life, however brief…to make things right and still the grief."

Thax looked at that motionless turtle for many minutes. Finally he lifted the turtle and carried it to the near stream. The shelled creature was placed in shallow water with care.

He watched in silence as the turtle swam slowly away with a flow of the current.

Wonderland

"This last month has indeed been most disturbing," said Sargon. He looked at the black-robed Angelina who stood silently near his side. "Firstly, your undependable boyfriend has not contacted me in regard to a supposed barter. Secondly, Mr. Thax is long overdue as to his arrival at the Wonderland. Thirdly, my empire on this earth is fading much too quickly. Lastly, there is a very, very, *very* strange aberration in the atmosphere of your puny planet. Here is a growing tingle of tension in the air which I have not sensed for several millennia.

"Such a tinge of expectation is a suspense you do not yet fully understand, but there is a feeling of exultation just before a hunt. Both the hunter and the hunted can feel a possibility of an oncoming triumph. There is the tremendous thrill of possible capture, but there is also the extraordinary ecstasy of possible escape. How I do love these games of continuing conflict...and I use the word *love* in an almost sincere manner."

Angelina had not responded to any of his conversation. She had not really reacted in any way since a light-green choker and a dark black robe had been placed upon her. Now she was immersed in a world of fear and ugliness. The Wonderland which Sargon often spoke about held no wonders for her. It was a depraved and deprived hazardous playground.

Labyrinths of caverns carved into these mountains only held the hideous creations of a deranged being. Fire was almost everywhere within the complex: torches burned with sooty flames; pools of oily fluid blazed as tiny infernos; hot embers steamed as they madly meandered about as walkways for the lost; smoke from those fires seared any interconnected rocky walls and roofs of the caverns. This entire place was a made hell on this earth.

Fierce fires also flickered around the many torture devices which littered a main cave. She had recognized The Rack and the Iron Maiden and even the ancient Persian torment of The Boats. Many other contraptions were scattered about which she could not even remotely understand. She did not want to comprehend the pain inflicted by such tortures.

Then there were uncounted creatures which existed in this fiery fiasco of evil: creatures half human and half animal; part human and part something else; partly alive, but mostly dead. Other creatures abounded which she did not have even the slightest clue as to what they had once been. They were hideous things, grotesquely scarred and deformed. All of these things never spoke, only emitting screams and howls and cackles.

Angelina found herself beyond speechless within this sprawl of misery. She also was made mute by many imagined bats which flew about her with increasing regularity. Her fear of bats had always been held since early childhood. Such a fear was a ridiculous phobia as bats were beneficial little flyers. And a childish fear is often the most difficult to overcome.

Her parents had taken Angelina to Bracken Cave when she was a young girl. The cave was a deep cavern on the edge of San Antonio which kept the biggest colony of bats in the world. Twenty million bats had made this rocky cavern their hidden home. These millions of bats would exit an arched opening of the cavern at the dusk of each day.

Clusters of bats flew out of an arc of the watched cave like an everlasting bat kingdom. Bats sped from the opening in continuing waves which seemed like they would never end. Angelina was frightened by the dark mass of a very natural spectacle. Both parents had tried to comfort her without success. Too many bats had stayed in her head as a prospering phobia.

Now any millions of dark bats only flew about in her mind. But they were attacking her with greater frequency. She was a helpless young girl again. Flapping bats were biting and clawing at her face and body. They were devouring her and her father and her mother with no way of escape. Her family was being torn apart by an airborne death.

Sargon more than sensed her distress. But an unrepentant being only smiled a leering smile. Such a monstrous master had always enjoyed the suffering of subservient slaves.

"My captured little angel," said Sargon, "I realize you are not yet accustomed to the restrictions of a choker. Eventually any fear you feel will become a permanent part of you and be more readily accepted after your completed conversion. You will finally leave a pathetically fragile human body behind. It will be remembered only as the remains of a lost frailty, abandoned as a residue of an inferior race.

"You will then stay as you are for many, many, *many* human lifetimes. Your beauty will never fade. Your eyes will stay bright. Your skin will not blemish. Your body will sing to a false marrow of its alloyed bones. You will not fear anything but a fear of your choker. You will walk down any alley or any street or any way of every world and never have to look back at following footsteps. For if any followers do catch you, they will find themselves the caught. No greater satisfaction exists in any existence than that of a conqueror."

Angelina still stayed motionless by his side. She sadly dwelled within this made hell on earth. Uncounted bats swirled about her. Vaporous images of her dead father and nearly dead mother also whirled around her. There must be a method to cause such hazy hallucinations to cease. Here must be a found peace to replace a screeching madness.

Sargon continued to look beyond the labyrinths of Wonderland. He searched a broad plain of a barren desert. Then he sought a vast expanse of an empty sky. Nothing was different except for a tiny tingle in the air. It was an almost lost sensation which made more than enough of a message.

"I do believe my weary wait is nearly over," said Sargon.

Now a remorseless being looked to a large connected nearby cave. Eerie flapping noises echoed from a chained creation. A wanting screech wafted from a wanton machine.

"It must be near the hour when my vicious pet should be released."

* * *

Driving from San Antonio to Chaco Canyon was a fifteen-hour trip. Adam and Aurelius could not take a flight to Albuquerque as the latter remained on the airline watch list. The firm former accepted such a restriction of the flexible latter with regret. But this former insisted on doing any driving without regret. No other test of tires of another rental car would be made.

Adam had been given the flight plan of Sargon's private jet from a friend at the bureau. Such an offered plan showed a nonstop flight from Brooklyn to Miami. This private jet was on such a plan when the F16 intercepted the jet off the coast of North Carolina. Then an F16 pilot reported that the private jet accelerated at an impossible speed, steadily leaving him in an airy dust far too easily. It disappeared south over the Atlantic Ocean in less than a minute.

Final radar contact with the private jet was at the Miami airport. The jet whizzed past the east coast of Florida on the same steady bearing. This bearing was extended upon a map projection of South America booted up from the internet. Then a probable final destination on this southern continent had to be determined. Yet an enigmatic end point was nowhere near where most people thought it could be.

Almost everybody knew that South America is *south* of the United States. But almost nobody realized that *all* of South America is *east* of Florida. The lengthy reach of Latin America is always to the southeast. Such a location leaves the southern continent nowhere near a western position where most people presumed it would be.

Extension of a projected path of the jet made its destination at the farthest *west* coast of South America. Desolate desert of southern

Peru beckoned as a final end point of the flight. Nothing seemed to be here except a deserted expanse of one of the driest places on earth.

Then Adam remembered what Angelina had told him about the Nazca Plain. Supposedly this isolated area was a landing spot for extraterrestrials many centuries earlier. He quickly googled several sites about Nazca. Soon he found that the Nazca Plain had not always been so deserted. Then he discovered that a people had once lived in the area who had constructed a group of amazing outlined images.

Here were 150 sketched images spread over three hundred square miles of an uninhabited land. Most of the images were so extensive they could only be completely seen from the air. None of these images were discovered until 1927. They had stayed completely unnoticed for hundreds of years, remaining as earthy reminders of an early past.

There were outlines of birds and animals and plants, outlines of fish and insects and geometric figures. There was also a humanoid figure a hundred feet tall on the side of a mountain. This figure was called *The Spaceman* or *The Astronaut* as it appeared to be wearing a space suit and a helmet. An extended trapezoidal outline reached for the humanoid figure like a waiting landing strip.

All of the images were made two thousand years ago by removing a top layer of small brown-reddish stones. Any removed stones were slightly banked on both sides of a revealed bottom layer of yellow soil. Those low banks protected the images from any winds of the terrain. Also an almost complete lack of rain had helped save the images. All of the images had stayed almost intact over several millennia.

Adam and Aurelius had to reach the Nazca Plain as quickly as possible. Aurelius suggested to Adam that a method concealed at Chaco Canyon was available to make a very fast trip to Nazca. No additional details were given about any means to such an end.

Soon Adam again stood aside a hidden doorway to an elevated Eden. Still no entrance was seen within such sheer cliffs of the butte. Then Aurelius waved his right hand near a face of the stone. Now a thin fissure appeared in otherwise solid rock.

"This entrance is made completely of holographic mirror rock," said Aurelius. "It is seen and felt as hard stone for an outside observer. But it is also seen and felt as a clear opening for an inside observer."

Those spiral stairs remained more rocks than steps. But up and up and up, again these stones did take them. Adam did not start counting any steps during his second ascent. He did begin a conversation with his now known companion.

"I can't believe you have been on this butte for more than two thousand years."

"You have to remember that your conception of Time has no absolute meaning for me. Your solar years and lunar months, your hours and minutes and seconds, make only a valid method of counting Time for this planet. They are constructions which help your species organize an existence upon a tiny piece of a universe. Yet they have no real significance for anything beyond a little earth."

"Okay, fair enough, but you still haven't told me how we are going to get to the Nazca Plain in any amount of time."

"In *due* Time, but first you must give me that Intergalactic Traveler which you have held too closely to yourself."

"Do you also want the laser gun?"

"No, I only want the Intergalactic Traveler."

Adam pulled out the dark Traveler and handed the star map to Aurelius. Then he watched in amazement as the ancient man crumbled the device to dust within closed hands. Now a wrought whirlwind formed as the hands were opened. Dust disappeared in an eerie vortex.

"Why would you destroy the star map? We needed it to save Angelina."

"Sargon has no intention of freeing Angelina. He will have you killed and enslave her no matter what you give him. My suggestion is that you have nothing available for such a supposed trade. You will still be killed, but nothing will be gained in return."

"That is really *so* very nice to know. You say I am only going on this trip to be *killed*!"

"That is not the only reason, but do not fear your death. You will be reborn after such a death. It is the way of any decent thing, in any place, within any measure of Time."

"Let us assume I accept what you are saying, and I am not saying that I do. Didn't you need the star map to return home?"

"Sargon's home is not *my* home. In any event, I need no map to find my own way. I have always known the right path. It has never wavered in the past and will never do so in the future."

Finally they reached the top of the wide butte: a spring-fed waterfall on the north side of the crater still fell to a clear pool; a little pueblo was still tucked under a layered ledge on the south side; chinquapin oak and western catalpa and other territorial types of trees continued to ring the reddened perimeter; colorful shrubs and ferns and flowers stayed speckled about much of the remaining ground. And a strange tingle of tension was still in the air.

The duo of beings entered the pueblo of stucco fieldstones and shown timbers. Pieces of rough furniture were still scattered around: a circular table made of planks firmly held the center of the room; low chairs remained close to that table like moons near a planet, but no bed or other creature comforts could yet be seen. An isolated monastic life still awaited on a very high butte.

"This place has been my wonderland on your earth, and I shall never forget it," said Aurelius.

"I have to admit this Eden is a beautiful place to be, and I promise never to tell anyone else about it," said Adam.

"It would not matter if you did tell anybody else. The top of this butte is covered in a dome of holographic mirror rock. Nothing can be seen from the air but a barren part of a desert."

"What about the entrance in the cliff?"

"Only specific vibrations from my right hand can open and close any holographic entrance. Such vibrations will never be able to be duplicated by the human kind."

"So nobody can ever return to this paradise?"

"No, not without my help."

Aurelius grabbed another white robe from a stucco wall. A dangling robe appeared to have hung at that spot by an unseen power.

Adam could not see any hook or any other protrusion on the empty wall when the robe was removed.

"You must put on this robe."

"Why?"

"Think of the robe as a pressurized flight suit."

"Okay."

Adam pulled the robe over his head. Then he and Aurelius walked alongside the ripples of the waiting clear pool. They went behind the flow of the wide spring-fed waterfall. Hidden here was the shuttle which had brought Aurelius to this earth many years ago. Its tinted glassed top and shimmering metallic sides were covered in a thick layer of dust.

"I haven't used this shuttle since my arrival on your planet."

"You don't really expect this shuttle to start after more than twenty centuries."

Now Aurelius waved his right hand slowly near the shuttle. Low rumbles started within the craft. Soon a rumble lowered to a soft and steady purr, sounding much like a contented house cat. But even such a faint noise fast faded to nothing.

"Yes, I certainly do. You have to love a cold fusion engine."

"Unbelievable."

No way was apparent to enter the shuttle. No seams of any kind were shown for any type of doors. Then a pair of door seams appeared after the engine had warmed for a few more seconds. The near door opened entirely when Adam reached for a shown seam.

Yet Adam had expected to see a series of complex instruments and monitors inside the shuttle. Absolutely nothing was on the empty expanse of the dashboard. Nothing else was anywhere else within the interior except a pair of identical seats.

Aurelius opened the far door. The white robe settled into the seat without a whisper of sound. "This shuttle works on a very advanced system which I cannot explain in a way you could really accept."

"Tell me, anyway. I've reached the point where I can believe almost anything."

"Okay, if you took all of the computing capacity from every computer which has ever existed on your planet, and added that power to the million most wise and intelligent human beings who have ever lived, you would still not have the equivalent reasoning abilities of this small shuttle."

"I surrender, you have gone far beyond my ability to understand many of the miracles you have told to me over these past weeks. I will just have to accept such stuff as absolute truths."

"Now let us continue our journey together."

Suddenly a silent shuttle lifted about a foot off of the ground, traveling a very short distance to the very wide waterfall. A waiting craft lingered for several watery moments, washing away any found dust of many lost centuries. Such a cleansing was more than complete.

Then the shuttle hovered over the clear pool for a moment more.

"Goodbye!" exclaimed Aurelius.

Adam winced as the shuttle sped over the top of the butte toward the ground below. The racing craft only flew a few feet above that ground at a rate of speed which could only be called incredible. It sped across the open desert at better than several miles a second.

"Shouldn't we fly at a higher altitude?" said Adam.

He could only assume they were going to crash into something somewhere in their immediate path. Yet any approaching objects were avoided even as an extremely earthbound route was continued.

"We'll stay low until we've passed beyond the southern border of the United States. We don't want NORAD to know a UFO is flying around the border."

"How long will it take us to reach the Nazca Plain?"

"Our trip will take about thirty of your minutes. We can only average eight thousand miles per hour in such a lower, denser atmosphere."

Adam knew they were traveling very quickly, but he had no idea they were traveling that quickly. No sense of motion was made for him except the scenery whizzing past. It was a flight without noise or vibration or any other indication of an extremely rapid rate of speed. An airy quiet was eerily deafening.

Arid brownness of the southwestern United States and northern Mexico was left behind after several handfuls of minutes. Then a calm grasp of the blue Pacific Ocean was held for several more handfuls of minutes. And then a northern start of the Andes Mountains was seen to the east. Many mountains flew past like fleeing pictures of peaks.

But an also fleeing shuttle suddenly began to pitch and roll, zigzagging as if on an invisible ski run. An escaping craft turned eastward to a relative safety of the mountains. Adam could still only know of such meandering maneuvers because of a sense of sight. His brisk heartbeat was the only sound which could now be heard. Ready red blood throbbed within his temples with a growing tension.

"What's the matter?" anxiously asked Adam.

"The shuttle is trying to avoid a predator. Sargon has sent a cyborg to intercept us," calmly answered Aurelius.

"Why can't the shuttle just outrun it?"

"Sargon has probably converted his large saved shuttle into a cyborg. This machine will have even greater speed than our shuttle. Such a mechanism has most likely been stripped down to a bare killing machine."

Then a kind of condor this world had never, ever seen swept past them. Brief tints of leadlium wings gleamed as the metallic condor dived at the shuttle. Such a dive seemed much like a deranged peregrine falcon attacking a puny pigeon. Now a crazed cyborg tore a hunk of metal from the tail of the shuttle. Violent vibration rocked the craft. Continuing tremors gave Adam a more than uneasy feeling.

"His cyborg is going to pick us to pieces!" yelled Adam.

"My shuttle will not allow such a conquest to happen," again calmly said Aurelius. "Our best possible outcome for a same confrontation will be computed. Any predator which seems too determined to pursue a prey is more than vulnerable."

Now a passive clawless shuttle went into a severe hyper drive for several seconds. Yet an aggressive clawing cyborg followed close behind. Then an elusive shuttle suddenly dipped a short distance and completely stopped in midair. But an accelerating cyborg could not as quickly adjust to such bizarre behavior. It also stopped, but a fraction of a second too late.

There was a brief moment for Adam when he thought his entire existence had exploded. The suicidal shuttle had forcefully smashed into the overhead belly of the beast, an impact much like a rocket flying into the middle of an airplane. Both shuttle and cyborg began to steadily disintegrate. Doomed machines plummeted ever earthward.

Adam had a brief glimpse of the faux condor swirling down like a broken kite. Pieces flaked off the descending cyborg like chunks from the tail of a comet. Pieces were also flaking off the shuttle in a similar way. They fell like very heavy rain.

Soon a dead shuttle ricocheted off the side of a mountain like a sailing pinball. The careening carcass soon after zoomed across an empty valley and hit another mountain. Then it skimmed down that valley like a flat stone on choppy water. Ever more hunks of the craft flaked from an eroding shell. Even more crumbling went on for miles across that rocky valley. Finally the collapsing craft came to a rowdy rest and completely fell apart.

Adam returned to reality after several more minutes. Aurelius was standing next to him with a smile. The white robe reached down with an ageless arm.

"I thought you told me the shuttle would compute a best possible outcome," said Adam.

"I told you that a best possible outcome for a same confrontation would be computed," said Aurelius. "An outcome of mutual destruction was the best possible choice for our circumstance. No other option existed in such a situation. Sargon knew that my shuttle was not weaponized. He constructed his shuttle to become a weapon made much too hostile for its own benefit."

"But how could Sargon know you were traveling here?"

"In the same way I know you are going to be killed here."

"Look, if I can live through a crash like this one, I'll be ready for anything."

"Do not be too sure of yourself. Any child could have survived such a crash. Look at the many tiny pieces about you, a shuttle was designed to disintegrate in such a manner. The wide valley behind you is also littered with such pieces. Each piece absorbed many newtons of force."

Adam looked around at the numerous fragments from the shuttle. No fragment was larger than a thumb. He quickly checked to make certain none of his own fingers were missing. Not even a scratch was on any of them.

"Thanks for the encouragement," said Adam with a grimace.

"You are very welcome," said Aurelius with a smile. "Now we can be on our way."

Aurelius waved a palm of his right hand over a swath of scattered fragments of the shuttle. Many broken fragments began to blend together very rapidly. They coalesced into a long linear form which grew ever thicker. Then a gnarled walking staff was waiting on the ground.

"Behold His mighty hand," softly said Adam.

* * *

Solomon Sage sat on the steps of his patio. He looked to the striations of colored light from another evening horizon. The far sun had fallen behind near palms and sycamores to end a solar day. It was a day which seemed to Solomon to be one of the very best days of his life.

No final photograph for the most recent Ultra Deep Field view from the Webb Telescope had yet been formed. Such a telescopic image for that speck of space would take months to be completed. But Solomon was confident those many faraway galaxies would eventually reappear. These swirling masses of trillions of stars in shimmering shapes and sizes would be again. Earth and all other earths could still be made whole.

Another spectrographic analysis had been completed for a thousand galaxies. Chosen galaxies were the same galaxies chosen for the analysis of three months earlier. Each and every one of these galaxies were no longer blue shifted. Each and every one of these galaxies were now red shifted again. Such a change meant they had encountered another celestial U-turn sign. They had turned back from their once contractive path.

Solomon wondered ever more often about the many wondrous things which Aurelius had told him. But such a forever expansion and contraction, a systolic-diastolic beat of a universe, could not be fully understood by the human kind. He had accepted his lack of comprehension of such things.

Perhaps existence will always be the conflict between the forces of lovely light and the forces of dreary dark; a struggle between harmony and entropy; a battle between good and evil…an eternal Armageddon between life and death. It has probably always been thus.

He had watched the seven o'clock national news this evening with more than a passing interest. How he had wanted to assure himself that no leaks had been made about the most recent spectrographic analysis. His colleagues had remained rock solid in their determination never to start a more than massive panic. Loyal as much as meek people should inherit any earth as far as Solomon Sage was concerned.

The news had also told an extensive story about the disloyalty of many former employees of Lanicrim Industries. Many of these employees were already spilling their guts to the authorities to salvage a more lenient prison sentence. Ten thousand corporate criminals had been arrested in an ever more completed worldwide crackdown.

Twenty of these conglomerate facilities had been permanently closed. The half dozen facilities which still remained open would not be sanctuaries for very many more days. Even the most autocratic regimes put self-survival above cold hard cash.

Then a very brief news flash was displayed across the bottom of the television. This written announcement did not even interrupt the continued speaking of the commentator. She continued ever onward with practiced words of her profession.

> *Director Hugo Buhner of the Federal Terrorist Task Force killed by lightning at golf course—story at ten o'clock.*

Solomon did not pay much attention to this news flash. He had become ever more calmed by an internal peace which had become a greater part of his self. Many disordered concepts were becoming ordered again for him. Now a hopeful man awaited any future discoveries of many future years like a dedicated schoolboy waits for a classroom bell. He hoped such a vibrant ring of knowledge would never end.

He recalled Einstein's most famous quotation: "God does not play dice with the universe." Solomon thought the great man would have quickly restated his quote under present-day circumstances.

"God does not play dice with *any* universe," murmured Solomon.

"What did you say, dear?" said Harriet.

She had walked out onto the patio with a pair of glasses of lemonade. Now she sat next to Solomon like he was the only man who had ever lived on this earth. They would love each other beyond such an earthly existence.

This husband extended his hand to this wife. Arching fingers intertwined with a firm and mutual embrace. An affectionate couple had complemented each other so very completely. Quantitative and qualitative portions of the human mind had blended perfectly for them.

Solomon and Harriet had become educated together. They had raised two children together. They had slowly prospered with the ready help of each other. A house had been hewn by their steady efforts; a little measure of an earth had been made their own.

One hundred billion human beings who had gone before had struggled in their own separate ways. They had strived to understand those things which could be understood. They had also attempted to understand those things which could not be understood. The ancient parade of the human kind had always held a breast of birth and a dirt of death. But what else did we have to hold upon such a tiny speck of dust?

Something far beyond humanity held the secrets of forever.

"I don't really understand our wonderland of life," said Solomon. "But I am more than grateful to be spending my years with you."

"Ditto," said Harriet.

Solomon tightly held his wife beneath a canopy of stars which covered the sky of an autumn night. He was more than thankful that those uncountable vibrant, vaporous suns would continue their expansive bloom. God and nature would end another cycle of existence in their own Time.

A Darkness of the Night

Sudden yelling began to awaken Consuela in the house of Rachel Herr. Now this dedicated employee and friend stayed almost constantly within this house. Visiting nurses gave her dual breaks of four hours, but she was otherwise a permanent fixture of the residence.

Personal prices had to be paid for such feminine devotion. Her husband had complained about the long absences from their own house. Consuela still cooked breakfast and supper for him each and every day. She also packed him a hearty lunch to help mute his construction complaints. Any way to the heart of such a marital man remained through his stomach.

Consuela reluctantly rolled over and looked at the dresser clock. Three bright digits showed a much too early 5:57 a.m. She glanced out of the window of the guest bedroom. Nothing was outside except a deep dark of an October night. Yet even louder yelling continued.

She arose from a welcoming mattress. There was no understanding why a group of perpetual pilgrims was making so much noise. Here was a pious group of people which had been a most peaceful nocturnal group. Her housecoat was put on for a brief walk to the living room.

Side curtains in a front window were slightly pulled aside. Now any constant night visitors were pointing to the west. She could not see the object of their attentions.

The front door was quickly opened to the warm air. Then Consuela saw a large meteor far on the western horizon, an enormous ball of fire lighting the skyline like a small sun. Already a fiery mass was almost out of sight, fleeing to the southeast like a meteor on a mission.

All of any night visitors were on their knees.

"It is a sign!" yelled one of the pilgrims.

"Yes, it is a sign from Heaven!" yelled another of the pilgrims.

Consuela watched as the meteor sped along its continuing path, appearing to be ever descending at a steady angle. Sparks stayed about its perimeter like the aura of an angered God. Finally the fiery mass disappeared beyond the skyline of her sight.

* * *

Adam did not think anything could amaze him after his earlier experiences with Aurelius. Quickly he discovered that astonishing amazements still abounded in their relationship. The white robe given to him to wear was an absolutely overwhelming garment. No thirst or hunger, nor heat or cold, was sensed within a bright whiteness. Only a growing sense of reassuring wellness was felt.

He had journeyed with Aurelius for seven days and seven nights. Many, many miles had been walked since the small shuttle had smashed into smithereens. Uncounted miles tread did not seem to really matter anymore. A wide valley with a scattered wreck had been left far behind them. An ever more enlightened man was on a more than major marathon from a distant wreckage of a life. But he was never tired and never needed rest and never wandered far from a path created by Aurelius. And what a straight and narrow path had been made.

They had steadily left the higher elevations of the craggy mountains, traveling along pretended trails which might have given pause to a highly skilled cliff climber. No such hesitations were within Aurelius, a leader gliding along any thin ledges of rock with the sureness of a mountain goat. Adam was swept along as a dedicated follower.

Finally Aurelius and Adam had reached the broad expanse of the Nazca Plain. They had continued their trek across an uninhabited land. Such a desert landscape reminded Adam of Chaco Canyon, but a major difference was those many outlined images carved into a soil many centuries earlier. Echoes of a living lost were scarred into otherwise empty terrain.

The morning sun was just beginning to arise on the eighth day of their journey. All outlined past images of all images passed began to be shown in a larger light. Pretended birds and animals and plants tried to live again. Imitation fish and insects and geometric figures strived to be made whole. Even a huge humanoid figure on a mountain seemed to shimmer.

"These early inhabitants of Nazca must have been a very hardworking people," said Adam.

"They most certainly were, but a fragile wheel of earthly existence must pass," said Aurelius.

"Their carved outlines seem to have survived the test of time."

"Nothing on your earth will survive the test of Time."

"You keep reminding me of such a fact."

"Humankind seems to require too many reminders of such a simple truth."

"I cannot defend my species anymore, and that includes myself."

"Have you ever read the history of Xenophon's Ten Thousand?"

"No, I was always interested in languages much more than anything else."

"Xenophon was a Greek mercenary, one of the leaders of a numerous number of other such mercenaries. These Greeks had joined Cyrus the Younger against Artaxerxes II at the battle of Cunaxa. Their furious fight was for the throne of Persia, but Cyrus was killed by a javelin during the battle. Then any surviving Greeks had to flee overland to their homeland, which was more than 1,500 miles away."

"This sounds like a happy story."

"These determined Greeks endured many hardships during their hurried and harried retreat from Mesopotamia. They marched for many days to return to their beloved Peloponnesus. Eventually they encamped among immense mounds of forgotten rubble. None of them had the slightest idea what those vast piles of wreckage had once been. Even Xenophon, a scholar and former student of Socrates, had no knowledge of the site.

"It was later revealed that the Greeks had slept upon the ruins of Nineveh, the once reviled capital of the Assyrian Empire, a city which had only two centuries earlier ruled the entire eastern Mediterranean world."

"Why are you telling me such a depressing hunk of history?"

"I am telling you such a history to show how fleeting is this human existence, how frail is an earthly memory, how flimsy a grasp of Time. Your kind has immersed itself in petty squabbles and complaints which quickly have no meanings even to yourselves. All such pathetic pettiness should end…and all such common complaints made mute."

"I wholeheartedly agree, but I don't—"

Aurelius held up his right hand. Ageless grey eyes searched a surrounding desert. A very strong tingle of tension was in the air.

"These nearby cliffs are partly covered in holographic mirror rock," said Aurelius. "There and there and there, perhaps several dozen spots in the immediate area. Sargon must be near and probably also Angelina."

"We have to find her as quickly as possible."

"Let us open the largest entrance in these pretended deserted cliffs."

Now Aurelius walked another several hundred feet in front of the face of the nearest cliff. The white-robed right hand was waved in front of a seeming stony slope. Then a large arch to a much larger labyrinth opened before them.

They edged up the cliff to the more elevated archway. The opened arch looked like an open invitation to the bowels of Hell. Putrid stenches seemed to pour from everywhere. Acrid smoke appeared to waft from everywhere. Echoes of strange screams and howls and cackles also started to echo from anywhere. Such sounds were the babble of the doomed.

Then the hulk of a huge starship was visible in the back of an immense cave.

"Sargon is almost ready to leave. He is only waiting for the Traveler to be traded."

"What about Angelina, do you sense anything about her?"

"Angelina is near, but she is like any others in this labyrinth, much more than tormented. Angelina has probably already been given a choker of slavery and a robe of servitude. No escape from such evil bondage exists without our help. Her chains must not be made permanent."

"What can we do?"

"We must reach her before a complete conversion is accomplished. I will remove that choker of the Prince of Death when we find her. You will then place your white robe upon her black robe, but stand back after you do so."

"And then?"

"And then you will be one of the very few mortal beings who have ever witnessed an Armageddon and lived to tell about it. Of course, nobody will ever believe you."

"I thought you told me that I was going to be killed."

"In due Time."

They walked to the far corner of the immense cave. Here was a long corridor lit by sooty torches which began at that spot. There was also a walkway made of fiery embers. All of these sooty torches immediately went out when Aurelius passed by them. All of those fiery embers immediately cooled and coalesced and kaleidoscope colored when Aurelius walked upon them. Any strange screams and howls and cackles also faded to silence. Then a natural phosphoresce made by patches of lichen lit the corridor. Soft light held the passageway in a steady glow.

This winding corridor led to a deeper central cave from which several dozen other passages fled. A broad, blazing pool of oily fluid was in the middle of this central location. Aurelius stopped for a moment as the burning, boiling pool steadily calmed and cleared. Only a welcoming cool spring of rippled water remained.

Aurelius looked at the start of many wandering passages. All of these corridors had those sooty torches on the walls, fiery embers on the ground. Now a white-robed arm pointed toward one of the passageways.

"Here is the way."

They entered another large cave filled with many torture devices. Aurelius briefly touched each device while walking among them. All of the mechanisms creaked their own brief conversions, disintegrating like small shacks in a tornado. Soon only tiny remnants were left of the shattered devices. Soon enough any remaining thin taints evaporated like shallow mud puddles beneath an unforgiving sun. Nothing endured except a purified stain of what had been.

Then Aurelius and Adam continued along the chosen corridor. But the thin passageway twisted back toward the cliff from which they had first entered the labyrinth. An acute corner of the corridor was turned and a motionless black-robed figure was suddenly seen.

Angelina was standing in the center of a low archway which was far above an expanse of desert below. Nothing else was in this narrow craggy cave except a purse and a valise. Her personal items had been thrown in a corner with an impersonal toss.

"Angelina!" cried Adam.

"Wait, do not touch her yet!" cautioned Aurelius.

The flowing white robe glided over to the motionless woman. Ageless eyes saw empty eyes which did not even really look back. No remaining glimmer of real humanity seemed left within her.

"We are too late," softly said Adam.

"We are not too late," strongly said Aurelius.

Then a white-robed hand gripped the dark symbol on the green choker around her neck. This whiteness grasped this darkness for a dear life. Momentary flurries of sparks emanated from the choker as this grasp was made ever greater. Finally an absolute evil was yanked from her soul.

"Now quickly put your robe completely upon her robe."

Adam pulled the white robe over his head. He placed the whiteness of his robe over the blackness of her robe. Even greater flurries of sparks were created when the covering was completed. Such a conflict was much like watching a brief struggle between matter and antimatter. Both robes furiously glowed and disappeared.

Now Angelina was held tightly as she collapsed toward the floor. Adam carried her over to a near rocky wall. He knelt in front of her like a nearly lost companion.

"What should I do?" said Adam.

"She will need a brief rest before becoming completely well again," said Aurelius. "Stay with her within this stony room. It will be the safest spot for what is about to happen."

"You are leaving us?"

"I am leaving to search for Sargon."

"Will you return?"

"In your dreams."

* * *

Thax struggled across the emptiness of the Nazca Plain. He wavered ever more erratically as the right half of his artificial body was on the verge of complete failure. His right arm already hung uselessly at his side. His right leg was more like a dragging weight than a useful limb. These injuries were the primary effects of a machine-made stroke.

Severely damaged sensors in his right electronic eye were adding to his problems. His eyelid had continuously opened and closed over the fading eye for hours. A brightness of a day and a darkness of a night were mingled together in a progressively faster succession. Any rapid opening and closing gave a view of his surroundings as if under a very fast strobe light. Every swift alternation only disoriented him ever more. Such spasms would not seem to cease.

Thax was also becoming concerned about the left half of his body. He was certain any remaining strengths had become more sluggish, any residual reflexes ever slower. Everything inside him seemed to be growing weaker. Everything outside him appeared to be growing stronger. His synthetic shell was becoming an emptier shell.

Yet no ready relief was readied for any of his rapidly increasing ills.

Ominous ocean salts had found more and more secret parts of him. Silent salts had seeped into mechanical nooks and crannies with evil ease. They ate away with the lusts of impersonal criminals. A murderer had almost become a murdered.

Now he welcomed a hot early morning sun of the desert. He was becoming somewhat dried out near the end of his long journey. Heavy rain and high humidity of the dense rainforests had only fed an accumulating mass of corroding creatures. Incessant airy moisture had nourished worsening watery wounds. But he was approaching the wonders of Wonderland, almost returning to the safety of his salvation.

Already Thax had wandered past more than a few outlined desert images around his most recent miles. But he never even glanced at any passing outlines marked into the skin of a soil. Only a single image was strenuously sought. The Spaceman was only a tiny standing figure on a distant side of a mountain. Each stressed step brought him ever closer to reaching, rescuing arms.

How he had once yearned for the smooth caress of such a welcoming embrace.

Somehow an empty stretch of an isolated desert gave him solace. Almost all of this planet had become a crowded and polluted sty of a world. Human pigs who lived upon this earth were the most hated of creatures. Their kind deserved whatever butcheries could be loosed upon them. Horrible atrocities had been apparently delayed until other days in other years. Yet a future reach of a dark revenge could be quite patient.

More personal sources of revenge also needed to be salved. Adam Hanson was at the very top of this hit list. Hanson's inquiries and investigations had become as destructive and devouring as ocean salts. He was a true man who had poured ever more salt into wasting wounds. Such a man truly deserved whatever torments could be inflicted upon his sorry self.

Thax touched the ragged gash on the side of his head where his ear had been. He also tentatively touched the bullet holes in his chest and abdomen. A solitary ear could be replaced; a pair of bourn holes could be made whole. But what would ever slake the hunger of a starving retribution. His machine mind raced with possibilities.

Any border of the nearly good had been completely crossed into a country of the absolute evil. Anything which had once been near human had become mashed into a back of his being. Morality had been crushed into an invisible nothingness. Mortality also seemed to be traveling toward a similar fate.

His memories of a very, very, *very* long time ago in a galaxy so very, very, *very* far away had totally evaporated. An almost dissipated warmth had been readily replaced by a continuing cauldron of coldness. Any failing fingers had grown ever more frozen in feeling. A lost heart had been replaced by a rusted chunk of found heartlessness. Nothing remained but a corroded clutch of a nearly ruined thing.

His right eyelid continued to violently flicker. And he tried and tried to control these ever more frequent flutters. But uncontrollable, unstoppable movements went on and on. No end was in sight for the spasms. Finally any growing anger was unleashed upon himself. Other collared victims were not available.

Suddenly he stopped his erratic walk on the stony ground. His still usable left fingers reached into that right eye socket. Six tiny metal internal sensors recessed around the socket were pressed in a necessary sequential order. Then a disconnected eyeball popped out like a small colored egg, falling to an ever more despised earth.

"*If your eye offends you, pluck it out*!" he said, laughing at his sad situation.

Thax continued his struggle across the emptiness of the Nazca Plain.

Armageddon

Now Sargon stood in front of the huge figure of The Spaceman. Expanses of a barren desert spread around him with a welcoming emptiness. Something about desolation still enthralled him. Some benevolence was in bleakness, a deeper desire for darkness. Such obscene objects of personal pursuits were the never-ending needs of a being beyond reasoned redemption.

Aurelius had glided down a stony slope with the gnarled wooden staff to confront Sargon. Two beings stood less than an earthly mile apart. Yet a vast void was really between them. Their voices to the other could still be clearly heard despite such a distance. Ageless adversaries had never been able to mend an ever-growing gap. They had been antagonists among uncounted vaporous stars, foes fighting within an infinity of galaxies.

"You are down here," said Aurelius.

"I have been down here. You are the intruder," said Sargon.

"You are still a twisted recluse, a hating hermit of too many carved caves."

"And you are still a pious prophet, a *Chozeh* of too many supposedly chosen."

"Your empire on this earth is crumbling. Your followers are fleeing."

"I will *always* be on this earth. Human hearts can be very hideous homes."

"What do you gain by inflicting such pain and torment on others? What is within you which continues to guide such evil tasks?"

"You sound like a celestial child. The thing which guides me is the same thing which guides you, a perpetuation of self. This is the preservation of what I am and what I always shall be, the contrary of you. Each coin of our realm will always have two sides. Every light day has a dark night. Each and every Paradise has an Armageddon."

"No Paradise made need ever end."

"You have always been a maker of such pitiful poems. But existence is not only the sweet birthing of poetic license, it is also the harsh dying found in many realistic documentaries. The history of any life *is* death. This saga of man and woman *always* ends. Your words are but soothing nonsense to a people waiting to be executed."

"I can see that nothing has changed, we are still opposites trapped in the orbit of each other. Our eternity of opposition awaits, but there can be no rest for the wicked."

"There can also be no respite for the pretended benevolent."

Sargon raised his left hand toward the stony slope behind him. Several dozen caves hidden by holographic mirror rock suddenly opened. All of many creatures of a labyrinth began to descend from any underground places. How they did pour upon an otherwise empty plain.

The monstrous mass was a mixed mess of beings: creatures half human and half animal; part human and part something else; partly alive, but mostly dead. Other creatures abounded which did not have the slightest clue as to what they had once been. They were hideous things, grotesquely deformed and scarred. All of these things never spoke, only emitting screams and howls and cackles.

"I can see you have brought your minions with you," said Aurelius.

"I did not *bring* them. I *gathered* them," said Sargon.

Soon thousands of scrambling creatures formed long lines of ready infantry. Soon enough such scowling creatures were in mangy rows ten deep. Their legions of the present were similar to their legions of the past. They leered and growled and waited for a taste of blood, holding a variety of bizarre weaponry. And too many meager minds were too much alike.

"You must know I would also not be so foolish as to journey here alone," said Aurelius.

"I do not see any of your flock anywhere in sight," said Sargon.

But Aurelius pointed his wooden staff toward the large meteor speeding from the northwest. This ball of fire had almost descended to this earthly sphere. Mass of a multitude began to break into dozens of fiery beams. Blooming beams further split into hundreds of blazing rays.

"Destroy Aurelius before the wrath of the Lord of Life is upon us!" commanded Sargon.

"You are too late!" countered Aurelius.

Then a white-robed hand threw the green choker which had harshly held Angelina far upon a waiting desert. Rectangular green stones and a dark symbol created a huge smoking crater as they disintegrated. Thin striations of green glass spread as verdant lines from a center of the crater. They looked like spokes of a fragile wheel.

Time temporarily stopped. A sun stayed in the sky like a motionless watcher. Any following hours became a wink of an eye. Many waiting cries and whispers within what was about to happen would never be heard beyond a blink of space. No tales could be told of such a battle, no books bound or blogs typed for such a struggle. Future historians would only have a blank page and an empty site for a brutal conflict.

Sargon led those thousands of hideous creatures which had charged with his command. They slithered into the crater like streams of dark poison. Their many weapons were raised with the vicious vigor of hatreds, battle cries hollered as the screams of the hateful. No sense of reason existed within such things.

Now Aurelius led those thousands of blazing rays which were taking shape and form. These rays morphed into individual foot soldiers and mounted cavalry. Foot soldiers carried sizzling swords and shining shields. Mounted cavalry on white horses held large bows with flaming arrows. All of them hit the ground as righteous runners. Nothing was going to keep any of them from their appointed tasks.

Those landed charging soldiers of Aurelius plowed into those massed charging soldiers of Sargon. Such a monumental crash was much like a pair of ancient armies smashing into each other. Fierce fighting was face-to-face, hand to hand. Eye looked upon eye to blind another sight. Mind gazed within mind to still another's will.

Aurelius and Sargon became the center of a savage conflict. Aurelius had broken the gnarled staff in half with a flick of white-robed hands. Both halves were now used as a pair of singing swords. Sargon used a dark stone as a black ball and chain. Opposing beings stayed in the center of a slaughter like perpetual warriors. Their struggle would never end. Their vigilance was eternal.

Clashing, clustering armies did not rest. Throngs of good and evil continued to gouge at each other without restraint. Heads were severed and arms lopped off and chests pierced. Hot blood splattered thirsty combatants and hungry ground. Only the sounds of weapon upon weapon, scream upon scream, were heard. Souls fled mildly while bodies bled wildly. No mercies would be given until after such an earthly catastrophe was completed.

All of the great white horses whinnied and snorted fire. These great horses reared, violently crashing down with a crushing strength. Their flanks were streaked crimson and their hearts skewered. They also fought valiantly and suffered silently and wept generously. Stallion weeping flowed like tender rain. Equine tears softly caressed a penitent planet.

Hours passed as determined adversaries fought on and on. Carnage continued with each passing uncounted minute. And a crater became littered with the bodies of broken creatures. They lay motionless or tried to crawl away. Their brethren continued the horrible fight.

Center forces of Aurelius seemed to be finally giving way. They slowly curved back in the middle of the line. Now a concave arch steadily became deeper and deeper. Forces of Sargon swept into a retreating breach like hungry predators.

"We have you now!" haughtily hollered Sargon.

"You have nothing!" calmly countered Aurelius.

All of any forces of Aurelius appeared to be on the brink of complete collapse. But mounted white cavalry of a seemingly retreating mass steadily became ever more extended. Whitened flanks readily began to encircle the forces of Sargon. Legions of predators were becoming legions of prey. Supposed victors were becoming vanquished.

Yet Sargon realized their plight too late. An unbreakable ring was closed upon them like an eternal circle. A balled mass became a restricted mess within which very few of them could actively fight. Then a relentless slaughter began as the circle became ever smaller.

Screams of the surrounded echoed again and again within cratered walls. No escape would be available for anything. No hope existed except as granted by the gaining conquerors. Their retribution seemed uncompromising. The terrible tragedy continued with bloodied efforts.

Growing masses of clouds began to form over this swirl of battle. Clutching clouds also became more and more swirled. They darkened with ominous rumbles of thunder, forming a ragged canopy covering the crater within which a battle still raged. But it was a struggle with waning strengths.

"You have trapped me!" screamed Sargon.

"You have trapped yourself!" stated Aurelius.

Massive blackened clouds filled with jagged lightning began to completely obscure nearly everything. Aurelius and Sargon were only fading outlines of images. Their armies were only disappearing sketches of dreams and nightmares. A terrible conflict was becoming forgotten by a forgotten land. Any remaining cries and crimes were evaporating into hot air.

Close clutches of pivoting clouds whirled more and more as a wild storm. Wanting winds steadily became much more like a twirling tornado. The tenacious twister continued to accelerate into a clawing cataclysm. Soon a dusty devourer of a seeking storm coveted everything held by the crater. Soon enough all things so seized started to disappear.

The immense twister coalesced these things together and sent them upward. Now a slender earthly storm became a black hole of a void. Its violent vortex swiftly ascended and blended into a higher atmosphere, completely departing to an otherworldly world.

Only a mysterious crater remained with a handful of thin striations of melted green glass. Saved spokes spread out from the center of a fragile wheel which continued to be. They dispersed a verdant benevolence across a waiting landscape, sparkling beneath a radiant suddenly seen sun. It was the reaching residue of myth and mystery and mayhem.

Then nothing else was left but immense towers of dust which slowly started to drift down upon an empty plain.

* * *

"They that sow the wind, shall reap the whirlwind," said Adam.

Somehow those ageless words of Hosea had been remembered. Such an ancient prophet would always be held in memory for the rest of a life. Yet even a pious prophet could be occasionally wrong. Adam had been more than awed by an Armageddon far below. But he still had not been killed.

He could not even see a remaining glimmer of what had just happened. A wink of an eye had ended; a blink of a space had closed. Uncountable specks of dust fell upon the sand of this earth as airy tears. Such shed tears had also been lost in the sands of uncounted other earths.

Angelina was slowly leaving a forced trance. Her gaining awareness of a real world was being made whole. Her growing number of words was really being mumbled.

Suddenly nothing but terror was shown on her furrowed face.

"It's okay, you're safe, everything is going to be fine," consoled Adam.

Then Adam saw Thax reflected in her clearing eyes. Adam pulled the laser gun from his belt very quickly. But Thax knocked the laser gun out of his grip slightly more quickly. The lost gun bounced against a far rocky wall of the narrow cave with a harsh clatter.

Now Adam was firmly held by a somewhat functioning left mechanical arm. He was tossed against the nearest wall of the cave with a brutal force. Adam was temporarily stunned as the machine man stood over him. Yet it was not a former version of an incredibly powerful Thax of yesterday. It was a latter version of a much weaker Thax of today.

"I am a most fortunate wreck," said Thax. "You mean more to my abandoned heart than any other aggravation."

"Lucky me," said Adam.

Thax had indeed become a wrecked thing: his right ear and right eye were missing; his right shoulder held a wide gash; his right arm hung motionlessly by his side; his right leg was dragged behind him like an unused attachment. He was only a remnant of what once had been.

The sight of him had become an almost failed vision. How a broken body did seem to have shrunk within itself. Faux skin appeared to have shriveled upon himself. He was a machine man headed to a junkyard. But he remained a more than formidable adversary for a true man. Any weakened physical state had not changed any state of mind. His hunger for revenge needed to be violently fed, a savage slaking salvaged by an artificial hand.

"I have missed you so very much," said Thax.

"I cannot say the same," said Adam.

Again Thax grabbed Adam, tossing him against the opposite wall of the restricted cave. Any pain could only be called almost tolerable. A true man was nearing the end of his life.

"I was feeling right badly," said Thax. "And yet I feel ever so much better."

Adam could not give a reply.

Now nothing except a continuing series of left-hand punches was felt by Adam. He would have also been kicked if Thax's right leg had not become too unstable for such an effort. Numerous punches continued without any added kicks.

A real world had spun into a blurred blotch. An ever more surreal earth had beckoned Adam and Angelina. Any causes of their dazes were different, but an effect was the same.

"Did you get it? I was feeling *right* badly!" said Thax with a smile. "How I do still enjoy a little comic repartee now and then."

Adam still could not give a reply.

Then Thax threw Adam to the edge of the cliff. One terrific backhand strike sent Adam over the brink of the precipice. A true man clung to a brink of life as a machine man mockingly stood over him. An excessive grin formed on the broken face of that machine. Even an empty eye socket seemed to jeeringly join a sickening smile.

But a groggy Adam tried to pull himself back over a hazy edge of existence. His efforts were beyond hopeless. No direction seemed available for him to go but down. A hunk of his hair was grabbed by Thax, strands severely stressed.

"Now you will be gone *forever*, a vast and ageless Time," said Thax with a glaring sneer. "And there will not even remain a distant whisper of your forgotten life."

The hunk of hair was pulled ever more back. Adam's head was strained backward with the force. Growing struggles were made to maintain his grip on the edge of the cliff, but a final blow was readied. Hard dying was nearly within reach of a hardened hand.

"Get away from him!" shouted a voice behind Thax.

Thax turned to see Angelina pointing the laser gun directly at him. Her trance had completely dissolved. Her world was almost a nearly completed reality. Yet it was a reality she could not yet fully accept.

"Hello, my lovely."

"I'm warning you, get away from him *now*!"

"My little angel, surely you would not harm me." Thax slowly moved away from Adam. Any laser gun would always more than hold his entire attention. Its biting bursts of energy could do a fatal fiery damage to him.

"Shoot him!" yelled a recovering Adam.

Thax walked closer toward Angelina. He looked intensely with his remaining eye at another additional victim. How he did yearn for an unrighteous retaliation.

For a fleeting moment, Angelina saw the smiling face of her father. "Remember what I told you," said a strangely familiar voice. The words sounded sinfully sweet.

Angelina was temporarily mesmerized. She stayed frozen with the sound of the faraway voice. "You told me that you would love me and Mom beyond the end of time."

"And so I will," said Thax. He had moved almost next to her. Soon the weapon would be within his greedy grasp. Then Thax could quickly crisp Angelina with that cursed laser. Another remaining human aggravation could be blasted into oblivion.

"It's a mind trick!" yelled Adam. "You told me your father would never harm *anything*!"

His warning words seemed to bring Angelina back to a completed reality. She clearly saw the monster of a man approaching as reflections of a lost father faded. But she remained the keeper of memories safely kept within the most secret, sacred part of her.

"You could *never* be my father."

"Yes, I could…the wondrous things I have seen…the taboo things I can tell you."

"You can't tell me a single word of your supposed wisdom!"

"Don't you want to know what really happened at Kalasasaya?"

Angelina only negatively shook her head back and forth. The monster man was upon her and began a tentative reach for the laser. But she retreated into a further reach of the cave with a ready realization of what she would have to do.

"I think I now know."

"Yes, but thinking and knowing are two very different things."

"Not anymore for Kalasasaya, not for me."

"I believe you are like your father. I do not think you could be a killer of anything."

"Yes, but thinking and knowing are two *very* different things."

"This cannot be the end of *me*!"

"Farewell, my ugly!"

Then Angelina pointed the laser gun at Thax's left side. Half a dozen blasts of the laser penetrated his synthetic skin. Bitter bursts burned through metal insides like tiny torches.

Now Thax reeled from the force of the impacts. Still an immense rage of anger overcame him. He attempted to charge her for a final chance at revenge with powers almost wholly gone. The staggering thing barely continued to exist.

She shot him with half a dozen more bursts of the laser, incendiary impacts sending him backward to his knees. He stayed motionless for a lingering moment, glaring at her with lost centuries of found hatreds. His final vulgar venom was spewed.

"*Assassin!*" yelled Thax.

Thax fell over the edge of the precipice, but he grabbed Adam while doing so. More than three hundred pounds of metallic weight was more than too much for Adam to bear. Both of them plummeted past the rim in solitary silence. They went down and down and down to a stony bottom of the cliff.

"No!" screamed Angelina.

She ran to the brink of the cliff, seeing the shattered body of Adam far below. Angelina began to cruelly cry. Watery regrets poured down her cheekbones like they would never end. How her tears did continue to flow.

"Please, no…" she softly whispered.

Suddenly Angelina remembered the Time distorter. She had never returned the distorter to Aurelius. This brilliant elliptical disc was still in her purse. Angelina ran to a craggy corner of the cave, recalling the words of Aurelius as she did so.

Anything touched by its ripple of light will go back in Time for a dozen of your seconds.

She frantically searched through her purse. The bright disc was under her cellphone and compact. Angelina raced to the edge of the precipice and pointed the clear end of the elliptical disc while pushing the indentation in its center. A pale ripple of light solely and soulfully engulfed Adam. An eternal sense of his future salvation awaited.

Then Adam was returned to the top of the cliff, holding the edge of rock as had been done seconds earlier. Thax had just fallen over the precipice was as much as Adam now knew, never knowing of his own fatal plummet. His readied rebirth of a life had begun. This day of destined deliverance awaited consummation with many waiting years.

Angelina helped Adam to the floor of the cavern, holding him closer than ever. They embraced in a way which would always meld them together. Neither would never let the other wander alone again.

"It's okay, we're safe, everything is going to be fine," consoled Adam. He could not understand why she was crying. Her tears were brushed from a forgiving face.

"I think you are now more than right," said Angelina.

* * *

Thax stayed motionless far below the opening of the deserted labyrinth. A taboo thing which could no longer remember itself as a true man was at the bottom of the cliff. An empty being remained almost emptied of being, unmoving upon the stony ground. His broken body clutched at the earth in a silent farewell. Ripped synthetic skin showed a cold glint of harsh machines. And a frail sheen of forever dreams.

The hoary head of an ancient thing faced a steadily higher morning sun. A remaining electronic eye reflected the rays of a rising star. An eyelid slowly closed upon any remaining wondrous light. There was a faint blink of memory and then only nothingness.

Finally a darkness which had been sought for so long a Time had been found.

Morning

The San Antonio River flowed past as it had done for thousands of years passed. Adam and Angelina sat with her mother on a restaurant patio near this river of life. They stayed beneath one of the large cypress trees which clung to the banks of the river like more than grateful children. How those waters still did quench a continuing thirst.

"Your boy is probably the cutest little baby in at least the State of Texas," said Rachel.

"Yes, Mom, I am certain no other grandmother in the world ever thought the same about her first grandchild," said Angelina.

"He is not so little anymore," said Adam.

"I cannot believe my grandson is already a year old and that I am still around to hold him," said Rachel.

"Here is his first birthday cake," said Angelina.

Their waiter walked toward the glassed table with a large cupcake, a small unlit candle placed in the middle of the chocolate frosting. Immediately a smiling child grabbed for the tempting treat put in front of him. He got a tiny finger of frosting before his mother pushed the plate beyond his reach.

"Let's be patient," said Adam.

Now an innocent child briefly looked at his worldly parents with eyes without regrets. The little amount of gained chocolate seemed to temporarily satisfy him. This bit of frosting was tasted with a dimpled grin.

"Senor and senoras, could I get any of you a dessert or something to drink?"

"You can get me a margarita, and don't be stingy with the tequila," said Rachel.

"Mom, you are setting a bad example for your grandson," said Angelina.

"I am more than certain he will be fine," said Rachel.

"Could I get anything else for anybody?" said the waiter.

"Thank you, anyway, but just the check when you get a chance," said Adam. "We're going to stay and talk for a while."

The waiter cleared any remaining dishes with a rehearsed efficiency. He quickly returned with a margarita and a check. Then he waited patiently while both women handed him the needed money. Each of the women insisted on making a total payment.

"I can afford to pay for a Sunday brunch in honor of my only grandchild's first birthday," said Rachel.

"I wish you would let us pay at least once for these after-church meals," said Adam.

Their relieved waiter quickly took the money from Rachel with a secret smile. He had become much too familiar with this particular mother and daughter. But any man should never disappoint any woman unless he has no other choices.

"And it won't be your only grandchild too much longer," said Angelina.

"Another grandchild already, praise be to God in Heaven," said Rachel.

"I thought we weren't going to say anything until we knew if it was a boy or a girl," said Adam.

"It's most definitely a girl," said Angelina.

"My daughter, the eternal fortune-teller. And how did you reach such a conclusion?"

Angelina felt the warm breeze that rustled through the cypress trees. She listened to the soft flow of the nearby water. How the current still held her so very close.

"The river told me this will be true."

Milton Keynes UK
Ingram Content Group UK Ltd.
UKHW040634090224
437425UK00003B/77